THE HIGHWAY MAN GAME

RYAN G. PEACOCK

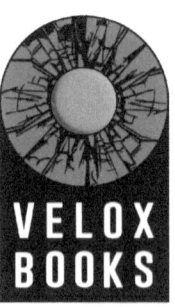

Published by arrangement with the author.

Copyright © 2026 by Ryan G. Peacock.

All rights reserved.

No part of this publication may be reproduced, distributed, or transmitted in any form or by any means, including photocopying, recording, or other electronic or mechanical methods, without the prior written permission of the publisher, except as permitted by U.S. copyright law.

The story, all names, characters, and incidents portrayed in this production are fictitious. No identification with actual persons (living or deceased), places, buildings, and products is intended or should be inferred.

YOU'RE READING ANOTHER TERRIFYING COLLECTION FROM

FOLLOW VELOX TO KEEP THE NIGHTMARES COMING:

CONTENTS

I Was Hired to Sleep Through a Porn Shoot	1
We Didn't Kill Aiden Pond	8
Fuck!	19
The Mall Game	26
YourBrittany	43
ED	52
Juicebox	66
Don't Use the Glory Hole at Roxy's Roadhouse	97
I Can Never Return to the Ocean	106
Premature Decay	120
Spacegirl	124
I Was Awake	124
My Organization Monitors Potential Apocalyptic Scenarios	124
The Highway Man Game	124
The Perfect Sin	124

I WAS HIRED TO SLEEP THROUGH A PORN SHOOT

Okay, let's be upfront about this. Yes. I'm a porn star. No, I'm not open to DMs. No, I'm not including pics or my actual stage name. I'm pretty small-time, and although I'm sure some of you have heard of me, I don't want this to damage anyone's professional reputation. I don't want to piss off the wrong people. I think the reasons will become pretty clear in a bit.

I don't think anyone really cares about my biography, but let me just say that I've been doing this for a couple of years and, for the most part, I like what I do. Like any job, it's got its ups and downs (lots of them), but I still end up having fun most of the time. There are a lot of good people in the porn industry, and even after this, I stand by that. But with what happened recently... I don't think I can work again.

The shoot was a pretty normal gig. It was a scene for a smaller website I'd never heard of before. But they paid, so I was fine with it. Admittedly, the pay was a little light, but money is money, right? Besides, the director told me that my role was going to be a little less porn and a little more actress, which I was fine with.

I know no one watches porn for the story, but the scene had a simple and kind of generic setup.

I was supposed to be having a sleepover with the actual leading lady of the shoot. She was a better-known actress than I, and I was honestly excited to meet her. I won't drop her name here, so let's just call her Pepper Petite. If you're smart, you can figure it out.

My 'Dad' would be played by a dude named Kevin Cawk. I'm sure by now you know where this is going. Kevin would come in, flirt with Pepper, and they'd fuck on the bed while I pretended to sleep soundly. Not exactly standard, but I was just happy for the easy money. Who wouldn't be?

On the day of the shoot, I got ready and drove to the set. It was an upscale-looking mansion that the director had rented for the week. I figured he'd probably been shooting almost constantly since he'd rented the place. It was clean, as most sets were, and there wasn't much of a crew there. Just the director, a couple of camera guys, and a boom operator.

I'd never worked with this director before. His name was Jackson Masters. I got the feeling it wasn't a stage name. Jackson didn't give me any odd vibes. He seemed friendly when he greeted me at the door, offering me a beer from the stash he kept in the fridge. I accepted, because I figured it would be easier to pretend to sleep if I was a little buzzed.

"So glad you could make it out today!" he said with a warm smile, as if we were at some summer beach party as opposed to a porn shoot.

"Oh, well, it's my pleasure," I said. "I've heard really great things about you and when I saw it was you, I thought it would be a lot of fun."

All complete bullshit. But he didn't need to know that. Why not make the connection, right? Especially if it might lead to more work in the future.

He actually blushed when I said that and took a sip of his beer.

"Ah, well. Y'know. I'm just starting out. Hey, we should go meet the rest of the cast! They're right upstairs!"

He gestured for me to follow and led me up to the bedroom where the other two actors were talking. Pepper Petite lived up to her name in person. I know her entire gimmick was being very petite, but damn. She was *really* tiny. Her infectious smile widened when she saw me enter the room, but I wasn't sure if it was genuine or not. She got up to greet me and exchange introductions. I'll admit, I was a little awkward about it.

"Nice to meet you," I said. "I'm a huge fan!"

What a great way to ruin an introduction. Good job, I thought to myself. Pepper didn't seem offended, though. She just laughed and tossed her golden hair back.

"Really? I'm so glad! I saw some of your work too, you know. You're really great! I'm glad you get to join us today!" Her smile beamed. "Maybe we can do another scene together sometime... I was a little disappointed when I heard it was just me and Kevin."

My heart fluttered a little at that. Pepper was attractive, but that wasn't what got to me. It was the idea of working with someone I truly admired. Now *that* was interesting!

"By the way, let me introduce you to Kevin," Pepper said, taking my hand gently. She led me towards the man in question.

Kevin Cawk was just about what I expected. I don't think I even need to describe him. He looked like someone who'd call himself Kevin Cawk. 30s, tanned, lean, and with the general short-cropped male haircut. I had a feeling I'd forget he even existed when I left that house later.

Pepper and I did a few run-throughs of our scenes together. Although none of it went all that well, I was kinda impressed by her as an actress. Obviously, she wasn't quite in the Hollywood league, but she seemed so full of energy.

"I've really been looking forward to this all week," she said. "We're going to have so much fun together!" She didn't even look at the script, not that there was much of one.

A finger brushed against her lips. She sucked on it seductively.

"Will... your dad be home?"

"I think he'll be in his office. So he won't bother us too much," I replied. My lines felt stilted. At least we weren't filming.

"Oh," Pepper sounded genuinely disappointed. She put on an exaggerated pout. "Well, hopefully he'll at least come to say goodnight to us!"

God, that writing was cringeworthy. Not even Pepper could have saved it.

We did a few more run-throughs before Jackson actually started filming. He only did a few takes. This wasn't what people would be paying the very fine porn site to see, after all.

The next shot was to be us getting into bed and going to sleep. My time to shine! Pepper went to get a bottle of water before the actual fun began, while I had another beer.

"Quick note before we start," Jackson said, coming up to me. I was halfway through my bottle.

"We're going to be moving the camera around a lot. I just want to make sure I'm reminding you. No matter what, don't open your eyes. You've got to sleep through the entire shoot."

I nodded.

"Yeah, sure thing," I said.

Jackson's smile faded.

"No matter what. Don't open your eyes," he repeated. "Promise?"

I nodded.

"I promise. I'll keep my eyes closed until you tell me to open them."

He seemed satisfied with that and let me finish my beer in peace. Pepper came back with her bottle of water and drank half of it before leaving it on a table out of the shot. I put my beer beside it.

"Ready to get paid?" I teased her. Pepper giggled.

"Always."

"We're going live!" Jackson said, while Pepper and I got into our positions. Jackson counted down and the scene began.

Pepper and I both climbed into bed. I pulled the duvet over me. I could feel her tiny body beside me, almost dwarfed by me.

"Goodnight, Pepper," I said.

"Goodnight!" she replied, chipper as always. Although the lights were still on, we both mimed sleep. I kept my eyes closed tight but listened intently, knowing what was about to come.

I heard Kevin's footsteps beside the bed and listened as he sat down on it. I felt his weight on Pepper's side of the bed.

"Mr. Smith, what are you doing?" Pepper asked with flirtatious indignation.

"It's alright. I just wanted to say goodnight," Kevin crooned. "After all, when my little girl brings my favorite of her friends over, I've got to say hi, right?"

"Oh, Mr. Smith!" Pepper giggled. "You're so nice!"

"Yeah? You wanna be nice to me, baby?"

"Oh yes, Mr. Smith!"

And that was when the kissing started.

I lay there listening as the two made out and let my mind wander. This bed was awfully comfortable. I liked the duvet too. It was really warm. I might have actually dozed off.

I heard the shuffling of Kevin's belt buckle and the wet sounds of work being done. It was all things I'd heard before, nothing special. I was busy thinking about how much I liked the pillows and focusing on not opening my eyes.

When the first satisfied moan escaped Pepper, I shifted a little to make room as the two bodies lay down on the bed beside me.

"But Mr. Smith, what if we wake her up?" Pepper asked.

"She sleeps like a rock. It'll be fine," Kevin assured her. Sure enough, the term "rock" was associated with what was happening in that bed. But it wasn't in relation to my fake sleeping.

Pepper moaned and swore under her breath as they did their job. I could hear his breathy dirty talk.

"You're such a bad girl. You're a dirty slut. I love how dirty a slut you are."

Real original.

For fun, I took everything I heard as out of context as possible and made up silly scenarios in my head as I feigned sleep. Everything seemed to be going according to plan and I'd likely be done in about 45 minutes or so.

Then I heard the first cry of pain.

"Ouch!" It was from Kevin, surprisingly. "Not so hard!"

Pepper giggled.

"Sorry," I could hear her smile in her voice. Kevin cried out again.

"Ow! No... What are you... No... No, NOOOO!"

His final word was broken down into a long, drawn-out, and horrified scream. The change was so sudden that it made me physically jolt. I almost got up and looked over my shoulder to see what was happening. But Jackson's words stuck with me.

No matter what. Don't open your eyes.

Was this supposed to be part of the shoot? I could feel Kevin thrashing on the bed, squirming and writhing as if he was trying to fight off Pepper. That shouldn't have been difficult, though. She was less than half his weight! Why was he struggling?

I heard nothing from Jackson or the crew... Just silence. Were they still filming? They had to be.

I curled into a tighter ball and kept quiet, letting everything unfold behind me.

Kevin's screams reached an awful, ear-splitting crescendo before they ended abruptly. I heard a low gurgling sound escape him before all movement ceased. Then I heard a wet, tearing noise. The sound sent shivers down my spine.

I wanted to look, but I told myself not to. Jackson was still filming! This had to be part of it! This was just some sort of fetish porn. That made sense, right? I didn't know much about the company, so it only made sense they were making some niche shit! I should've asked more questions. This was my fault.

The tearing sound came again, and the awful wetness of it made me want to vomit. I remained still, keeping my eyes closed and pressing my hands over my mouth.

The world around me was silent except for the tearing of flesh and... chewing. That had to be it—chewing. I heard it clearly now. Was... was something eating Kevin? Where were Jackson and the crew?

I almost opened my eyes but thought better of it. What if what was behind me was something I didn't want to see?

Slowly, my reluctance to open my eyes turned from professionalism to fear. I don't know how long I lay there, listening to that sickening tearing and chewing... but it felt like it went on for hours.

Then I felt the weight on the bed shift. I felt something climbing on top of me. Pepper?

I could feel her lips close to my ear. I could smell her rancid hot breath and feel the blood and saliva dripping from her mouth. Her breathing was heavy and feral. I kept my eyes closed.

Pepper seemed bigger than I remembered. Her arms were over my head. Her legs extended past mine. Maybe it was because I was curled up, but she seemed longer and spindly. My eyes remained closed tight. Whatever horror I imagined was standing over me, I only wanted to imagine it. In my heart, I knew that seeing it would only make things worse.

Pepper continued to stand over me, still letting her heavy, rancid breath wash over me. The silence ticked by. She didn't move.

Then, at last, I felt her weight shift. I heard her step onto the floor as she left me there. Her footsteps traveled farther and farther into the house as I lay there feigning sleep, too afraid to open my eyes out of fear of what I'd see.

The police found me in that bed, curled into a ball and shaking, my face wet with tears. When I felt the officer's hand on my shoulder, I cried out and curled up tighter.

"NO!"

"Shit! We've got a live one!" the cop called. I heard other movement and felt hands on me, easing me up out of the bed. My eyes remained closed.

"Honey, are you okay?" a man asked me. I shook my head. I still didn't want to open my eyes.

"No... No, please get me out of here..." I whispered. He did as I asked. I never actually saw the state the bedroom was in. I'm glad I didn't.

Down at the station, the police asked their questions. I told them the same story I've told here. They showed me the pictures of the crime scene.

Oh God.

Body parts all around. Pieces of meat. Blood coating the floor... I don't know what happened. I don't want to ever know, because I already know too much.

I know that all the bodies found in that room belonged to men. There was no sign of Pepper Petite. There was no evidence that she'd ever even been there. I told the police that I may have been mistaken. I don't know if they've tried to reach out to her. I don't care either.

I don't think I'm ever working in the porn industry again.

WE DIDN'T KILL AIDEN POND

It was just supposed to be a prank. A fucking joke. That was it! Hell, it was all fucking Derek's idea, not mine and not anyone else's!

We just wanted to fuck with him, y'know? Screw around. That's it! I swear!

I swear...

Fine, fine. Let me start from the beginning.

There was this guy back in high school, Aiden Pond. Everyone knew that he was kind of a... shit, what's the word here? I dunno. Whatever. He was prone to tantrums, though. Like, you could push this guy just a little bit, and he'd flip out on you. I'm talking about a full meltdown here. It was funny as shit! He'd start screaming, swearing, and getting all red in the face. Sometimes he'd even cry.

My buddies Derek, Jeremy, and I used to tease him a little. We were just having some fun; it wasn't that serious or anything. He just blew it all out of proportion.

Like that thing with the mouse! We just wanted to screw with him a little. Jeremy had caught a mouse outside. We thought it would be funny to put it in his desk. So yeah, that's what we did, and it was fucking funny!

Aiden got in, opened the desk to put his binder in, and started losing his shit when he saw the mouse. He must've jumped like a foot in the air. It was hilarious!

Then he saw us laughing and put the pieces together. He started crying and yelling at us, telling us what assholes we were.

That's what got the teacher involved, and naturally, Aiden squealed.

We got detention for the next three days. I still figured it was all worth it, but Derek was pissed.

I guess he thought that Aiden had overreacted or something. I dunno. But he wanted to get even with him.

So he suggested we egg his house.

We'd gotten some eggs and were heading over a little after school when we saw Aiden.

There was a path that ran along the woods out behind the school. I knew that Aiden usually walked home that way, so it wasn't that surprising that we saw him. It was kind of late to be leaving school, but he was part of a few after-school groups, so I guess it wasn't that weird for him.

I remember that he saw us up ahead on the trail. We didn't have any time to hide without looking more suspicious, and he just sort of slowed down once he recognized us, watching us carefully as he did. I knew that he *had* to see the egg carton in Derek's hands. And I remember thinking that the gig was up.

But I guess Derek wasn't ready to give up just yet, though. Nope. Like I said, I think he took the whole detention thing a little too personally.

Once Aiden saw us, Derek probably figured that he'd catch on to what we were up to and squeal on us. Even if we hadn't done it yet, he'd still squeal. That was just the way he was...

So I imagine he just thought: *'In for a penny, in for a pound.'*

Before he even threw the first egg, Aiden was screaming like a little kid for him to stop. Derek didn't care. He just kept fucking throwing eggs at him like a goddamn caveman.

Aiden put his hands up to try and cover his face. He backed away, stumbling towards the woods for cover. I saw him spitting out bits of yolk in between his angry screams, saying shit like:

"FUCK YOU GUYS! I'M GONNA FUCKING KILL YOU! FUCK YOU!"

Derek didn't give a shit. He just kept throwing eggs. By that point, Jeremy and I had gotten in on the action, too.

Aiden kept trying to blindly run towards the woods. I don't think he realized how steep the incline off the path into the forest was.

Maybe we could've stopped him from falling. Maybe.

Truth be told, though, I don't think any of us cared... I think we wanted him to fall, just because it would've been funny to watch.

I think we all just expected Aiden to tumble down into the woods, get up, and start screaming at us again, then we'd run off and probably get in more trouble later.

God... We were all so fucking stupid...

Aiden fell, all right. He went right down that incline and into the woods.

Derek, Jeremy, and I all watched, laughing our asses off the whole time. We laughed, and laughed, and laughed...

And Aiden just lay there in a heap of limbs on the ground...

We looked down at him, our laughter slowly fading until it stopped being so funny.

Aiden should've gotten up by then. He should've been red in the face and swearing at us...

But he wasn't.

He was just lying there... still. Silent.

Jeremy was the first one to call out to him. But there was no response.

After a few seconds of trying that, he went down. I followed. Derek stayed behind, watching in the vain hope that Aiden would simply get up, get mad, and everything would be okay again.

We made our way down the incline. We turned Aiden onto his back...

He wasn't moving. His eyes were closed. His nose was bleeding.

That's when we started panicking.

We didn't know what a dead body looked like, so we couldn't be sure. We didn't think to check his pulse or check to see if he was breathing. We just panicked.

Derek came down around that point while we freaked out, thinking we'd just fucking killed Aiden Pond!

We didn't know what to do. Should we just leave him there? Let someone else find him? Play dumb?

No! No... what if they caught us? We'd seen enough crime shows to believe that an entire FBI squad would hunt us down individually if we just let them find the body.

We considered just dragging him deeper into the woods, but that didn't seem much better. The 'woods' were really just a small patch of forest separating the park from the nearby road. It wasn't exactly the ideal hiding spot for a body. Someone was bound to find him.

We had to get rid of the body somehow. And it was Jeremy who gave us the idea.

"My Dad's not home..." he'd said. "We could take him to the backyard..."

Jeremy's Dad owned a landscaping company. He lived on a fairly rural property a few miles away. It wouldn't be that long of a walk to get there, and he kept most of his heavier equipment in the backyard—lawn mowers, chainsaws, hedge trimmers... and a wood chipper.

We'd helped Jeremy's Dad with the wood chipper plenty of times. When his clients wanted brush taken off their property, he'd usually load it into his truck, bring it home, and toss it into the wood chipper.

We knew how to use it. And considering the predicament we were in, it seemed like a good idea at the time.

We carried Aiden all the way to Jeremy's house. Well... I carried him. I was volunteered for it since I was the biggest.

I put him on my back like it was a piggyback ride... I remember feeling the uncomfortable weight of him as I carried him. I remember feeling the disgust in my stomach as I thought about how Aiden was probably already decaying...

We cut through a few fields and patches of woods to avoid running into anyone. Looking back at everything, I don't really know how the hell we didn't get caught. Dumb luck, maybe? Or maybe the world's just a quieter, less nosy place than we all think it is. When you're trying to hide something, you'll always feel eyes on you, even when there aren't any.

Once we got to Jeremy's house, we worked fast. He got the keys to his Dad's shed, and we wheeled the wood chipper out. We took it into the forest for some privacy.

Then we did what we came to do.

Jeremy started up the wood chipper, and once it was going, Derek and I lifted Aiden up. We were going to put him in feet first.

Just as we were ready to let him drop into the spinning blades, I saw his face move. I saw his eyelids flutter.

And in the moment before we put him in... I felt a spike of horror rising from my stomach as I realized that we didn't kill Aiden Pond.

I wish I could've said something... I wish I could've stopped it... But I didn't have time...

No... no, that's bullshit...

I know it's bullshit.

I could've said something. I could've stopped it. Any fucking one of us could have.

But as soon as Aiden's feet went into the wood chipper and he started screaming, we all knew that we weren't going back. We'd already gone too far. Sure, we could've stopped it. Maybe we could've saved his life.

But the fact that we'd gone this far already would've ruined our lives. We were only fifteen, and we knew that much to be true.

So we did the only thing that made sense.

We let him go.

Aiden struggled and thrashed. He tried to grab the edges of the wood chipper to keep himself from going in. But we forced him. He screamed and he cried. The sounds he made...

Oh God...

The fucking sounds he made...

The sounds the wood chipper made as it tore him apart.

I won't ever forget those. Not for the rest of my life.

We spent almost an hour out there. By the time the wood chipper had gotten through his legs, Aiden was long gone. His body was pale and limp.

There was so much fucking blood... we didn't realize there'd be so much of it.

By the time the wood chipper started tearing into his guts, I couldn't take it anymore. I had to run off into the woods to vomit.

It tore through his ribcage, gooey chunks of him sticking to the blades...

Shortly after that, it jammed.

When we couldn't get it to start again, we panicked. Derek took what was left of the body out.

Fuck... the mess he made... the bits of Aiden coming out of him.

The memory makes me sick.

We didn't know what to do. We eventually settled on just burying it.

Then it came time to deal with the wood chipper. We hadn't thought this through. We'd thought that maybe there wouldn't be that much blood.

We couldn't clean it off, not without taking it back to Jeremy's place, and his Mom was definitely home by then. She would've seen us.

We decided to just leave it in the woods.

Then there was the matter of our bloody clothes...

Christ! We didn't know what to do about that. We considered just stripping them off and leaving them in the woods, but no luck...

Eventually, we agreed we'd just sneak into Derek's house, borrow some of his clothes, and go home.

It didn't work.

His mom saw us coming in, and when she did, I remember the way the color drained from her face. She stared at us, covered in blood and shaken from what we'd spent the evening doing.

Then she started screaming.

I don't blame her.

Considering what a piss-poor job we'd done of covering our tracks, the case was closed pretty quickly.

Derek refused to talk to the police, but Jeremy and I both cracked almost immediately. No point in lying and digging ourselves into an even deeper pit.

The three of us were tried as adults. And that was it.

Derek got twenty-five years—a life sentence. Jeremy and I got fifteen each.

We served our time in the same prison. But we rarely ever saw each other.

I consider myself lucky that I was ever considered eligible for parole.

I served eight years of my sentence... eight years of my life, gone. But I still had my youth, more or less.

I don't want to talk about prison... I don't want to think about that.

I deserved what I got, I know that. We all did.

Jeremy and I both tried to shut up and serve our time. Get it over with as painlessly as possible. Juvie wasn't so bad, but when we got transferred to an adult correctional facility, things were a lot rougher.

We just kept our heads down and tried to be as close to model prisoners as either of us could be.

Derek, on the other hand, chose to be as big a pain in the ass as possible.

He was enough of a bastard in juvie that Jeremy and I both started avoiding him, and he only got worse after we were transferred.

I didn't see much of him, but I know he spent a lot of time in solitary confinement. Whenever he was allowed back into general population, it was only a matter of months before he'd end up in another fight that would send his ass right back to solitary.

Naturally, I wasn't that surprised when he eventually turned up dead.

The way I heard it, somebody had gotten into his cell in solitary and fucked him up. Nobody knew who. Nobody even had a good guess. The guards just heard him screaming one night and came in to find him damn near gutted and bleeding out. They couldn't save him (assuming they even bothered to try).

I can't say I shed any tears for him. If anything, I was almost glad he was dead.

We'd all taken part in what we did to Aiden. We all deserved the blame. But Derek had been the one who'd fucking started it. It had all originally been his idea. And in the years since, I'd always figured he didn't regret what we'd done. He just regretted that we didn't do it *better*.

Me? I just wanted to put it behind me. Move on with my life. Start over and just become somebody else. I knew it wouldn't change the past... I'd always know what I'd done. I'd never, ever get away from it.

I suppose some dumb, juvenile part of me sort of hoped that at the very least Jeremy might get released around the same time I did... I hadn't heard anything about him possibly being up for parole, but who knows, right?

I suppose in the end it didn't matter...

Two months before I got out, they found Jeremy lying dead in the showers. I never saw the body. But I heard about the state he was in.

Someone had gone to town on him, carving deep gashes in his stomach and legs. They'd apparently damn near torn him open. There was more blood flowing down the drain than there actually was inside of him.

They'd figured that someone had jumped him in the shower. Jeremy wasn't really the confrontational sort, but there were some real psychos in that place. All he'd have needed to do was rub the wrong person the wrong way, and that was it.

I was sad to hear what had happened to him. But unfortunately, he wasn't the first guy I'd known in that shithole who didn't survive to see parole, and by then we'd drifted apart enough that I only barely recognized him when I saw him.

I still mourned for him a lot more than I did for Derek… But what happened, happened. I accepted it for what it was.

After they finally let me out, I started trying to get my life together. I checked in with my parole officer, got a room at a halfway house for guys like me, and started looking for work. I picked up a shitty job washing dishes and made enough money to get by.

Honestly? That was good with me. This was what I wanted.

The guilt never really went away. Most nights, I'd dream about Aiden.

The screams he'd made…

The sound of the wood chipper.

The blood…

The gore…

God… Just the memory of it still turned my stomach.

But I'd long since learned to live with all that.

I've been out of prison for about eight months now.

I've been trying to get by. Trying to get my life in order and salvage what I've made of it.

But now, I don't think I can.

I came home from work a couple of days ago at around midnight. I walked up the stairs to my room at the halfway house, changed into my pajamas, and tried to relax. My evening plans were to eat, jerk off, sleep, and get up somewhat early the next morning to jog. Same as I did just about every day.

I'd made myself a PB and J and was getting comfy on my single bed as I looked out my little window onto the street below. I watched some of the cars pass on the street and let myself zone out a little as I decompressed after a long shift.

I didn't pay much attention to it when I noticed movement on the street. I just sort of stared thoughtlessly into the void for a bit before realizing that there was something down on the road, crawling around.

I figured it was just a dog at first, since the first glimpse I got of it was it passing behind a car parked on the street. I watched it for only a few seconds before deciding it wasn't anything worth paying attention to and going back to my sandwich.

About a minute or so later, I saw whatever it was coming out from under the car, and I looked down to satisfy my mild curiosity.

Although the longer I looked at it... the less sure I was as to what it was. It only had two legs... It couldn't have been a dog or a cat. Some sort of bird, maybe? No... Birds didn't move like that.

Whatever this thing was, it crawled along on the ground, and the shape of it looked... almost looked like the top half of a person...

I blinked in disbelief, trying to make sense of what I was seeing. There was no way that could be true! No fucking way!

But the longer I looked, the more sure I was...

It was the top half of a person, dragging itself along the ground. A man, by the looks of it. No... a teenage boy...

I felt a sense of dread growing in my stomach as I realized that what I was looking at wasn't just a trick of my eyes...

Looking back, I'm not sure how I didn't recognize him immediately. Maybe the sheer impossibility of it had made me dismiss it outright, but I couldn't deny what was staring me right in the face.

Aiden Pond was crawling towards my building...

Half of him was, anyway.

I watched him move, my eyes widening in disbelief as my stomach tied itself in knots.

I saw his face, pale and bloodless as he looked up at me, his eyes wide and sightless.

I watched as he reached the wall beneath my window and began to climb.

That was when I finally moved, stumbling back and tripping over my own two feet to land on my ass.

I stared at the window like an idiot, half expecting this to all be some dream. It had to be! I'd probably just dozed off on my bed! Yeah, sure. That had to be it...

Please, dear God, tell me that was it...

I saw a pale hand with skeletal, clawlike fingers reaching up towards my window.

I knew it was real.

Aiden Pond rose up to press his face against the glass. His vacant eyes seemed to stare at me. His mouth hung open in a silent scream. God... I could... I could see bits of him hanging off the tattered remains of the bottom half of his torso.

I watched him fumble with the edge of my window and realized that he aimed to open it.

I stood up, sprinting to the window to try to stop him. I pressed the lock closed.

It didn't make any difference.

Aiden forced it open.

I heard the metal of the lock break. I saw cracks spiderweb across the glass. Aiden lurched forward, almost touching me as he fell into my room.

He didn't speak. Didn't say a word... didn't even pause to reorient himself. He landed in a graceless heap on the ground and just kept moving... reaching one pale, dead hand out to drag himself even closer.

I tried to run. I stumbled back out of my room, looking back at him as I did.

He just got closer and closer. Slowly but surely, he dragged himself toward me.

I took a few more steps back without thinking.

I didn't even realize how close I was to the stairs... not until I was falling.

I tumbled backward, my head slamming against one of the steps as I flopped over, crashing against every step as I fell.

When I finally hit the ground... I lay there, waiting.

I could see Aiden at the top of the stairs, watching me with his cold, dead eyes.

I tried to move my legs. But the pain was too much. All I could do was scream.

White bone jutted out of my broken skin. I wouldn't be walking again anytime soon... So, using my arms, I pulled myself forward, dragging myself away from the sight of Aiden hunting me, tears streaming down my cheeks the whole time.

I didn't move nearly as fast as he did. And though he didn't make a sound, I knew he was getting closer...

Down a nearby hallway, I could see lights come on. I could see doors opening as some of the other guys came out to investigate the noise.

I vaguely remember screaming at them to run when one of them approached me to ask if I was okay. I tried to point to the ghost behind me...

But when they looked, there was nothing there.

Aiden was gone.

I've spent the last few days in the hospital. The doctor says I'll make a full recovery.

I don't believe that.

I don't think I'll leave this building alive.

He's never there when anyone else is in the room, but when I'm alone, I can see him... in the shadows, under beds, in the corners...

Watching me.

Waiting.

I think about Jeremy and Derek a lot. I wonder if this was how their final days were...

I wonder why he saved me for last. But I suppose it doesn't really matter why.

I'm scared of what will happen soon. I'm afraid to die. But I know that this is what I deserve... I did something terrible. I was just as much to blame as Derek and Jeremy were. Aiden deserves his revenge.

FUCK!

Jesus Christ, what the fuck? How do I even... FUCK! Where do I even fucking start...

Maybe with her profile? Yeah. Yeah, her profile sounds good. That sounds about right.

Her screen name was PizzaCat98. She was young, cute and clearly down to fuck. Her pictures all had filters on them to give her cat ears, flower crowns and sparkles, but beneath all of that, I'd say she was still genuinely cute. Not 'ugly from every angle except one', cute. She had long, wavy brown hair and round plastic glasses that made her eyes look bigger than they really were. I've got to admit, that was something of a turn on. But what really got me was her bio.

HEY there! I'm Halee, and I'm just looking to meet new people. I'm the kinda girl you can bring home to DADDY, but I know how to have fun too! I'm really down to earth and not difficult to PLEASE. I don't really give a FUCK if people judge ME because I just live the best life I can, and that's what I'm going to keep doing UNTIL I can't anymore. If you're okay with that, I really think we'd get along fine! Just coming off a bad Breakup. So not looking for anything too serious right now. But what happens, happens!

You go and find me one guy who wouldn't have slid into her DM's, and I'll find you one liar. This girl was looking to get fucking railed, and she couldn't have possibly said it any louder. Fortunately for her, she and I had a common interest. I was looking for something casual, no strings attached, no long-term commitment. Just a little bit of naughty fun between two consenting adults. Nothing wrong with that, right?

Well, I messaged her, and she got back to me almost immediately. I don't have our chat logs, since her profile's long gone by now. But there wasn't much to discuss between us anyway.

She told me her name was Halee, we flirted for a bit, and she asked if I was busy that night. I wasn't, and I already had a raging hard-on, so when she asked if I wanted to come over, I probably made it there in record time.

This isn't my first rodeo. Most girls at least want to chat for a bit or meet up first. I'm fine with that. But my heart always went out to the ones who didn't even bother with the formalities. They wanted to fuck, and then they wanted me out. That was fine by me. Honestly, I like it better that way. At least we both know where we stand.

Halee lived in a fairly nice apartment building downtown. I had to buzz in and everything, and I spotted cameras watching me from the lobby to the elevator.

She said she was on the 4th floor, apartment number 415, and I made my way there as if I'd been there a thousand times before. I remember shooting her a message as I got into the elevator, something like:

'On my way up.'

It was something of a fair warning, just in case she got cold feet at the last minute. She just replied with:

'The door's unlocked, Daddy <3.'

I took that as a green light to proceed.

Sure enough, the door to her apartment was unlocked and slightly ajar. I stepped inside and was greeted by the smell of incense with something both sweet and a little sour underneath. Not exactly the nicest smell, but I've hooked up in worse places. The apartment was fairly clean, and the lights were a little dim.

"Hello?" I called.

"Be right there!" I heard a voice say from deeper in the apartment. I closed and locked the door behind me, then waited to meet Halee in the flesh.

She bounced around the corner, and my God, was she a sight to see. She was every bit as cute as her profile pictures suggested, standing at about 5'5 and curvy in all the right places. She'd dressed up for me, too. She wore a tight black turtleneck with no bra underneath, and it looked good on her. I could see her nipples through the fabric. Her skirt just barely covered her thighs, and she wore black nylon socks that reached her knees.

She had a sweet, million-watt smile that was downright adorable and the little giggle that escaped her as soon as she saw me suited her just fine.

"Hey there, Jakey," She purred as she sauntered closer to me and pulled me into a kiss. Her arms wrapped tightly around me. I couldn't help but think that she felt awfully cold to the touch and her skin felt. Well, it felt a little bit weird. Maybe she'd just gotten out of the shower or something, but I swear her skin felt cold and kinda slippery.

She pressed me up against the door, kissing me long and deep before resting her head against my chest.

"You kept me waiting," she teased.

"Sorry! I came as fast as I could!"

"Don't worry. You're going to make it up to me."

She gave me one quick, gentle kiss before pulling away from me and beckoning me to follow her, flashing that million-watt smile as she did.

I wasn't going to say no to that—no way in hell. I was rock hard at that point and looking forward to what was to come.

As I followed her down the hall, she gave me a little tease as well, flipping the back of her skirt up and showing me that there was nothing underneath. She had an absolutely perfect, heart-shaped ass.

She disappeared into a bedroom just ahead of us and when I got there, she was lying on the bed, waiting for me.

Straight to business, just the way I liked it.

Her bedroom was tidy and lit with some erotic red lamps. She'd drawn the curtains to her window, but I could still hear the traffic outside... for the time being, at least. I imagined that in a few minutes, she'd be screaming so loud that we wouldn't notice.

She patted the spot on the bed beside her, and I was happy to lay down. As soon as I did, her hands were all over me. She moved one down between my legs, palming my crotch and riling me up even further as she leaned in to kiss me again.

"You look good enough to eat, Daddy," she crooned, "I'll bet you can't wait to feel my mouth around you..."

"Not one more minute..." I replied. I put my hand on her thigh and slipped it under her skirt. Her skin still felt cold and slippery. It made me pause for a moment, but Halee hardly even seemed to notice.

"Oh yeah, Daddy... I'm gonna take all of you so deep... I want it so bad... so fucking bad..."

She grabbed me by the wrist, and with her eyes locked to mine, she made me move my hand further up her skirt. Normally, I wouldn't need encouragement... but my enthusiasm was starting to fade a little bit.

Something about the way she was looking at me didn't seem right. She didn't blink. Her eyes didn't even seem to move at all.

"I'm gonna put you inside of me, Daddy... I'm gonna squeeze you so hard. I'm gonna hump and pump and grind. Yes Daddy. I'm so ready for it..."

"Whoa. Let's... let's just calm down, alright, babe?"

I smiled sheepishly and tried to pull back. Her grip on my arm didn't break. If anything, it was starting to hurt.

She still wasn't blinking. She kept her eyes firmly planted on mine.

"Grind and squeeze, Daddy, until you pop, and pop, and pop, and pop..."

She lunged for me, pinning me to the bed as she climbed on top of me. The hand she'd forced up her skirt felt... wrong. It was as if I'd immersed it in a bucket of cold oil, and that cold was starting to burn a little bit.

I tried to cry out, but Halee leaned down to kiss me again. Her lips felt ice-cold against mine.

I tried to push her off of me. But she wasn't moving! If anything, she seemed to be sinking ever closer to me.

I could feel her tongue in my mouth, cold and slimy. Her eyes were still staring into mine, dead and empty. Unblinking. Inhuman.

I tried to scream. I tried to bite down on her tongue but nothing helped!

The hand under her skirt was burning! It hurt more than anything else had ever hurt before!

I screamed, struggled, kicked and thrashed, but Halee wouldn't move. She just sank down onto me, lower and lower as if she were melting. Her features seemed to grow further apart. I could feel... Jesus, I could feel her going down my throat... cold and slimy with a horrible sour taste. I couldn't breathe and felt my eyes watering.

With a desperate pull, I finally pulled my 'hand' free of her iron grip and ripped it away from her skirt.

I only caught a glimpse of what was left... a jagged bone at the end of my arm with clear slime, dribbling down the skin, burning it away.

Oh God! Oh dear God... what was she doing to me?

I could feel that cold, burning sensation on my stomach as she melted onto me. I could feel my body burning. Being digested by whatever the fuck she was...

I panicked. I cried.

I didn't want to die like this! I didn't want to fucking die, period! With my free arm, the one that no longer had a hand, I tried to push her off. I wasn't used to not having a hand there anymore. Maybe that worked out in my favor. The burned, jagged spear of bone that now protruded from my arm was shoved through what had once been Halee's head.

I could feel her entire body violently tremble on top of me. Horrible waves radiated through her. The slimy tendril she'd forced down my throat expanded, then pulled back at long last as I finally got her to move!

With every bit of strength I had, I pushed her. She moved less like a person now and more like some pudding being dumped out of a bowl. When she toppled off of me, she rolled... no... poured off of the bed. She hit the ground with a wet splat and coagulated on the floor in a vaguely human mass.

I could see shapes that resembled limbs moving in amongst that mass and I could've sworn that I saw her face starting to form back together.

I didn't stick around to watch and see how long it would take her, though.

Clutching my mangled arm to my chest and coughing up a substance like thick mucus, I dragged myself off the bed and collapsed to the floor.

My lungs were burning. Breathing was difficult.

I tried to stand, but my legs failed me. Every part of my body hurts. I felt dizzy and disoriented.

I tried to look upwards towards the bedroom door but I could already see the viscous mass that had introduced itself as Halee was crawling to block my way.

"Don't go, Daddy! I wanna feel you inside of me. I wanna take it all!" Her voice still sounded human, although there was a slight reverb to it as if there were two of her speaking at once.

Still in agony, I tried to crawl back towards the window.

The slimy mass pulled part of itself up onto the bed. A humanoid shape that looked like Halee's smiling face rose up from the disgusting mass before me and with tears streaming from my eyes, I backed against the wall.

"Kiss me, Jakey. Come kiss me now. Kiss. Kiss. Kiss. Kiss..."

Her lips puckered as she blew kisses at me, yet her body oozed over the bed and advanced on me like a rolling, shapeless wall.

The window was at my back. Nowhere else to go. I threw the curtain aside and frantically pounded on the glass. It didn't budge.

Desperate, I tried to look for something that would break it. I spotted a lamp on a table nearby and grabbed it, ripping the cord out as I did.

Screaming in exertion, I slammed the lamp against the glass. The window cracked. I struck it again and again, watching those cracks desperately spiderweb out.

I looked back to see Halee's face just a few feet away from mine, a sweet smile plastered across her lips.

I hit the window one last time. The glass broke, and without thinking, I threw myself through. I felt the white hot pain of a thousand shards of glass raking against my body. I felt the wind rushing past me as I fell.

I didn't feel the ground rush up to greet me, though. Maybe I got lucky and passed out before the pain could register.

I guess when people watch a man throw himself out of a fourth-storey window, they tend to worry. Someone called an ambulance and I somehow survived the trip to the hospital.

I lost a hell of a lot of blood and needed a hell of a lot of stitches. But I guess I'm as stable as I'm going to get. Where my hand once was is now nothing but a bandaged stump. The doctors say it could be months, if not years, before I walk again.

But I'm alive, and I'll take that over the alternative.

I told the police everything. They didn't believe me. According to them, Halee's apartment was an empty unit. They think I'm crazy. But I know what happened. I've got the scars to fucking prove it!

My phone survived the fall. The screen is cracked, but it still works. I've had some friends send me texts to get well, and some old hookups send me their best wishes. But among all those texts, I saw a few from a number I didn't recognize...

Hey Jakey!

Sorry you had to leave so suddenly, but I really would like to see you again. Maybe we can even finish what we started ;)

Hope to see you soon!

Jesus... I can't get it out of my head that I only just delayed the inevitable. Every time I wake up, I'm afraid that I'll see her standing over my bed and smiling at me. Every time the nurse tells me I've got a visitor, I'm afraid it'll be her.

But the worst part?

I can't get that fucking burning feeling out of my chest and my stomach. Every day, I swear it gets a little bit worse and no matter how much water I drink, it never goes away.

I'm afraid that she left part of herself behind... I... I'm afraid that it won't go away and I'm afraid of what's going to happen to me.

I don't want to die...

But I don't think I have a choice anymore.

THE MALL GAME

Have you ever lost someone you loved? Someone who was such an important part of your life that losing them ripped everything out of you and left you as nothing but an empty husk?

I have.

Grief does things to a person. It can destroy them, and the scars will never heal, not really. Suddenly, the world seems like a darker place. You wish you'd had more time, and you cling to the memories of what time you did have. You wish that you could go back and have just one more minute with them. Just one... that's all you want.

That was all *I* wanted...

Abigail Swann believed that the world was a magical place. She'd been obsessed with mystery and seemed so certain that if she looked hard enough, she could pull back the veil to see the things that humanity was never meant to see.

When I first asked her out, I did so before Halloween, and our first date was during a local ghost walk.

Seeing how excited she was as we followed the group from place to place, listening to the horrific tales of pain and suffering that haunted our lonely city streets, only made me fall deeper in love with her. She had the most wonderful, mischievous grin that made her dark eyes sparkle, and that night led to many others.

Abandoned cabins, deserted theme parks, quiet forests—we visited them all together as we grew from a cute high school couple into young lovers, planning our future together. As time went by, we talked of marriage, mortgages, and even children. (She wanted to get married in an abandoned church.)

Abigail was a force of nature. An unstoppable person who saw magic and beauty everywhere she went... and she made me see it too.

Maybe if I'd taken a different route that day, I'd still have her with me.

Some local kids decided to mix booze and daddy's fast car. They ran a red light and hit me on the passenger side before I could react. The boys were fine. I spent two weeks in the hospital, and Abigail... she didn't even make it that far.

The months after her death were the hardest. My body might have healed, but it was the only thing that did. I felt her absence in every waking moment. I pored over her old photographs as mutual friends offered me empty condolences.

I knew they meant well, but their support didn't change what I'd lost. They didn't cushion the pain that I felt. Nothing really could.

I would have given anything to undo what had been done or to even have one more minute with Abigail... *anything*.

That's why I did it. It's why I played the Mall Game. I didn't know if it would work, and I knew that in the unlikely event that it did, I'd probably end up killing myself in the process. But given my state and what it promised, I couldn't say no. As I mentioned earlier, grief can have a profound impact on a person. It sends them to dark places, and in those places, there are often other things waiting.

I'd first heard about the Mall Game through Abigail. It's not a well-known ritual. I'd never heard of anyone who'd completed it successfully, but with all the details out there, someone must have.

Those who attempted it usually failed to even start it correctly, although if you dig deep, you might find some rumors of people who tried to play it and disappeared.

Supposedly, if you manage to beat the Mall Game, you will be allowed access to another world. There, you would have your choice of prizes: worldly possessions, riches, knowledge, and if you so choose, an opportunity to speak to the dead.

The catch is, you can only take one prize, and if you were to beat the Mall Game, you can never, ever play it again. You have one chance to play and one chance to win.

In order to even play the game, you must have recently lost someone close to you; otherwise, it won't work. However, if you have, and you are still reeling from the grief, you need to visit any large indoor mall of your choosing. It doesn't matter where it is. It just needs to be a large indoor mall. A strip mall won't work.

You need to enter the mall first thing in the morning and ensure that you are the first one to set foot inside that day. Then, approach the nearest kiosk and ask the person working there, "What time does the mall close today?"

Their answer is very important. If they do anything other than smile at you and say, "Stay and find out," then you have failed. However, if they smile and say those words... then the game begins.

My city has a very large mall near the highway that I knew would serve my purposes perfectly. I made sure to be there bright and early on a weekday, when they might not be as busy in the morning. I thought it might be easier to be the first person inside that way.

The mall opened at 10:00 a.m., and when the doors were unlocked that day, I was already inside before they had fully opened. The underpaid employee who I'd pushed past shot me a dirty look as I made a beeline for the nearest kiosk: a cell phone provider.

Common sense told me that this wouldn't work. Even if the Mall Game was real, it was such a long shot that I'd actually trigger it.

But if I had a chance to speak to Abigail one last time, I needed to take it. I needed to see her again.

The kiosk sat just ahead of me, and the employee there looked over at me as I drew closer. They probably thought I was there to browse or buy. There was no way they'd have expected the question I asked.

"Excuse me, what time does the mall close?"

Their initial expression was one of surprise, and I felt my heart sink. I was so sure I'd failed at the first step... and then I saw their smile. Their eyes met mine, their gaze both knowing and mocking.

"Stay and find out," they replied. Their tone was almost condescending.

Those four words sent a chill through me. For a moment, I wasn't sure I'd actually heard them correctly.

The kiosk employee chuckled and turned away from me, leaving me standing dumbfounded by their counter. Finally, I pulled away as I realized that it had worked.

I'd successfully begun the Mall Game.

That knowledge filled me with both elation and a quiet dread. Elation because for the first time, I felt just the slightest spark of hope.

Dread because I knew what would come next.

The Mall Game is fundamentally a game of tag. By beginning it, you invite something else into the mall with you. What exactly it is, is up for debate. Most people just call it the Hunter, though.

Some people said that the Hunter would look like any other mall patron, and they'd be difficult to pick out from a crowd. There would be subtle things to distinguish them, but it was never specified exactly what those things might be.

What is agreed upon is that once the Mall Game has begun, you cannot exit the mall at any time because the Hunter will continue to follow you if you do. The only way to get rid of it is to win the game, which is easier said than done.

In order to win, you need to remain within the mall until it closes. You cannot be caught, and you cannot leave. You must avoid the Hunter until the hour before the mall closes, and then you begin the next step of the game...

The mall I was in closed at nine p.m. That left me with about ten hours until the game was finished. I knew that the Hunter would be entering soon, and I had every intention of avoiding them when they arrived.

I figured that I'd try a pragmatic approach. Obviously, the Hunter was going to come straight for me. So why not find a place where I'd be able to see it coming? Somewhere open and central, such as the food court.

I could feel nervous palpitations in my chest as I headed there, keeping a distance from any other shoppers I saw. No one that I passed stuck out to me in any noticeable way. They were just average people going about their business.

The food court was more or less empty when I got there. Some of the restaurants weren't even open yet. The few that were didn't interest me. I doubted I'd be able to hold down any food that I ate. My stomach churned too much, and I hadn't had much of an appetite in the past few weeks, anyway.

I found a table where I could look out on the rest of the mall and waited, drumming my fingers impatiently on the table as I watched strangers pass by.

I figured that anyone traveling in a group was probably safe. Everything I'd read suggested that there would only be one Hunter, so I waited for them. I don't think I waited long, either.

My fingers drummed anxiously on the table as I saw a pale, bald man in a suit walking slowly past the food court. I expected him to look at me, but he remained stoic and looked straight ahead before he disappeared from my sight.

I spotted a young mother and her two children entering the food court. The kids looked at me, but they didn't seem all that threatening. I spotted a lonely old lady with a walker around the corner and didn't linger on her for long.

My fingers kept drumming on the table as I eyed a group of teenagers passing by and watched as they entered the food court. They were all pierced and dressed in black, although I noticed that one of them trailed behind the others. They looked at me. As they did, I realized that the air around me felt a little colder than before.

My eyes remained locked on the androgynous teenager who frowned before looking at their phone and jogging to catch up to their friends.

I watched them for a moment longer before conceding that they weren't the Hunter. Although that new chill in the air made me uneasy.

The room seemed darker than before, and I looked over to the other side of the food court, hoping to catch sight of any newcomers, before I noticed the old woman again.

She wove slowly through the tables as she approached me. Her serious eyes never left me, and that intense glare made me feel uneasy.

She couldn't have been more than ten feet away from me, and as she slowly came closer, I felt the room getting colder as the lights around me dimmed. Her very presence seemed to cast a shadow and suck all the warmth from the air around her.

My every instinct told me to get up, but my body would not obey. As the old woman closed the distance between us, I could feel the world around me going dark, and in that dark, I saw her features begin to change.

Where once an old woman had stood, now stood something else entirely. It lurched towards me, its skin clammy and gray, its eyes sunken and skeletal. What was beneath that rotten skin was only barely human.

I saw blistered lips curl into a grin as fresh pus dribbled from the sores. My nostrils were filled with an overwhelming stench of coppery blood as the Hunter drew nearer.

I had foolishly come in believing that the Mall Game would be easy to play. I had thought I could easily evade the Hunter once it revealed itself to me. No doubt I hadn't been the first to think that.

Running sounds simple in concept, but when faced with what hides behind the veil, your body doesn't respond. You sit there, like a deer in the headlights, watching it come for you, throat full of gnashing rotten teeth and the stink of rotting flesh wafting from its threshing maw.

I knew at that moment why others had gone missing. Either they hadn't seen the Hunter coming or they'd been paralyzed with fear when they saw it, just like I was.

I sat in that seat in the food court, pulled into whatever cold darkness the Hunter had brought with it as it advanced on me. I knew that when it took me, no one would notice. I would be dismissed as another disappearance… and I would be forgotten.

In what I was sure would be my final moments, I pictured Abigail and hoped that maybe I might see her on the other side.

I imagined her mischievous smile and her sweet laugh. A laugh I would've done anything to hear again. Even that game.

With the Hunter only feet away from me, skeletal hands reaching for my throat to snatch me and drag me into its mouth, I found the strength to move.

At last, I screamed and launched myself backward, off the chair. As I put some distance between myself and the Hunter, I saw the world around me get brighter. A few strangers noticed me and looked over in my direction, but I paid them no mind.

As I stumbled away from the Hunter, I saw that it seemed more human. The further I got, the more it looked like a harmless old lady.

The effect was similar to those images you sometimes see, where movement causes the image to change into something else. Lenticular printing, I think it's called.

Yet even with its harmless disguise back up, I still knew what that creature really was.

I suppose in a sense, my plan had worked. In fact, it had worked too well. I knew what was after me. I knew exactly what it was, and even once I'd turned to run, I could still smell the rotting flesh of the idiots who'd tried and failed to play the Mall Game before me.

I must have looked like an idiot, taking off at top speed out of the food court and away from that harmless-looking old lady, but I didn't care. No one else would have seen what I'd seen, and if they did, God help them.

I looked back only once as I left the food court, and I saw the old lady several feet behind me. She'd moved faster than I'd expected, but I'd still put some distance between us. I rushed up one of the nearby escalators to the second floor, where I was sure I'd be "safe" for the time being.

From the second floor, I watched the old lady following me towards the escalator. She kept a steady pace, and her gaze was always fixated directly on me.

I looked back at her before turning to leave. I didn't run, but I kept a brisk pace, intending not to let her catch up to me again.

The first hour was only barely done. I had nine more to go.

Part of me considered heading for the mall door, catching the bus, and heading home. But the warnings I'd read had been clear.

Leaving the mall at any time would not get rid of the Hunter. The game would end, and the Hunter would continue to pursue me until it inevitably caught me.

To leave would be to die, plain and simple. Judging by what I'd seen behind that harmless old lady facade, it would be a very painful death, too.

No... I wasn't going to leave. Not at all.

Hiding was out of the question, too. The Hunter would know where I was immediately, so I'd only be wasting my time and possibly cornering myself as well. On the subject of cornering myself, going into any of the stores would probably also be a mistake. Mall stores generally have only one entrance, which is also the exit. I didn't know how smart the Hunter was, but if it happened to catch me in one of the smaller stores, all it would need to do is wait by the entrance for me to come out, and it would have me.

A better strategy seemed to be to simply keep moving. The mall had a circuit I could follow. I could move between the upstairs and downstairs, and it would allow me to stay ahead of the Hunter.

I'd just do laps around the mall for the day until it was time to find a store and end the game. I could do that, right?

For the first couple of hours, things went well. I kept a close eye on the Hunter, who I kept at about a thirty-foot distance.

It followed me up and down escalators, keeping its steady pace as it pursued me. Its eyes never once left me.

Despite its appearance as an old lady, I figured that it moved just about as quickly as I did. Despite how terrifying my first encounter with it had been, I caught myself feeling confident that I might just win this after all.

By the time noon had rolled around, my confidence was starting to wane.

I'm not exactly a health nut, but I consider myself at least somewhat in shape. Keeping a brisk pace to keep the Hunter away from me, though, was far more trying than I'd expected.

As I felt myself starting to tire, I made myself get further ahead in the vain hope that if I put some distance between myself and the Hunter, I might just buy myself some time to rest.

It didn't take long to leave her behind as I headed back towards the food court. I was hoping that I might grab a drink or something to keep myself ready to go.

There were no rules in the ritual explicitly forbidding you from stopping to eat or drink at any point in time. I'd even heard some people encouraging you to eat or buy food during the game. There would be no opportunity to eat for some time once it was all over.

I was on the second floor and was getting close to the escalator that led down towards the food court when I felt a familiar drop in the temperature around me. I paused and looked backward, expecting to see the Hunter behind me, but there was no one.

The lights around me were starting to dim again, and I remained frozen, unsure of what was close to me.

Was there something else nearby? A second hunter, perhaps? The descriptions I'd read hadn't said anything about that.

Then, from the corner of my eye, I saw her.

I'm not sure when she got down to the lower level or when she'd caught up to me, but there she was. That same little old lady was riding the escalator up to me. Her eyes were fixated on me like they always were, and I could see something shifting behind her human facade.

I recoiled on instinct away from the escalator and broke into a run, putting some more distance between us. Not too much this time. I didn't want to lose track of her again.

I watched as she reached the top of the escalator and resumed her steady pursuit of me. I could hear my blood pounding in my ears, and I could've sworn I saw a wry smile on her lips.

Suddenly, I wasn't very thirsty anymore.

Over the next few hours, I kept moving. Whenever I got tired or wanted to stop, she was there.

I learned very quickly that if I got too far ahead of her, she'd find a way to get close to me again.

About five hours into the game, I saw her come out of a store in front of me when I was sure she'd been behind me.

Not long after, I saw her coming straight for me when, again, I'd last seen her twenty feet behind me.

As the day went on, she became more and more aggressive. The mall itself began to feel... wrong.

I was sure I'd followed the circuit that led around the mall exclusively. However, every now and then, I'd find myself disoriented. Routes that had looped around last time seemed to end in doors out. Stores that I'd passed before began to pop up in the wrong places.

Maybe it was just the exhaustion, or maybe it was something else entirely.

Through it all, that goddamn old lady behind me kept up her brisk pace, and so did I. I made myself move just a little slower, choose my paths more deliberately.

Near the end of it, my legs felt sore as if I'd been hiking all day. I was thirsty, hungry, and tired.

Every little group of benches or chairs I passed looked so inviting that I considered resting for just a moment. I only actually tried it once.

As soon as I sat down, I felt the air grow colder and saw the lights around me growing dim.

The first two times, it had frightened me. This time, it angered me.

From the corner of my eye, I saw the Hunter approaching, and I growled in frustration. Something deep, primal, and angry in me made me want to lash out at it. A far more rational part of my mind told me to run.

Despite my mind telling me to fight, I chose to run anyway.

When I finally heard the announcement, I can't tell you how tired I was.

"Attention shoppers," a voice said over the intercom, "the mall will be closing in one hour."

I wasn't sure how much longer I'd be able to keep moving. It had been ten hours at that point, but it felt like days.

At the sound of the announcement, I looked back towards the Hunter behind me. The old lady just continued her stoic march towards me, and I moved away from her with a renewed vigor.

Just a little bit further... a little bit further, then I could rest.

To win the Mall Game, you need to find a store. Preferably, a large one with a bed, although in theory, you could probably use any store.

Once you get there, you'll need to tell an employee that "You are invited," and no matter what they tell you or how much they plead, you must answer their every question with "Yes."

After that, they will take you to a safe place where you can sleep, and you can finally claim your prize.

Thoughts of Abigail filled my mind as I made my way to a local department store. It was large, and I knew they sold mattresses. It seemed like the ideal place to go for the final part of the game.

As I stepped inside, I looked back towards the Hunter behind me. It had kept up its steady pace, and though I'd been told I wouldn't have to worry about it for much longer, I was still worried.

They were still about forty feet back by the time I entered the store, and with the last of my energy, I made myself jog over to a nearby customer service counter.

The kid working there couldn't have been older than 16. He was tall and plain-looking with glasses and acne. He seemed a little annoyed that I'd come up to him.

"How can I help you?" he asked crossly.

"I am invited," I replied, my eyes meeting his and hoping desperately for a reaction.

He stared back at me and frowned before he nodded.

"Okay," he said. His voice was softer now. Understanding, even. He left the desk and headed further into the store, gesturing for me to follow.

I looked back; the old lady had followed me inside and still tailed me, although she seemed slower than before. She seemed to be watching me instead of hunting me now.

I let the young man lead me to the bedding department, where several mattresses waited. He stopped in front of one of them and looked back over at me. His expression was dour and uncertain.

"Are you sure about this?" he asked. "If you accept, you may not like what you find."

"Yes," I replied. I kept my tone even. The kid didn't seem to like that.

"I don't think you understand," he said. There was more urgency in his voice now. "Look... you won. That's obvious. Why don't you take the win and go? I really don't think this is worth it. Are you really going to accept the invitation?"

"Yes," I replied again, and I saw frustration rising in the boy's eyes.

"Why? What could be so important that you'd actually accept? Do you actually know how much danger you're in? Are you fucking stupid? Suicidal? What? If you do this, you may not come back anyway! Those 'prizes' have a price, and one day, they must be paid back! Are you really going to accept the invitation?"

"Yes," I replied again as I saw the boy's frustration turn into rage.

I wasn't offended by it. This was all part of what needed to be done. A final test of resolve before I could claim my prize. It was trivial compared to what I'd already been through.

"Fuck you! I hope you get ripped apart! What do you think is so important that you'd go this far? Money? Knowledge? Something else? It's not worth it!" His expression hardened.

"Abigail is dead, Michael."

The fact that he said my name sent a chill through me, and he knew he'd caught me off guard.

"Oh yeah. I know who you are, Michael Warren, and I know you're wasting your time. Why would you torture yourself by going down to see her? What do you think she'll say? Is this worth it, dipshit? Huh? Is it? Are you going to accept the invitation?!"

"Yes," I repeated.

"FUCK YOU!" Angry tears began to stream down the kid's face. "Don't do this. Please... Don't do this... Don't... You don't need to throw your life away. I'm telling you, you're going to die if you accept."

He grabbed me by the shoulders, his tearful eyes meeting mine. I stared back without emotion. This too was part of the test, and when all was said and done, the kid probably wouldn't even remember a word he'd said.

"Are you going to accept the invitation?" he asked one last time.

"Yes," I said.

He looked into my eyes, tears still flowing, before wiping them away.

"Fine..." the kid spat. "Fine... do what you must..."

With that, he pulled away from me and took off.

From the corner of my eye, I saw the old lady standing there. She was close enough that I should have felt a drop in temperature, but instead, she just stood still and watched me calmly. Her expression was stoic and impossible to read.

I stared back at her, and she let out a huff of approval.

"Decently played, I suppose," she said. Her voice was deeper than an old lady's should have been. There was a coldness to it.

I didn't reply. I didn't know how to, and I suspect I didn't need to.

Without a further word, the thing that looked like an old lady turned and walked away from me.

I was alone with the bed, and there was only one thing left to do.

My body was exhausted from the day. The bed was soft and welcoming when I lay down on it, and as the mall closed, I shut my eyes and drifted off into a dreamless sleep.

When I awoke, the world was quiet. The lights were off, but I could see a pinkish twilight shining through the windows of the department store.

As I sat up and got out of the bed, I noticed a stale smell in the air.

I knew that it had worked... I was in the other world.

I made note of the bed I'd been in before I approached the door of the department store. I didn't dare open it. Leaving the mall while in the other world would prevent me from ever returning home.

I saw a few idle cars waiting in the parking lot, and on the street beyond them, I thought I caught glimpses of dark figures moving about. I didn't try to look too closely at them.

The sky above looked to be an ominous pink. I stared up at it and felt as if it was staring back into me before I pulled away from the door and headed back towards the interior of the mall itself.

The whole place seemed to be in a state of disrepair. Broken glass and debris littered the floor. Food I passed in some of the aisles was spoiled, and silence enveloped the place like a cloud.

I could hear my footsteps echoing off the walls as I walked through the hallways of the mall and looked for a pathway down to the treasure I so desperately sought.

It didn't take me long to find it.

Over the past several hours, I had become very familiar with the layout of the mall. It was easy to tell when something was out of place, and the stairway on the ground level that inexplicably led downward was certainly out of place.

I approached it slowly, and I could see a dim red light shining from down below. It pulsated like a heartbeat.

I began my descent, unconsciously holding my breath as I did.

My footsteps echoed off the marble floor beneath me as I set foot down into the "lower level."

I'm not sure exactly what I expected to see down there. Another mall level wasn't it. In fact, what I found seemed mundane compared to what I was expecting.

I could see countless storefronts, most of them recognizable. The only catch was that they were empty.

Neon signs and posters advertised video games and movies. I spotted what looked like some sort of kiddie ride in one corner and some sort of "massage parlor" in the other.

This was what I'd come so far for? No… no, not quite.

The accounts I'd read of the Mall Game said that there were a few different prizes one could choose. The first was worldly possessions, and everything I saw before me certainly seemed to fit the bill.

While there were things that tempted me, shallow things like games, rides, and movies weren't what I had come so far for.

These prizes have a price, the kid had said before I'd slept. No doubt if I touched anything, I'd need to give it back at some point.

I looked straight ahead and began to walk again. In the distance, I could see another staircase leading down, and I jogged towards it before I began to descend again.

The next floor was more drastically different. This one only barely resembled the mall I'd been through. The layout was the same, but the "storefronts" were gone. In their place were alcoves filled with things that made me pause.

Great golden statues with jeweled bodies watched me like silent shopkeepers. I saw golden coins and ingots scattered about and piled up amongst the nooks where the stores once were. Jewels as large as my head were dotted amongst the gold: emeralds, rubies, sapphires, even diamonds.

Just one would be enough to see me set for life, and I caught myself approaching one of them before stopping.

I didn't let myself lay a hand on anything there. Like the kid said, there was a price, and as wonderful as those treasures were, I suspected it would be higher than I'd care to pay.

Besides, this treasure, marvelous as it was, wasn't what I had come for. If I took anything, I wouldn't be able to go deeper. I wouldn't be able to see Abigail again.

It took more restraint than I'd expected to pull myself away from some of the treasures I saw and look straight ahead again.

Sure enough, I could see another stairway in the distance, and I made myself go to it. I wanted to take one final glance at the treasures behind me… but didn't let myself. I just forced myself to go down the next set of stairs.

The fourth level was truly massive, larger than it appeared at first glance. It bore no resemblance to the mall above me and barely resembled any library that I'd ever seen. Massive shelves jam-packed with books seemed to span onward into infinity. As I passed them, I skimmed some of their titles, and many of them gave me pause. They promised secrets… truths about the universe that anyone would want to know. Are we alone? Why were we made? How did the Universe begin? How will it end?

If I were a weaker man, I would have given in to the temptation, but I'd already come so far. I could stand to go a little further.

As before, there was one final set of stairs up ahead, and I knew what was waiting for me beyond them.

I tore my gaze away from the books as I approached the stairs and began my final descent, and there... there I found myself on a city street.

The street was a familiar one I'd seen before. It stretched onward into the night, and when I looked up, I could see the stars above me. When I looked back, I could see stars.

This place made no sense. But after all I'd gone through, I can't say it surprised me much.

The street looked just as it had on that Halloween night, several years ago... the night that Abigail and I had taken that ghost walk around town. Our very first date.

"There must be someone very important to you if you've come all this way," a voice said, and I turned to address it.

The old woman who'd hunted me through the mall stood patiently before me. Her expression seemed a little softer than before.

"Yes..." I said. "Yes, she is very important."

The old woman cracked a knowing smile.

"Very well then. I'll leave you to it. But know that of each reward here, you may only have one. One luxury, one treasure, one secret, and one more hour with the one you've lost..."

My heart sank for a moment, but I nodded.

"I understand..." I said. The old woman nodded back at me before she took off down the street. I watched her go.

I didn't realize I'd been holding my breath until I heard her voice.

"Mikey?"

She was behind me. I knew that voice. I knew her.

Slowly, I turned to face her, and when I saw her standing on the sidewalk, dressed as she'd been the day she'd died, I broke.

Tears filled my eyes as I ran to her and scooped her up in my arms, holding her so tightly that I was sure I'd never let her go.

I felt Abigail's arms close around me in turn, and in that moment, I knew I was home.

I looked up at her and cupped her cheeks as I kissed her.

"Mikey, what are you doing here? Did you? No... you're not...?"

"I'm alive," I promised her. "I-I played the Mall Game a-and I won! I get to see you again..."

I saw her eyes widen for a moment. Disbelief, fear, and finally excitement crossed her face and culminated in that smile I loved so dearly.

That smile made everything worth it.

"You actually played the Mall Game?!" she asked. "Oh my God! You dumbass! You really did, didn't you?"

"I really did," I said. "I had to see you one more time... I... I had to say goodbye..."

She caressed my cheek, her smile fading slightly. She didn't speak. She didn't need to. I could see the tears welling up before she kissed me one last time.

We talked. For one last time, she and I sat at the place where we had begun, and we talked. Maybe it wasn't much... but it was enough for me.

I told her I loved her. I told her I was sorry... I told her that I didn't know what I'd do without her, and as I spoke, as I cried, she held me close.

"You're going to be all right," she promised me. "Death is... scary. But it's peaceful too. I'm okay. You don't need to worry about me. So just worry about you, all right, Mikey?"

She brushed my hair from my eyes.

"I know it's going to be hard, but when you get back up there, keep going. You've still got a life to live. Don't waste it. I'll be down here when you're done. I promise."

I almost laughed at that. She giggled a little bit, too.

"I just don't know if my life will ever be the same without you, though," I said. She shrugged.

"Who says that's a bad thing? Look. I... I know we didn't get to do everything we wanted to while I was up there. But that doesn't mean you should give up on it. It's okay if you need some time, but when you're ready, find someone. You deserve to be happy, Mikey, and I don't want you lingering on me. Like I said, I'll be here, and when we see each other again, I want to hear all about the things you did! Go out and live your life, baby. Do it for me."

Her cold hand closed over mine. I squeezed it affectionately.

"All right…" I promised. "When I'm ready, I will."

She kissed my cheek as she wrapped her other arm around me. We cuddled close as our time ran out.

In the distance, a clock chimed, and I looked up. Our hour had passed; we both knew it.

Abigail let go of my hand and stood up.

"You should go… I'll see you soon, I guess. Hopefully not too soon."

She forced a smile, and I did the same.

"Hopefully…" I replied. "Take care of yourself, okay?"

"I always do. You too, Mikey. You too."

She walked me to the stairwell. I gave her one last parting look, and she offered me a reassuring smile before she let go of my hand.

Part of me wanted to beg her to come with me… but I knew it wasn't possible. There was no undoing what was done. All I could do was live with it.

I began to ascend the stairs, tears still in my eyes.

At the top, I found the first floor of the mall. Not the library.

I looked back down towards the stairs only to see that they were gone. There was only a plain tile floor behind me.

Tears streamed down my cheeks, but I still found it in myself to smile. Whatever price I'd have to pay one day, it would be worth it for that one moment I'd gotten. It wasn't enough. It would never be enough. But it was better than what I'd had.

I returned to the department store where the bed waited for me and lay down once more. I wiped the tears away one last time before I drifted back off to sleep…

When I awoke again, the mall was opening for the next day.

As the doors unlocked, I stepped out of them and looked up into a familiar blue sky. The cool air was crisp in my lungs as I walked away from the mall.

My grief still felt heavy in my soul, but the burden felt a little lighter.

As I left the mall behind, I walked towards an uncertain future. I didn't know what lay ahead of me, but for the first time since Abigail died, I felt hopeful, and I knew that one day, I would be all right again.

YOURBRITTANY

"What the fuck is wrong with you, Brittany? I thought we were friends?"

That was the voicemail I woke up to.

"*You're fucking sick, okay? Fucking sick! I don't know what the hell your problem is, or what's going on with you, and I don't want to know! Fuck you, you sick, homewrecking whore!*"

The recording ended, and I sat on the side of my bed, wondering what the hell had just happened.

When I'd gone to bed, Michelle and I had been friends! I'd gone out to dinner with her and her boyfriend, Rick, just a few days ago, and everything had been fine then! I didn't know what had changed!

I tried calling her back, of course, but I couldn't get through. She'd probably blocked my number. She certainly seemed to have me blocked on every other kind of social media! Facebook, Instagram, *and* Twitter.

I'd messaged a few of our mutual friends, but most of them either didn't respond to me or had also blocked me.

What the hell had just happened? What the hell had I done? Why were people suddenly refusing to even talk to me? It didn't make any sense!

'*Fuck you, you sick, homewrecking whore!*'

Homewrecking? Did Michelle think that I'd done something with Rick? She couldn't possibly believe that, could she? I wasn't exactly open about how much I hated Rick, but it wasn't much of a secret either. I'd always known that Michelle could do better than him. I mean, seriously, she worked as a paralegal. He worked for some no-name mobile game developer that published the kinds of disgusting low-brow 'games' you see advertised all over the internet. He was twenty-seven and looked forty-five. He had a forehead that took up most of his face and overly red skin that looked to be covered in grease. You couldn't have a conversation with the man without him either talking about his NFTs or pushing whatever crap game his company had recently launched (such gems as *Fart Cloud Massacre* and something called *Love Match* that advertised itself as some puzzle/makeover game but was *literally just Bejeweled with a different fucking color scheme!*)

I had literally no idea why Michelle ever bothered with him, and I had no idea why she seemed to think I'd done anything with him!

But since nobody else seemed to want to give me any answers as to what the hell was happening, Rick was starting to look like the best person to contact.

If I'd supposedly done something with him, then maybe he'd know what it was.

So I bit the bullet, swallowed my pride, and sent him a message on Facebook.

"Hey, what happened between you and Michelle? She's pissed at me! What did I do?"

Unsurprisingly, it didn't take him all that long to respond.

"Hey, Brittany! Sorry about that... she's pissed because she found some of your videos on my laptop. Shouldn't have let her borrow it! Love your stuff, though..."

My videos?

What the hell was he talking about? My mind immediately searched for something that I might have filmed with Michelle at some point. Our high school graduation, maybe? There weren't a lot of videos of me out there. I've never really liked being on camera. Why would Rick even have videos of me on his computer anyway, and why would Michelle be mad at *me* about it? Maybe this was a case of mistaken identity? Although, how many other Brittanys could she possibly know?

While I sat in bed, mulling all of this over and still trying to wake up, I got another message from Rick.

"Hey, since we're talking... I wanted to know if you did custom requests! I was looking for some more specialized fetish content. Like... I wanted to

purchase a video of you pooping, but like... more. Doing stuff with it. Would you be open to that?"

I stared at the screen, reading over the words that Rick had just sent me and trying to make sense of them. For a moment, it was almost like I was reading something in another language entirely. I hadn't had my coffee yet, so my brain was not working at full capacity.

Custom requests...

A video of me pooping...

'More...'

Slowly, every little bit of the meaning behind the message I'd just read clicked into place. As I read it again and again, I was forced to accept that I had in fact read what I'd just read.

What the actual fuck?

"*EXCUSE ME?*" I messaged back, and I really don't think that those two words fully encapsulated the barrage of complicated emotions that his message had incited in me.

"*It's cool if you don't!*" Rick said. "*I know you don't really interact with fans but like... I like your stuff. It's kinda intimate, you know?*"

No! No, I didn't know!

"*What videos?!*" I demanded, before shaking my head and just pulling him into a call.

Rick took a while to answer, and for a moment, I was almost afraid that he wasn't going to. But after a few minutes, I heard him pick up.

"What videos?" I asked. "Rick, what the *fuck* are you talking about? Is this some kind of fucking joke?"

"N-no!" he said. "I swear it's not! I thought... the videos, on YourBrittany! That's what I was talking about!"

"What the hell is YourBrittany?"

"It's... it's... you know, it's..." His voice was faltering, as if he was slowly piecing something together. He trailed off, going silent.

"Rick?" I asked. "Rick, what the hell is YourBrittany?"

He didn't answer, not at first, and his silence just made me all the more uneasy.

"Can we meet?" he asked. His voice sounded a little different than before. Smaller, almost shaken. It did absolutely nothing to put me at ease.

"I-I swear to God it's not for anything weird! I swear to fucking God! But... shit... shit... shit... I think you need to see this..."

I could feel my heart beating faster and faster in my chest.

"See what?" I asked, already dreading the answer.

Half an hour later, I was pulling into Rick and Michelle's driveway. She wasn't home, and I wasn't particularly thrilled by the prospect of showing up at their house while she was away after she'd accused me of having some kind of fling with her boyfriend. However, he'd insisted that I go there, and I didn't have a whole lot of other options.

I'd brought a can of pepper spray from my apartment, just in case this somehow went south. When I went to knock on the door, I found it unlocked.

Rick was in the kitchen on his laptop, looking a hell of a lot paler than usual, and when he saw me, his grave expression didn't do much to calm my nerves.

"Rick, what the hell is going on?" I asked. I wasn't really in the mood for formalities at the moment.

"It's... it's better if you see for yourself," he said quietly, before turning the laptop to face me.

I was greeted by a website with my face all over it.

There were photographs of me that I'd taken in various places. Most of them had probably been ripped right off of social media. At the top of the website was a header that read:

Welcome to YourBrittany! The object of your secret admirations!

"What the fuck?" I said under my breath as I scrolled through the site. On the left side was a short blurb that I read through.

'Hi! My name is Brittany Murphy, and I love the feeling of being watched! So here at YourBrittany, I want to share all of my private moments with you! With a membership, you can watch me anywhere, anytime, doing anything, and you can purchase my highlight videos to enjoy at your leisure! Nothing is off limits, I'm your naughty domestic girl and I'm ready to put on a show for you!'

"What the hell is this?" I asked as I scrolled through some of the highlight videos that were available. Just the names of them turned my stomach...

Shower fun!
Shitting in the morning!
Private time with my vibe <3
Shower pee!
Bedtime for Brittany!

The thumbnails all displayed different vantage points from inside my house. My bedroom, my shower... from inside of my fucking toilet!

I looked over at Rick in disbelief. He couldn't even make eye contact with me. Up until recently, I didn't think that this guy was capable of shame, but he was proving me very, very wrong.

"I... I found it a while ago," he stammered. "I saw one of your videos on a site I like and I... I didn't know! I thought you were making this!"

"You thought I was making *this?!*" I asked.

"It's got your name and face all over it! It says it's you! So yeah, I thought you were making it!" he said. "I figured it was like an OnlyFans or something... I mean, the money had to be good! The subscription isn't exactly cheap!"

"So you thought I put *a camera in my toilet* for money?" I demanded, in complete and utter disbelief.

"Look, there's good money in weird porn," he commented. "And I'm not exactly in a position to fucking judge, am I?"

"You knew about this and never said anything to me?" I asked. "You didn't say anything to Michelle?!"

"How exactly was I supposed to tell either of you that I found your secret porn site!" he asked. "I mean, it's not exactly *normal* porn! I didn't want to call you out!"

I just shook my head and tried to move on from the subject.

"How long has this site been active?" I asked.

"About a year," he said. "I've only known about it for a few months, though."

I scrolled a little further before I couldn't do it anymore. With trembling hands, I closed the laptop.

A year...

A whole year of my life, broadcast to strangers as... as fucking porn...

I kept trying to wrap my mind around it, kept trying to make sense of it. Part of me wanted to break down laughing at the sheer *stupidity* of this entire situation. But the other part felt eyes on me at that very moment. My skin felt like it was crawling. I felt like I wanted to bury myself in a little hole and just stop existing.

Who else in my life knew about this? Who else did I know that had been watching me in the shower? Watching me in the bathroom? Watching me sleep?

How many people had been watching?

How many people had recognized me? How many people had tried to find me?

"Brittany?" Rick asked, though I barely heard him. My breathing was getting heavier. My chest felt tight, as if something were crushing me. I could feel myself starting to cry.

Rick just sat quietly beside me, unsure what to say for a while before finally choosing something.

"We should call the police," he said. "You're renting, right? You should give them the name of your landlord... maybe he's the one who..."

My landlord?

I felt a fresh stab of panic in my chest. My landlords were a middle-aged couple who lived across town. I'd been renting from them for about three years and couldn't imagine them having set any of this up, although who else would have had access to the house?

After another moment of hesitation, Rick got up. He took out his phone, but I stopped him.

"N-no... don't call," I said. "I want to go there in person."

He paused before nodding.

I think he could see in my eyes just how scared I was at that moment. Just how *violated* I felt. And even though in a sense, he'd been one of those violators, in that moment, he felt like the only person I could trust. I still hated him. But he at least seemed to understand the horror that I felt, and I wondered if he shared it in his own way.

I believed him when he said he'd only... indulged in those videos when he'd thought that I'd been the one producing them. At least in the scenario he envisioned, there was some measure of consent there. Some belief that I'd *chosen* to share those videos as opposed to having the choice made for me.

"Let's go to the police then," he said, before picking up his laptop and getting ready to leave.

We didn't speak during the entire ride over to the police station.

I don't actually remember much of the ride over. I just kept thinking about my house, trying to imagine where the cameras might have been. I would have thought I'd have noticed some hidden cameras! I would have thought I'd have seen them at some point!

Wouldn't I?

At the station, Rick showed the police the website, and I gave my statement. I don't know what I expected them to do... I don't know what I'd hoped for them to do.

Time passed in a blur, and I don't remember most of what happened at the police station. For the most part, it's because I stayed in one of their interview rooms, sitting quietly and waiting for time to pass. They said they'd send some officers to my home, although while those officers were doing their investigation, there wasn't much for me to do.

Rick had stayed with me for the first hour or so, ultimately leaving when it was time for work. He'd offered to stay longer, but I'd told him that it was fine.

A couple of hours later, a detective walked into the room with me, a fairly grave expression on his face. I could see the collection of wires gripped in his hand, along with the small camera hanging off the end. It had been painted to match the wall, making it easy to miss.

He spoke to me like a friend, making small talk and introducing himself. Unfortunately, most of it just went in one ear and out the other. Just because he spoke like nothing was wrong didn't mean that nothing was wrong. My eyes remained fixated on the camera he'd set on the table in front of me, and the longer I stared at it, the deeper the dread in my chest seemed to sink.

"This was one of the ones from your bedroom," he said, as he noticed me staring down at the camera. "We found others in the bathroom, kitchen, living room... just about every other room in the house. We've still got a couple of officers there looking to make sure we got them all."

I stared down at the camera, feeling hollow inside and unsure what to even say. The blank lens looked right at me, and even though the camera should have been off, I still felt watched.

"T-take it away, please..." I said.

The detective just gave a curt nod before pushing it off to the side. He was kind enough to move the lens so that it wasn't facing me.

"We've spoken to the owners of the property and will be questioning them shortly," he said. "We're also looking into our options regarding taking the website and the video content down, although I can't promise you any immediate or lasting results. We don't have any way to gauge how often these videos have been downloaded or where else they may have been uploaded."

I looked up at him, a fresh wave of horror washing over me.

"It could have been uploaded elsewhere?" I asked, my voice quaking a little bit.

"Your friend, Rick Wilson. He indicated that he'd first discovered the content on another website when we spoke to him. We asked him to provide the relevant links so that you can contact those websites to request a takedown."

I could feel my entire body trembling again. My chest felt tight. Breathing felt difficult. I felt myself finally starting to fully break down. The panic attack hit me like a train, and there was nothing I could do to stop it as I started to cry.

I tried to sleep in a hotel that night, although really, I only barely slept at all. I kept getting up to inspect the corners of the room and check the bathroom up and down.

I didn't find any cameras... but I hadn't found them before, so why would I start finding them now?

Over the next few days, the police cleared my landlords of any charges. They determined that they weren't the ones who'd installed the cameras, although that wasn't much of a comfort to me.

I told them I wasn't going back to the house, and they let me out of my lease without argument. Not even a week later, the house was for sale.

YourBrittany was taken down the day after I'd talked to Rick, although I know that it wasn't the police who did it. Without its star, the show couldn't go on.

Again, that wasn't much of a comfort to me.

My life was already ruined.
There was no going back.

I've moved out of the state and started a new life.

I've changed my name, shaved my hair, and gotten some tattoos. Anything I can do to make myself unrecognizable. But it isn't enough.

I still look for the cameras everywhere I go.

I'm still waiting to find another video of me online.

That's why I've hired you.

They say that you're the best... that you can do anything.

Anything.

It's been a few years since YourBrittany went down, but I guess if anyone could find out who put it up, it's you.

I've saved up every penny I have, and it's all yours. All of it.

I just want to know it's over.

I just want to know that whoever did this to me is dead, and I don't care how they die. Do it however you want.

I just want to feel safe again.

ED

It's been ages since I've talked about the man I'll call Patrick Hearst.

I've been a therapist for almost twenty years, and I've dealt with a lot of troubled people in my time. I don't judge; everyone has their issues. But Patrick was a unique case.

Let me make it clear that I don't make a habit of talking about my patients. It's a violation of both patient confidentiality and the trust they put in me as their doctor. I know that in Patrick's case, he wouldn't mind. But if anyone found out I was doing this, I could lose my license. For that reason, I'll refrain from identifying myself. I'd also like to note that the name "Patrick Hearst" is an alias. Don't try to look him up. Chances are you won't find him.

Patrick's problem wasn't all that unusual. The root of it was medical, as these things often are, so there wasn't much I could do to address the cause. Instead, my job was to help him deal with the effect it had on his mind and self-image. That was why I'd been assigned to his case.

Patrick was a gruff man in his mid-thirties. He was tall with stubble and had a build like a LEGO man—not overweight, but with a heavy build and thick, muscular limbs. He was unmarried, smoked and drank often, and was the middle child in a household of three brothers. His family was all blue-collar, and Patrick was no different. I won't say where he worked; that might disclose too much. But I will say that it was at a warehouse, and that was where the accident occurred.

Patrick would tell me the details during our second session together. Six years before he started seeing me, he'd been moving a skid for storage. Apparently, in the aisle beside him, a forklift had been driving. Supposedly, the driver was drunk and had been a little reckless. He'd grazed one of the large shelves that some of the packed skids were stored on and knocked out the support. The shelf had collapsed, and Patrick had been under it when it did. Before he even knew what had happened, he'd been buried alive under falling boxes and pallets and stayed there, crushed under their weight and screaming for help for hours until they finally managed to dig him out and send him to the hospital.

He'd broken several bones, and it apparently took him months to recover. It was a miracle that he'd survived at all, but he didn't get out of his ordeal unscathed, and that was why he'd come to me.

It wasn't the claustrophobia that got to him. Patrick considered himself tough. He shook that off like a bad hangover. Something told me that he'd been through his fair share of shit in the past, and this would have been just another lump in a life full of them. But his accident had left scars, the most prominent of which was between his legs.

I won't mince words here; it's better if I don't. After the accident, Patrick couldn't get an erection. He hadn't had one since, and that was why he came to me. Something had hit him when all of those boxes and pallets had fallen on him and caused enough damage that his penis no longer worked. For a man like Patrick, that was unacceptable.

I'm sure it sounds funny when you think of it upfront. *Ha ha. His dick doesn't work. That's hilarious!* But think of it from another angle. One accident, and you'll never reproduce, you'll never feel sexual pleasure again, and worst of all, you'll feel like some part of you is missing. You've lost a part of your manhood, and you'll never get it back. Imagine living like that, only seeing yourself as a broken man.

Imagine spending years like that.

That was the state Patrick came to me in.

The loss of his manhood was something that weighed on him. Masculinity had defined him for all of his life. With that suddenly gone, what was left?

He told me that he'd tried everything he could think of. Medication didn't work, and his efforts to make do anyway had failed. He was attractive enough to charm a few women into his bed and to attempt a relationship, but the fact that he'd been unable to satisfy them was ultimately what killed it. His impotence had led to alcohol abuse and had caused him to be arrested twice already. It was after the second arrest that we first met.

The man who came into my office was fidgety and clearly uncomfortable. When I offered him a seat, he hesitated before taking it.

Our session wasn't all that productive. We talked, and I took notes, profiling him and trying to understand him better. He didn't mention his injury until near the end of our first session, and when he brought it up, I knew from the tone in his voice that he blamed it for all of his problems.

"Everything keeps on getting worse and fucking worse..." he'd said. "I can't be with anyone. I can't do jack shit. I hate it. I'm stuck here, feeling like I'm barely even a man anymore! Nobody'll fuckin' say it to my face, but I know they're laughing at me. Even Chuck, that motherfucker who was driving the forklift. He thinks it's a goddamn hoot."

"Is he a coworker of yours?"

"Yeah... forklift driver," he murmured. "Real asshole..." He folded his arms and glanced at the clock on the wall.

"Is my time up yet?"

"Yes, Patrick. Your time is up. I think we're off to a good start. I'll tell you what. Why don't you come in again next week, and we'll talk more about the accident."

"Why? So you can fuckin' laugh at me too?"

"I'm not here to laugh at you, Patrick," I said. "I'm here to help you get things back on track."

He stared at me, a little mistrustfully, before sighing.

"Fine... I'll talk to the lady out front," he murmured and lumbered outside to book his next appointment.

When he came back, we picked up where we'd left off.

He recounted the accident and went on about how Chuck had treated him afterward.

"That motherfucker nearly killed me!" he growled. "But he doesn't give a shit. He tells the supervisor that it was an 'accident.' So they play back the footage, and you can see him swerve on it! Hell, I could smell the fucking liquor on him that day! They just nodded their heads, shrugged, and agreed it was an accident, though. They didn't give a shit. Chuck's been there too goddamn long, and they all know him. Nobody wants to fire him."

"That sounds very unfair," I said.

"No shit, it's unfair! Now he just fucking laughs at me, like this wasn't his goddamn fault! Thinks it's so fucking funny... I can't have a fucking normal life now! I can't... I can't be a fucking man in the bedroom! The last girl I was with, Lana, was there for three weeks before she left. Three weeks! I'm lucky if they stick around that long."

"Why did she leave?" I asked. Patrick just scoffed.

"Why the fuck do you think? She said it was the drinking... but I saw that bitch match me drink for drink. No... She left because I couldn't fuck her like a man. She kept asking me what she could do, and I just didn't have a fucking answer for her. It just doesn't work, and I knew it bothered her."

"There are plenty of people out there who aren't interested in sex," I said. "Maybe you need a relationship where the foundation isn't based on that."

"And what, date some cold femnazi?" he scoffed. "I don't think I'd get along with someone like that..."

"You can't just dismiss all asexual partners as 'cold,'" I said. "Some people just don't feel sexual arousal."

"It's not about whether or not I wanna fuck!" Patrick said. "Trust me. I wanna fuck. I just... I can't. I'm sick and fucking tired of it! I'm tired of it! I'm tired of being broken! I'm not supposed to be like this! I'm supposed to be a Man!"

I don't think he realized he'd started screaming at me until his voice hit a pitch, and he paused, going quiet.

"Sorry... It's just... Sorry..." He avoided eye contact, and I waited for him to calm down and keep talking. He looked at the clock, hoping that his time would be up. He still had almost fifteen minutes, but just looking at him, I knew he wouldn't stay.

"I think I'm done for today," he murmured and got up.

"If you'd like to go, you can go," I said. "Just talk to Katelynn out front to book a new appointment."

"Yeah, sure," he murmured before shuffling out the door.

For six months, I saw Patrick, and most of my other sessions with him turned out the same. He shot down most of my suggestions and would grow angrier the more he talked about his own impotence. Truth be told, there wasn't much that I felt I could do to help him. He just seemed so determined to be miserable and helpless. When he eventually stopped booking his appointments, I wasn't surprised, and I thought that maybe that would be the end of it. He wasn't the first person to give up on therapy when they didn't get the results they wanted, and I knew he wouldn't be the last.

What I didn't expect was the call I got about two months after Patrick had stopped seeing me. I was in my office at the time, waiting for another appointment, when Katelynn, my secretary, patched him through to my line. Patrick sounded like he hadn't slept in days. His voice was hoarse, and I barely even recognized him.

"Doc..." he murmured, "it's Patrick Hearst here. I was coming to your office up until a few months ago."

"Hi, Patrick. I didn't forget about you. Don't worry," I said. "What can I help you with?"

"I'm not doing so great," he murmured. "I don't know who else to turn to. I don't have a lot of people left..." He trailed off, as if struggling with what he was about to say.

"I'm at a police station right now. I was... I was arrested. I don't have a lawyer, and I dunno what to tell these people, and I'm fucking scared, man!"

I listened to his every word. His fear was obvious, even without him saying it. Worse than that, though, he sounded shaken.

"What would you like me to do?" I asked.

"If you come down... maybe they'll let you talk to me. I don't know what I should say to anyone else. I thought—I was hoping that you might know what to do."

"If you'd like, I can come down to the station tonight," I said. I wasn't about to leave my upcoming appointment, but I knew I couldn't just abandon Patrick either. In his darkest hour, he'd turned to me. It would be wrong to refuse his call.

I headed down to the police station he'd told me he was at after my appointment. By the time I got there, the cops had already discussed whether or not to let me in to see him. The decision had been "yes," but I recall the officer who led me to him mentioning that this was a little unconventional.

"Can't say I've ever heard of someone asking to talk to a shrink they haven't seen in months," he said to me. "But whatever. I can't say if there's a precedent for it, and it's hardly my problem, I guess. It is what it is."

"He sounded upset when I spoke to him," I said. "He didn't say what he was charged with. May I ask what exactly happened?"

The officer paused before deciding that there was no harm in telling me.

"Seems he's a bit of a firebug," he said. "About a week back, his apartment burned down. A lot of people died in there. It didn't look like arson, but someone caught him trying to set fire to the motel he was staying in after the fire. We're looking more into the case now, trying to see if there's anything else we can tie him to."

A firebug? I'd never gotten that vibe from Patrick. Then again, I could hardly say I was a close friend. There were easily things he could have never told me.

The officer unlocked the door to the interrogation cell where Patrick was waiting for me.

"You've got thirty minutes," he said. "Hope he makes it worth it."

"So do I," I replied as the officer let me in.

Patrick looked like he hadn't slept in weeks. He was fidgeting more than usual and looked up at me with big, dark circles under his eyes.

"Doctor..." he said, sounding utterly broken. "You really came!"

"Hi, Patrick," I replied as I pulled up a seat across from him. "Looks like you're not doing so great."

"Shit, you could say that again..." he scoffed. "What did they tell you?"

"That you're suspected of starting a few fires, that's all."

"Fires? Fuck, it's worse than that. People are dead, Doc! I don't know what to do!"

"You can start by telling me what happened," I said. I reached into my pocket and took out a tape recorder. I made a habit of recording most of my sessions for my own personal notes. Of course, they'd never see the light of day, but it was nice to be able to go back over them to better understand my patients.

Patrick looked down at the tape recorder, already knowing both what it was and why it was there. He waited for me to start it up before he spoke again.

I've transcribed most of what he said here, although I will note that there were some modifications made to the transcript. These were done to protect Patrick's anonymity as well as my own. The transcript reads as follows:

"Still recording, huh, Doc? Old habits die hard, I guess. This... whole thing's been fucked, ever since it started. I'm scared! I'm really fucking scared, because I don't know what I've gone and got myself into!"

It's at this point that I ask Patrick what exactly happened. He pauses for a moment before officially starting his story.

"Right... Right... It mostly started after I stopped seeing you, actually. No hard feelings, right? I'm sure you're a great doctor, but nothin' you said was really for me. Still, it did get me thinking. I mean, my little injury is the source of half my problems, right? So I started thinking that maybe there was some way to fix that.

I talked to my doctor again, and he just told me I was good and fucked. He said there's no fix, and so I figured I'd talk to someone else. I asked around a bit and tried a few different things. This one guy I spoke to told me about some herbal shit I could try. It ended up being a bunch of hippie nonsense, but I still tried it. I ended up repeating a lot of things that already didn't work, and I was running out of hope. I started getting kinda low and... well... I thought about maybe taking that gun from my nightstand and putting it in my mouth. Might as well, right? Why even live if I'm forced to continue through life as half a man?"

Patrick chuckles nervously.

"Still, I kept looking into hippie stuff because I was really fucking desperate. I start talking to some real whack jobs and asking what they thought might work, and I come across this one lady. Ginseng. Dunno if that was her real name, but that was what she called herself. She starts hitting me with all sorts of herbs and crystals and shit. None of it worked, so she told me that I need a 'more powerful magic.' Sounds like a real crock of shit, right? But whatever. I figured I'd give it a go. Not like I had much to lose...

Anyway, Ginseng introduces me to this guy named Alistair. Skinny goth-looking bastard. He starts talking to me about revitalizing my spirit and whatnot, and I figured he was batshit crazy. But again, not like I had anything left to lose. He tells me to meet him at his house in a couple of nights, and I do it. I didn't know what to expect, and I figured he was probably gonna wave a magic fucking crystal over my dick and hope that was just the sorta fucked-up spirit viagra that I needed. I didn't have high hopes.

Still, I went, and when I got there, he took me up to his guest bedroom. He had arranged some candles and placed a big mirror in the corner of the room. He tells me to undress and lay on the bed, because he's gonna summon a succubus. Yeah. You heard me right. A fucking succubus. I almost turned around and left, but he told me that he'd seen this work before. See... according to Alistair, a succubus has an unnatural power over men. If you use the right ritual, you can summon one through a mirror. He told me that it was the best fuck of his life, and that if a succubus can't fix me, nothing can. I really shouldn't have believed him, but there was something in the way he said it...

This guy believed his own bullshit. He would've put money down on that, and I hadn't exactly paid him anything yet. I thought it over and figured it was worth a shot. So I took my clothes off and let Alistair show me the ritual. We performed it together. Foreign chants and lighting the candles in a certain order. Stuff like that. Then, when it was done, he left, and I lay down on the bed with nothing but the candlelight there.

While I was lying there, I heard someone moving. At first, I thought that Alistair had come back, but then I saw her... Jesus, Doc... She was something else. Tall with long dark hair, wide hips, perfect tits. She could've been a supermodel or an actress. She was the most beautiful woman I'd ever seen in my life!

She gave me this smile, and I could feel my heart racing in my chest.

She knew my name, Doc. She knew what I wanted, and most importantly, she fixed my fucking issue. Let me tell you, everything Alistair promised me... she delivered, and then some. I felt like a man again! Just the feeling of her beneath me, screaming and crying out in pleasure... It was amazing! Then it was over...

I went home, still feeling like a million bucks. But it wasn't all that long until I realized that my problem still wasn't fixed... See, while She was there, I was the fucking man! But as soon as she was gone, I was just me again. A broken man with a broken cock... and now that I knew what it felt like to be a real man again, I didn't want to go back!

It took me a while to recreate the ritual properly. My pronunciation was a little off, and I damn near had to beg Alistair to help me. He told me not to fuck around with it. Fed me some sob story about a guy who tried to make a deal with a succubus to cure his cancer and tried to cheat it. Apparently, it didn't end too well for him. Thing is, I wasn't looking to cure cancer. I just wanted to fuck, and I told Alistair that he'd either help me, or I'd beat the holy hell out of him. That was enough to make him agree.

He showed me how to do the ritual again, and when I got home, I tried it. Just like I'd hoped, she came again. The same girl, and the second time was just as good!

After that, whenever I needed to see her, I'd summon her. Every time, she came and we'd fuck like there was no tomorrow. Just the feeling of her hand on my shoulder was enough to get me hard. God, she was something else...

That's why I wanted to keep her, Doc.

See, after every meet-up we had, I'd always doze off. When I woke up, she'd be gone. That bothered me. I asked Alistair about that, and he said that all Demons and Fae returned to where they came unless they were bound to this Earth. I think you see where this is going, don't you?

With a little bit of 'persuasion,' Alistair showed me how to bind. He kept bitching and moaning about how I shouldn't do it. But the thing is, I just didn't give a damn. That girl, succubus or not, gave me back what I'd lost. She fixed me! She made me into a man again. I couldn't let that go.

So when I summoned her next, I did what Alistair told me to do. I surrounded the room with salt and kept a hammer nearby to shatter the mirror so she couldn't escape. When I summoned her this time, I watched as she appeared out of the mirror. When she came towards me, I saw the look on her face change. She watched me and started screaming as I got out of bed and destroyed the mirror.

'What have you done?' she asked. 'What is this?'

I told her exactly what I just told you. I was tired of being broken. I was tired of being just half a man, and I wasn't going back! I told her that she was mine now, that she always would be! Then, I took her to bed. This time, she fought. But she still was able to get me going..."

Patrick pauses here; I suspect he noticed a certain look on my face at this point in the audio.

"What? Don't you dare fuckin' judge me! You didn't have to go through what I went through! Besides... she was a succubus. She was basically the equivalent of a Demon whore. You can't tell me that she didn't like it. That's what she was made to do, after all!

When I was done, I removed the mirror pieces and kept her in that room, just in case. I slept in another room because she kept threatening to kill me. But the salt across the door meant that she couldn't get out. I was planning to take the next day off work and spend it with her. I figured that maybe she'd calm down after a little while. Sure, she had some fight in her, and maybe she was a little pissy that I'd trapped her. But she'd get over it. See, I'm a good guy. All the other girls I dated thought so. I figured she would too. She seemed to be close enough to human, at least.

During the night, though, I woke up to the sound of the smoke alarm and the smell of something burning. By the time I made it to the bedroom, she'd already set the bed alight and was standing buck naked in front of it, glaring at me.

'You thought you could hold me?' she asked. 'I cannot be held. Not by you.'

The fire was already spreading, but I didn't know what to do! I didn't have an extinguisher, and the fire was already spreading! You never realize how quickly a fire spreads until you see it.

I panicked. I started running and got the fuck out of that building. I was one of the first ones out, and I watched from the street as the flames spread from my apartment and outward.

Most of the people made it out. Some didn't. I think they said it was 32. Mostly those on the top floors. The smoke got them.

I was there when the fire trucks and the cops came. I watched them treating people and pulling others out. I remember as the flames got really bad, I saw her in the lobby. She was standing there in the thick black smoke, naked and calm as ever. She looked right at me with the angriest eyes I've ever seen, then turned and walked back into the smoke. Nobody even fucking noticed her. But I knew she was telling me that she wasn't done. No, I'd gone and I'd pissed her off.

I went to the motel after that and tried to keep my shit together. I already had the next day off, so I used it to get my bearings and then went back to work like I was supposed to. Aside from the fact that I didn't have anywhere to fuckin' live now, things were quiet. I was spooked, but nothing really happened.

Then, a few nights later, I woke up at the motel and she was standing over me. I looked up at her, and I dunno what to say. But I felt my heart fucking racing. She climbed on top of me and held me down. She looked me in the eye and pressed her hands down onto the pillow, one on each side of my head. I could feel it heating up, and I realized that she was gonna set the whole fucking thing alight! I started squirming and fighting, trying to push her off of me. She was a hell of a lot stronger than she looked, though. I felt the pillow combust the instant I finally got free. I wiggled out from under her, and I could hear her laughing.

I looked back, and there she was. Lying on the bed as it started to burn and fucking mocking me! I watched as the flames swallowed her up, and I ran. I grabbed my keys, got in my truck, and got the fuck out of there! I was sitting in a parking lot a few miles away, trying to figure out what to do when the cops found me. Someone else had noticed the fire and saw me getting the hell out of Dodge. After that, they put me here and started building a fucking case on my ass... I thought about trying to tell them. But when I think it over in my head, it just sounds so fucking stupid. They wouldn't believe it. They'd think I was crazy or making it all up! You don't, though, do you, Doc? You know I'm not crazy, right? Right!"

As he finished his story, Patrick looked at me with wild eyes. His recollection had been a bizarre one for sure. A succubus, the occult—this was almost too crazy to believe. But the conviction with which he told me all of this was hard to ignore. I'd dealt with my fair share of liars in my profession: people who pathologically couldn't help themselves, people who were so insecure that they needed to hide behind something, and even people who were full-on delusional. This could have been the latter, but it didn't feel like it.

"Please... believe me..." he pleaded. "I dunno if anyone else will, and I dunno what to tell these cops. I didn't start those fires, though. It was her!"

I went over his story again in my head and looked down at my tape recorder. No matter how sure he'd been, this all seemed like too much to believe. After some thought, I turned the recorder off.

"Patrick, I understand you believe that the fires were started by something otherworldly. But you have to understand how all of this sounds."

"I do fucking understand it!" Patrick snapped. "I told you, nobody else would fucking believe me! But you should! I don't know what to do here! I dunno how to make them understand that it wasn't me!"

"Well, the obvious question is, do you have any proof?" I asked.

"Proof?! She burned up all the fucking proof! That's what she does!"

"What about Alistair?" I asked, and that gave him pause.

"W-what? Yes! Alistair! He'll know! He told me everything! Shit, we can get him! We can talk to him, right?"

"I suppose. Let's say I humor you and look for him. Where would I find him?" I asked.

Patrick seemed to barely be able to contain his excitement as he rambled off an address.

"Go get Alistair!" he said. "He'll explain everything! He can back me up! I know he can!" He was grinning wide from ear to ear, his hope newly restored, although I still had my doubts about his story.

I left him soon after and went home for the night. I listened to my recording of his story again. It sounded no more believable the second time I heard it, but at the end of the day, I had to follow up on what he said about Alistair.

The next day, I called Katelynn to reschedule my morning appointments and took a drive down to the address that Patrick had given me. It was a run-down shop just outside of the city, in a little town just off the highway.

The sign out front said: *Nightblooms Metaphysical Shop*.

I glanced at it and at the display of crystals in the window before I went inside. The shop was a fairly dreary building, but I spotted a young woman behind the counter. She looked to be in her early thirties and had long black hair. She wore a simple black dress that was tight in all the right places. She only glanced at me before returning her attention to the TV she was watching. I could see the local news on the screen, but I couldn't tell what the story was.

"Excuse me," I asked. "Do you know where I can find Alistair?"

She raised an eyebrow and looked back at me.

"He's not in right now. I'm not sure where he is, actually. But maybe I can help you." She tipped me a small, seductive smile.

"I just wanted to ask a few questions," I said. "You wouldn't happen to have met a man named Patrick Hearst, would you?"

I could see the recognition in her eyes, and her smile grew a little.

"He stopped by once or twice," she said softly. "I heard he was in jail."

"He is, and he told me a pretty interesting story about how he ended up in there."

She leaned against the counter.

"Do tell!" she said wryly. "Something about demons and all that?"

"Yes, actually."

"Not sure what I can tell you," she shrugged. "One of Alistair's friends brought him in. I only spoke to him a few times. He seemed to believe some really crazy shit, though. I think he said he was trying to summon a demon or something like that. Wouldn't be the first time. Alistair knows a fair bit about that kind of thing."

"Do you know if any of it worked?"

"I really can't say. I did tell him not to mess around with that kinda shit, though. Look where it got him."

She gestured to the TV screen, and I looked to see an image of the police station I'd been in the other night. She turned up the volume and cracked a knowing smile as the news anchor spoke.

"*...Thankfully, all of the staff was able to make it out without any major injuries, although a man in the holding cell was pronounced dead at the scene. Officers have stated that they suspect he started the fire in an attempt to escape.*"

"Shame..." she said with a wistful sigh. I saw her take a box of cigarettes out from under the counter.

"I can't say I liked him much... But burning really is a terrible way to die." She took out a cigarette and put it between her lips before setting the pack down. Her eyes met mine as she pressed her middle finger to the tip of her cigarette. I watched as the cigarette began to smoke, and she took a deep drag, her gaze never leaving mine. I took a step backward, a deep unease in my stomach as she stared into my soul and spoke.

"Still... I'd say he got what he deserved, wouldn't you?" She chuckled softly as I backed out of the shop and hurried back to my car. I could hear her laughter behind me.

She was right. He did get what he deserved.

JUICEBOX

"*What I'm looking for is to optimize myself,*" Shay said during our initial phone call. "*I see so many new directions I can go in... I'm just not sure if my current approach is the right one. Is that something you can help with?*"

"W-well, yes!" I said. "Absolutely! I've helped over forty clients rebuild themselves into more successful—"

"*Save the sales pitch. That's all I need to know. We'll discuss the details in person tomorrow evening at my place. I presume you have no issues having our first meeting there?*"

"None at all!" I assured her.

"*Good. Now, I will ask for your discretion in this matter. I like to keep my private development private. Given the position I'm in, I'm sure you understand.*"

"Oh yes! Absolutely! Trust me, you're not the first client I've had with an interest in discretion!"

"*I would expect as much. And to be clear, I do mean absolute discretion,*" Shay said. "*Keep my name out of your address books, and you are to tell no one that we are meeting. I recognize that this level of precaution may seem... unnecessary, but I've run into problems before. Once again, I'm sure you understand.*"

I told her I did. Sure, it was weird... but I didn't really think too hard about it.

People made weird requests all the time, and it made sense that she'd want to be discreet. Not everyone takes life coaches seriously. Maybe Shay was worried that looking for guidance would come across as a sign of weakness? Judging by her reputation, she wasn't the sort of woman who showed a lot of vulnerability.

"I completely understand," I said, and Shay seemed satisfied by that.

"Excellent. We'll meet at my penthouse at 8 p.m. sharp. 2011 St. Theresa Street. Top floor. The doorman will give you access. Supper will be provided, so there's no need to stop elsewhere beforehand."

"Sounds good! See you tomorrow at 8!"

"Be early if possible. I don't like to wait."

That was the last thing she said before she hung up.

Once I set my phone down, I let out the breath that I'd been holding. I felt a little shaken after that conversation... but by all accounts, that was just part of the experience you got when talking to Shay Blackburn.

Shay's reputation preceded her in just about every imaginable way, and going off our initial conversation, she was easily one of the most intimidating women I'd ever spoken to. Even over the phone, she had this aura of power about her. I'd never once seen a picture of her smiling, and during our call she'd been curt and to the point... although I suppose that wasn't really surprising given what she did for a living.

It was odd that she'd reached out to me of all people, though...

As stated before, I'm a life coach. My job is to help people build a path to achieving their goals. Find their ambitions, find what drives them, break it down into steps, and guide them along the way! I'd like to think I'm pretty good at it, too.

I try to use a sort of gentle touch with my clients. I find that I get the best results if they see me as an advisor, not a leader. It allows them to more naturally grow into a leadership role, which they can bring to other aspects of their lives. I help them find their passion and use it to drive themselves forward. My clients are people who have dreams but aren't sure how to follow them. People who want to be more ambitious but don't quite know how yet. People who just need a little nudge to help them achieve their best selves!

Shay Blackburn was not one of those people.

Shay was the head of Blackburn Strategy, one of the fastest-growing financial services firms on the East Coast. She wasn't the sort of person I would've expected to get hired by. Most of my clients are people who dream of one day becoming someone like her. They're people who want to achieve their goals, unlock their potential, and find the best versions of themselves! Not people who already did that ten years ago.

Still, I wasn't going to turn my nose up at such a high-profile client... especially not one offering such a hefty payday, and I figured this would probably be great for my career! I already had a few high-profile clients, but no one like Shay Blackburn. I told myself that this was going to be the start of something incredible!

God... I was so naive...

As promised, I arrived at Shay's building around 7:45, and the moment I entered the lobby, I was greeted by a tall, somewhat imposing-looking doorman.

"Name?" he asked. His voice was low and booming.

"Um... Emily. Emily McGuire!"

He sized me up for a moment before nodding and gesturing for me to follow him. Our footsteps echoed across the plain granite floor as he led me to a private elevator. He scanned a keycard to open it for me before gesturing for me to step inside.

"Enjoy your evening, Miss McGuire," he said coolly before the elevator doors closed. I never got the chance to reply to him.

I quietly looked over at the buttons. There were only two. One to send the elevator up and the other to send it down. I pressed the button to go up.

As it rose, I felt a quiet anxiety gnawing away in my chest. As I said before, Shay's reputation preceded her, and I fully expected her to live up to it. I'd seen pictures of her before, and she struck me as the sort of person who was in control of every single nanosecond of her existence. Her long, blonde hair was always perfectly coiffed; her clothes were always immaculately clean, and despite their designer brand, they had an almost Spartan uniformity to them. Plain blazers, pencil skirts, and leggings. She preferred black, but I'd seen her venture into shades of charcoal gray, slate, obsidian, onyx, and even sable. Her shoes were always the most expressive part of her wardrobe, but even then, she rarely deviated from some variation of black six-inch heels.

For a moment... I almost wondered if I was a little underdressed for the occasion. Maybe I was? I wasn't exactly wearing rags; I'd picked out a professional but nice blouse for the meeting and a comfortable, matching skirt. I'd wanted to make a good first impression, but was this going to be enough? God, I couldn't remember the last time I'd been this nervous to meet a client! On the phone, she'd been curt and to the point; I had no reason to expect that would change!

Maybe it would be fine? She was asking to meet at home, after all; maybe she wouldn't be dressed for the office? I couldn't exactly imagine her walking up to me in sweatpants, though.

The elevator doors opened. I exhaled the breath I'd been holding and stepped out before freezing at the sight of the penthouse before me.

Her penthouse was probably one of the most decadent buildings I'd ever set foot inside. I'd expected something fancy, but I couldn't have even begun to imagine anything like this.

The floor was polished pale marble, with a sweeping grand staircase coming down from the left side. The walls were white plaster, lovingly carved. Various paintings adorned each wall, adding a uniform splash of crimson to the white of the walls. I wanted to get a better look at them, but then I heard the sound of high heels clicking against a marble floor, slowly getting closer to me.

She rounded a corner just ahead of me... and was more or less exactly what I was expecting. Her clothes were professional to a fault and immaculate, with not so much as a fiber out of place. Her eyes were cold and focused. Her expression was stoic. It was hard to tell if she was staring me down with contempt or if that was just her default facial expression.

"Miss McGuire?" she asked coolly.

"Y-yes. That's me!" I said. "Pleased to meet you, Miss Blackburn!"

I offered a hand to shake, but she ignored it, simply turning and gesturing for me to follow.

"Come. I've had a place set up in the dining room for us to talk."

I obediently followed her through the penthouse—which looked more and more like a mansion the deeper I went. Most of the surfaces were an unblemished white, with only a few splashes of color here or there. This place hardly even looked lived in. It felt more like walking through an Ikea showroom than somebody's home.

"I don't suppose you have any food allergies or nutritional requirements?" she asked.

"Oh, I can't have nuts…" I said. "I've got my EpiPen, but—"

"Understood. Just let James know what you can and cannot have. He'll take care of you."

"James…?" I started to ask, but before we entered the dining room, I saw exactly who she was talking about: a young man in a black chef's jacket and apron. Probably her private chef. Of course a woman like her would have a private chef.

James just offered me a gentle, albeit nervous smile.

"He's a master of a variety of wonderful dishes," Shay noted. "Although I do enjoy his pastas… speaking of which, I'm in the mood for fettuccine alfredo. Chicken, mushrooms, and spinach—extra garlic, please and thank you."

"Of course, ma'am," James said, before looking over at me.

"Um, fettuccine sounds good!" I said. I wasn't sure if it would've been bad form to order anything different, and I did like fettuccine alfredo!

James gave a nod before taking off. As he did, I watched Shay open a bottle of wine. She filled a silver wine glass before looking up at me.

"Will you join me?" she asked.

"Sure, just a little!" I said.

She filled a second glass and offered it to me. It felt like real silver. I looked up at her, watching as she took a long sip before sitting down.

"So… about what I'm after," she began.

Straight to business. Just like I'd expected.

"Yes, you mentioned seeing some new places you wanted to take yourself. I wanted to get a better idea about what you had in mind."

"Diversification," she said. "Finance is a promising enterprise, don't get me wrong. I've done well. But there comes a time when one has no more dragons left to slay, as it were. I need a fresh challenge… I was thinking about a few potential investment opportunities. Small businesses. It's worked out quite well for a pair of sisters who've started running in the same circles that I do. They've made some impressive money off of their current portfolio: coffee chains, sports drinks, chocolate…"

I looked up at her. That description sounded awfully familiar.

"The Delaneys?" I asked.

Shay paused. She seemed a little caught off guard.

"You know them?" she asked.

"Yes! We've actually worked together before," I said.

Technically, I'd only ever worked with Alanna. She'd been a client of mine a few years back. I'd met her sister, Ashley, on a few occasions as well, but she'd never had any interest in a session. They were decent enough people! Alanna was soft-spoken and had struggled a bit with her confidence but was overall an intelligent and capable young woman. Her sister, Ashley, on the other hand, seemed a little more bullish. She was the sort of person who knew what she wanted and went after it. I wasn't surprised that Shay knew them, too. They'd done quite well for themselves over the past year, and while I didn't want to claim credit, I liked to think that I was able to help them achieve their success!

"Interesting..." Shay said. "It's a small world, I suppose. How were they to work with?"

"Oh, they were wonderful!" I said. "I'm really happy to hear they're doing well!"

Shay nodded thoughtfully and took another sip of her wine. Her eyes shifted back toward me, and she seemed to contemplate something for a moment before speaking again.

"Yes... well, they *are* doing incredibly well," she said. "Well enough that it's got me thinking about doing the same, although I'm not sure if that's just a passing fancy or something more."

"Well, you're in a good position to start making investments," I stated. "You've already got a wealth of knowledge when it comes to finance, so you're already ahead of a lot of others. Why don't we break things down a little further? Why don't we take a look at some of the KPIs you're looking to hit?"

Shay's answer to that question was, unsurprisingly, incredibly detailed... although to be honest, I don't remember much about what she said after this point. I was taking notes at the time, but I imagine any notes I had from that night are long gone by now.

What I do remember is that we spent almost an hour reviewing her investment goals before being interrupted by James, who brought out a feast: a chicken fettuccine alfredo that smelled like a garlicky piece of heaven, complete with a side of freshly baked breadsticks.

"Finally," Shay seemed to sigh as the food was brought out. "We can resume this discussion later... I'm sorry if I'm rushing you to eat, but I haven't had much of an opportunity to stop for a meal today. I'm sure you understand."

That didn't seem healthy—but I wasn't in a position to criticize. I just gave her a soft smile.

"One hundred percent," I assured her. The food did smell amazing, and I couldn't wait to dig in. I looked over toward James to thank him. He just gave a half nod... although he didn't make direct eye contact with me. Looking back, I remember that there was a strange look in his eyes, and it's only now that I realize it was probably guilt. At the time, though, I thought nothing of it. I was hungry, the food smelled amazing, and Shay was already eating, so I did the same.

The first few bites were incredible. They were absolutely swimming with flavor. The garlic didn't overpower any of it; it just made everything better. James really knew how to cook!

I noticed Shay staring at me as I ate, watching every bite like a hawk as she pushed her own food around the plate. When she realized I'd noticed her, she started talking again.

"He's a talented chef, isn't he?"

"He's amazing! I don't remember the last time I've had anything this good!"

"Well, your health is influenced by what you put into your body," Shay said. "It's part of why I enjoy a little extra garlic. It's especially good for the blood, you know, reducing the risk of clots, clearing out toxins, the list goes on."

"Really? I never... ne... v..."

The words slurred in my mouth, and I tried to correct myself.

"Never k... knew tha... t..."

A half smile tugged at the corner of Shay's mouth.

"Are you all right?" she asked, her tone bland and betraying nothing. I tried to tell her I was, but I didn't feel all right... I felt... dizzy...

James was staring at me now.

Shay's knowing smile only grew wider.

"You're looking a little out of it, Miss McGuire... why don't you rest your eyes for a moment? Let yourself recover..."

I didn't want to. That would've been unprofessional, but I couldn't help myself. My eyes drooped, and the next thing I knew… I was falling.

The last thing I remember thinking was: *Did they put something in my food?*

When I woke up, I was in a room I didn't recognize. I was lying in a cot, pressed up against the far wall of a small bedroom. My head was swimming. It was hard to focus… I felt so out of it… so tired. And I could feel something pressed against me.

Someone.

Their thick perfume filled my nostrils as they buried their face in my neck. It was almost suffocating. I tried to push them off but felt hands gripping my wrists, forcing me against the cot. That was when I finally noticed the pain in my neck. A sharp stabbing sensation, I could feel lips pressing against my neck. It felt almost like they were kissing me… but at the same time, that didn't feel like an accurate way to describe it either.

The figure looming over me pulled back, exhaling in satisfaction as she did.

Shay looked down at me, and I watched her lick her lips clean.

"Mmm? Awake already?" she mused. "Don't move, darling… you're still bleeding a little. Can't have that. Waste not, want not."

She picked up something off the floor. It looked like a bandage with some gauze. I couldn't do much to resist as she pressed it against my neck.

"The bleeding should stop shortly," she said. "For now, get your rest. I need you to build your strength back up for me. I'll need you again in a few days."

"W-what is this…?" I rasped. My voice felt weak. I was fighting to stay awake.

"Your new living arrangements," Shay replied. "Don't worry… I'll tie up the loose ends, and I'll ensure you're well taken care of. It really is in my best interest to keep you in top shape."

"What…?"

I pressed a hand to my neck. The spot where she'd bitten me still hurt.

"What were you doing...? I... I wanna go home..."

"I'm afraid that's not convenient for me. I need you here where I can keep a close eye on you," she said. "As promised, I'll take good care of you. Now, rest up. I'll have James send something in to help you recover soon. Again, I won't need you for another few days, but when the time comes, I need you nice and healed up for then."

With a calm, knowing smile, Shay stood up and turned to leave.

"Wait..." I rasped. I fell off the cot, trying to go after her. *"W-wait... please... wai—"*

My voice died in my throat as Shay began to close the door to the room I was in. It looked more like the kind of door you'd find on a safe or a vault. Thick and made of metal. I could only watch and silently plead as she closed it with a thud of finality, leaving me all alone in that room.

I lay helpless on the floor, unable to speak for a few moments before finally starting to cry. I was so scared... I didn't know what to do. I didn't know why she was doing this, I didn't know what she wanted... none of this made sense.

Slowly, I dragged myself back toward the cot, but I didn't have the strength to pull myself back onto it. Instead, I just curled up on the floor beside it and cried.

I don't know how long I stayed like that... but when eventually the tears finally stopped coming, I did manage to pick myself up off the ground and take a good look at my new surroundings.

The room I was in was sparsely furnished. It resembled a prison cell more than it did anything else... although I suppose it could have been considered a luxurious prison cell, so there was that.

The floor was plain hardwood, and the walls were a sterile white. There was a doorway off to one side that led to a small bathroom with a sink, a mirror, a toilet, and a shower stall. The doorway had no actual door... but that wasn't entirely surprising.

I took a few staggering steps on trembling legs to approach the mirror above the sink. I looked like an absolute mess. My skin was pale, and my glasses were askew. I tilted my head to look at the bandage Shay had put on my neck. Reluctantly, I peeled it back. Somehow, part of me already knew what I'd see under there. But that didn't mean I was ready for it.

Two small pinpricks were there on my neck. A bite mark... like something out of a Hollywood horror movie. My fingers brushed against it. The skin was still tender, and it was still bleeding a little.

My heart started to race faster. This didn't feel real... I struggled to think of a more logical explanation for this, but I just couldn't.

She'd been drinking my blood... and she was going to do it again.

Panic started to set in. Was she just going to keep me here? Was she just going to keep feeding on me? I thought about the way James had avoided looking at me... he must've known. He must've been the one who drugged me.

I had to get out of here. I was going to die if I didn't get out of here!

My breathing was getting heavier. My heart just kept racing. I stumbled back toward the metal door. I tried pounding on it. Tried screaming for help. Tears streamed down my cheeks as I begged for someone to let me out.

But no one came.

No one helped me.

I screamed for hours... hours... but nothing happened.

No one came.

When the door finally opened a few hours later, I was too tired to move. I could only look up from the wall I was slumped against with a halfhearted hope that someone had come to help. But it was just James with a tray of food. Steak and spinach, with a cup of orange juice. It all smelled great... although I didn't have much of an appetite.

He didn't say anything, just set it on a small table by the bed and turned to leave. He only stopped when I spoke to him.

"Please... please let me go..."

He hesitated in the doorway for a moment before quietly looking back at me.

"I'm sorry..." was all he could say. And as he turned away, I noticed a set of faded scars on his neck. They would've been easy to miss before... but now that I knew what to look for, I saw them.

Old bite marks.

My heart sank. I knew at that moment that James wouldn't help me. He couldn't.

He closed the vault door behind him, and just as quickly as he'd arrived, he was gone. I stared at the food he'd left behind, and with nothing else to do, I ate.

The next few days passed in a blur.

I'd often hear Shay moving around the penthouse outside—but I never saw her, and I was never allowed to leave my room.

That room was just about the only thing I knew during my time there... and beyond the bed and the small bathroom, there wasn't much to it.

I knew I wasn't its first occupant. There were old bloodstains on the mattress, and on the side of the bathroom mirror, someone else had carved a message into the wood.

Break it and be free.
Megan Dinh 2021.

It took me a moment to understand what Megan had meant by that... and when I figured it out, I did consider it for a moment. But ultimately, I didn't have the stomach for it.

Two times a day, James would bring me food. Nothing fancy. Always just meat, beans, and greens. We never spoke much after that first conversation. I'm not sure if he wasn't supposed to talk to me or if he just didn't know what to say.

I did make one attempt to push past him and get out—and I actually made it. I got through that vault door!

But I only found myself in a plain office, with the door locked. It wouldn't open no matter how much I struggled, and I stopped when I felt James's hand on my shoulder.

"Don't..." he said softly. His eyes were stern... pleading, almost. "She'll kill us both."

I wanted to argue, wanted to fight. But I already knew that there wasn't any point in attacking James, and something in my gut told me that I didn't stand a ghost of a chance against Shay. So instead of fighting, I just quietly allowed myself to be led back to my room. It was the first time I'd ever seen what the door to my room looked like from the outside.

I'd expected something like the door to a safe... and maybe there was such a door behind it. But a bookshelf had been built over it. I had no doubts that when closed, the doorway was impossible to notice.

No one was ever going to find me in there, I knew that much for sure. I hesitated, not wanting to go back inside. But I didn't linger for long.

I had nowhere else to go, after all.

After a few days, Shay returned for me.

The moment she opened the door, I found myself shrinking back in fear. A coy smile tugged at the corner of her mouth when she saw me.

"Well, well... nervous, aren't we?" she teased, stepping into my room and closing the door behind her.

"Please..." I said. "Please don't bite me... not again, please..."

"Shh... just relax, dear," Shay crooned as she closed the distance between us. "Fighting isn't going to get you anywhere. Trust me, things like me can't die."

She loomed over me as I shrank into the corner, trying to make myself so small that she couldn't hurt me... but it didn't change anything.

"Don't struggle. If I bite wrong... you could bleed out, and neither of us wants that..."

She gently moved my hands out of the way, tilted my head to the side, and sank her teeth into my neck. My body tensed up as she bit me, and for several minutes, I could only sit there in silence as she fed.

When she finally pulled back and replaced the gauze on my neck, I asked the question that had lingered in the back of my mind for the past few days.

"W-why... why are you doing this to me?"

"We all need to eat," Shay replied matter-of-factly. "My dietary needs are simply... different. Hunting is time-consuming. Not that time isn't something I have in abundance—a little perk of immortality. But I'd rather use mine productively. Besides, most of my kind rely on seduction to get close, and that always comes with certain *expectations*. Frankly, I've got better things to do, and I'm not about to start paying for it like some do either. What a miserable way to exist. I've spent the past 400 years as an apex predator. Why would I consent to live as anything less now? No, I prefer having a juicebox or two on hand for the sake of convenience. It's much easier this way."

Juicebox... the casual way she said that word made me sick, as if that's really all I was in her eyes. A quick and easy snack.

"*Why me?*" I asked.

"It's easiest to take people no one will miss," she said. There was a cruel implication behind her words that didn't escape me. "James, for example. I found him working as a sous chef at a rather lovely restaurant downtown. He was talented, of course, but that's not why I hired him. He had no one: just a small one-bedroom apartment and delusions of white picket fences. When I offered him the chance to work for me, he couldn't have said yes fast enough. Granted, I was a little more up front with him than I was with you. He knew going in that this would be a live-in position. You... well... I suppose you'll learn. If you keep up your best behavior, maybe someday you'll graduate to a proper bedroom too."

"*I... I don't want a bedroom... I want to go home!*"

Shay laughed.

"Home to what, sweetheart? What exactly have you got going on in your little life? I did my research on you, you know. You live alone in a modest two-bedroom apartment. No close friends. No pets. Nothing. For a so-called life coach... your own life is pretty pathetic. Honestly, though, I never put much stock into that kind of thing anyway—no offense. But I always thought that if someone doesn't understand how to set basic goals, they don't deserve success. Trying to teach them things that anyone with a brain should already know just seems like a waste. Then again, most self-help stuff always struck me as something of a scam... so which of us is the real vampire here?"

"*You are...*"

Shay's brow creased slightly. She pursed her lips before deciding not to dignify that with a response. She stood up, smoothing out her dark charcoal blazer and exhaled through her nostrils.

"Get your rest. I'll be hungry again in a few more days," she said calmly, before turning to leave, locking me in that room once again. I just stayed in the corner, unable to move.

I didn't know what I *could* do.

This was my life now.

Shay's visits and the meals James brought me soon became the only way I could really mark the passage of time. I had no windows. They'd taken everything off of me except for my EpiPen. James had given that back to me after I'd told him that I could die without it. I omitted the fact that I'd only really need it in the event that I was exposed to peanuts, but he hadn't asked about that.

Everything else was gone, though. My phone, my notebook, my pens. There was nothing I could really do.

As the days went by, with only the meals and the feedings to keep me company, I was sure I could feel myself starting to decay.

I thought about breaking the mirror in the bathroom and slitting my wrists, just like the note carved into the wood had recommended, but I still couldn't bring myself to go through with it. I was more afraid of dying than I was of Shay. She'd said that maybe someday, I could have my own room, right? It got me thinking that maybe if I behaved, maybe if I didn't fight, maybe I'd be okay in the end?

James didn't seem to be suffering too much. Maybe I could be okay, too?

Maybe...

I don't know if I really believed that or not, but it was something to tell myself as I lay curled up in bed. Something to keep me going.

Shay came for me early on the day of the party. She was dressed down compared to what I usually saw her in, wearing her bathrobe as opposed to her usual outfit. She didn't drink as much either.

"T-that's it?" I asked as she pulled away from me. She licked the blood off her lips as she stared down at me.

"I only need a little top-up," she said. "I'm having a little get-together this evening. I prefer to eat light beforehand. It's best not to be seen as too ravenous. Especially since they're bringing in volunteers."

She said that final word with such disgust.

"It's a pathetic way to live, if you ask me. Lying to yourself that you're anything more than prey… or worse… getting off on it. Believe me, darling. There's far more dignity in your position than theirs."

I didn't really follow her logic, but I wasn't about to argue with her.

"You just rest and keep quiet," she said. "I'd prefer not to have to dispose of a body tonight."

She patched me up as she usually did before getting up to leave me. Soon after the door closed behind her, I heard the shower running as she prepared for the party.

The music started maybe an hour or two later. A live band, by the sound of it. I suppose I wasn't surprised that Shay was going all out for whatever gathering this was.

I could actually hear everything pretty well from my little room… and that was when I finally started thinking, maybe someone might be able to hear me?

I knew it was probably a long shot. The music and the mingling guests would probably drown me out. But I still needed to try.

I waited for a while longer until I heard more voices downstairs.

Then, I started to make noise.

I kicked at the door. Stomped on the floor. I screamed for someone to come and find me.

I kept waiting to hear Shay come in to shut me up… but she never did. Maybe no one heard me? The thought had crossed my mind a few times. But I couldn't give up! I couldn't stop trying! Someone would be bound to find me eventually! They had to!

They had to…

So I screamed.

I screamed until my face was red. I pounded on the floor and kicked at the door. I begged for someone, anyone, to help me.

And when I finally heard the door to the office outside open, my voice died in my throat. I could hear someone just outside my door. Footsteps.

I wasn't sure if it was Shay or not… I was terrified that it was. I listened, hoping that whoever was out there might call out… and they did.

"*Hello?*"

My heart skipped a beat.

I knew that voice.

Alanna Delaney!

Immediately, I stumbled toward the door and pounded on it.

"I-I'm in here!" I cried. "It's the bookcase, it's a door! P-please, please just get me out of here!"

"Emily?"

Alanna sounded closer now. She was right outside the door. I could hear her fumbling with the bookcase before I heard the telltale creak of the door unlocking.

Alanna pulled it open... and oh God...

I'd never been so happy to see another human being in my life.

"Alanna..." I sobbed, tears streaming down my cheeks. "Oh God, Alanna..."

I crashed into her arms, hugging her tight.

"What the hell is this? What are you doing in here?" she asked. She looked over my shoulder, into the room where I'd been held captive. I could sense her body tensing up.

"Oh my God..." she said under her breath. Her eyes settled on the gauze patch on my neck. "Has she been...?"

"I-it's Shay..." I stammered. "She's been keeping me here and I... oh God, I don't know how long, I... she... she's..."

The words barely came out. Terror and hope didn't leave me very articulate.

"It's okay," Alanna said. "It's okay..."

She stroked my hair as she held me.

"We're going to get you out of here, okay? We're going to get you out of here right now..."

Then I heard it.

Footsteps out in the hall. The familiar, distinct sound of high heels on hardwood.

"No..." I sobbed, as Alanna turned toward the door to the office, moving to stand in front of me protectively.

The door opened slowly, and we both watched as Shay stepped in. She gingerly closed it behind her and sized us both up, her cold expression difficult to read as always.

"I thought I told you to rest and keep quiet," she said.

"Shay, what the hell is this?!" Alanna demanded. "You're keeping a blood slave?"

"You and Ashley don't?" Shay asked, her tone dismissive. "Don't tell me you two actually go out and hunt... or God forbid, pay for it..."

Hunt? Pay for it...?

I looked over at Alanna. The way she phrased it, it almost sounded like Alanna and her sister were vampires too!

"It's Imperium Law!" Alanna argued. "You could be *executed* for something like this!"

"Come now. You think the Council doesn't do it too?" Shay asked. "We're vampires, dear. The Imperium may like the sound of paid blood farms and willing donors... but that is not what we are. You and your sister are still young, so a little bit of idealism isn't unreasonable. They do paint a nice picture! But be realistic. We're not just going to deny our natures. Nothing ever can."

"You want to test that theory?" Alanna snapped. "What happens if I bring her out to everyone out there? What do you think they'll say?"

Shay's brow furrowed. I saw a flash of rage in her eyes.

"That would be extremely ill-advised," she said, her voice as calm as always. "I was extremely generous in inviting you and your sister out tonight, and I would not recommend rewarding my generosity with provocation."

"Provocation?" Alanna repeated. Her eyes narrowed. "I think we're way past that."

"Do you? Because I don't. I'm more than willing to be reasonable here, so long as you are reasonable in turn. Why don't you return Miss McGuire to her room, and we can discuss this like civilized adults, yes? I'm sure we can reach an understanding. There's no need to escalate this into a full-on confrontation."

"Then get out of my way, Shay!"

Shay remained still.

"That's not an option for me. I'm going to ask you one last time, Alanna. Don't make me escalate this."

Alanna remained still. Her body seemed tense, though.

She was scared.

I could see it. So could Shay.

Still, she held her ground. She sized up the vampire in front of her... and then she made her move.

"ASHL—"

Shay crossed the room in just the blink of an eye, seizing Alanna by the throat before she could finish calling for her sister. Alanna struggled as she was dragged to the ground, clawing at Shay's face. Shay did briefly let her go, giving her a chance to try to scramble away. But she only made it a foot or so before Shay seized a handful of her long, auburn hair and locked her arm around her throat, keeping her from screaming. Alanna struggled against the chokehold, fighting hard to escape. Her pale face flushed red as she tried to breathe.

Shay just held fast, her expression calm and placid. She braced one hand against the back of Alanna's head, then moved the other hand to her chin, jerking her head violently to the side.

I could hear the crack of her bones... and I watched as Alanna's struggles stopped. Her eyes widened before going vacant. Her limbs twitched. Her breath hitched... and she was gone.

Shay sighed in exhaustion.

"I did try to avoid that..." she mused, before her eyes settled on me.

I stood, paralyzed on the spot. I knew I needed to run, but the fear kept me in place. Tears still streamed down my cheeks.

Shay's eyes never left me as she lugged Alanna's body through the door in the bookcase.

"Now for you... you know better than to run right now, don't you?"

I weakly nodded my head.

"Good girl. I'll tell you what. Go back to your room. Sit quietly... and you'll live past tomorrow. Does that sound fair to you?"

"P-please..."

"That was a yes or no question, Emily."

"Yes..."

"Then go... and if I hear any pounding or screaming, I'll kill you on the spot. Am I clear?"

Again, I nodded and allowed myself to be shepherded back into the room. Shay closed the door behind me once more, leaving me in silence with Alanna's body.

I could still hear the party outside... but I didn't make any more noise.

I was too afraid of what might happen if I did.

My eyes wandered to Alanna's lifeless body. Her eyes were still open. Her lips were slightly parted, revealing her fangs. I stared at her, hoping that maybe she might get up, maybe she might still be alive somehow.

But there was no doubt in my mind that she was gone.

I slowly approached her and took the time to close her eyes.

"I'm sorry…" I whispered and sat quietly by her body, as if the company would be any comfort to her.

I'm a little ashamed to admit that I did try to search her body for anything useful she might have had on her, like a phone. But her red party dress had no pockets. If she had a purse, she hadn't had it on her when she'd found me.

There was nothing that could help me.

So I just sat with her.

The sudden brutality of her death lingered in my mind. The way Shay had just so effortlessly snapped her neck… I'd never seen anyone die before, and the suddenness of it was what scared me the most. One moment she was there and the next she wasn't.

Hadn't Shay said that vampires like her couldn't be killed so easily?

She had, hadn't she? And yet she'd snapped Alanna's neck like it was nothing. Was that even a way vampires could be killed in stories? I didn't think so.

Then again… did any of the old vampire myths apply to Shay? I'd seen her eat garlic, I'd watched her touch silver. I knew she could ingest things other than blood, and I'd heard her in the shower before, so I knew she wasn't averse to running water. I personally hadn't ever seen her in direct sunlight, but I'd seen pictures of her outside before, so odds were that sunlight wouldn't kill her.

No… none of the weaknesses from the old myths applied to her.

Come to think of it, they hadn't applied to Alanna either. I'd seen Alanna and her sister out during the daytime plenty of times, and neither of them had ever once given any indication they were put off by garlic. Christ, I hadn't even realized they'd been vampires! They'd both just seemed completely normal!

But if those traditional weaknesses didn't apply to vampires… was the same true for their strengths?

I thought back to what I *had* seen Shay do.

She hadn't really hypnotized me. I was relatively certain she couldn't turn into a bat, and while she had been remarkably fast when she'd attacked Alanna... it hadn't seemed supernatural. Even the way she'd killed Alanna... she'd just snapped her neck. It was so *mundane.* So simple.

"Things like me can't die," Shay had said. But here I was, sitting next to a dead vampire.

Of course, she'd said she couldn't die.

She didn't want us to think we could kill her.

She didn't want us to think she was vulnerable.

I stared down at Alanna.

I knew Shay wouldn't leave her here to rot. She'd need to get rid of her. Odds were that she'd be back in the morning... and there was a risk she'd get rid of me too, when she returned.

I needed to be ready.

I quietly got up and went over to my bed. I stripped the pillowcase off the pillow, then made my way into the bathroom. I'd left my EpiPen by the sink. I slipped it into my pocket without thinking, before wrapping the pillowcase around my hand and punching the mirror as hard as I could. Cracks spiderwebbed across its surface, and with a trembling hand, I hit it a few more times until I was able to pull a shard of glass free from the rest of the mirror.

It would work as a makeshift knife.

I knew there was a good chance Shay would still kill me... but after sitting in that room, helpless and afraid for so long, it felt almost freeing to finally choose to fight back. If I had to die, I didn't want to die afraid.

I slipped the broken shard of mirror under my pillow and then sat down on the bed to wait.

The party went on... and slowly died down.

The guests departed, leaving everything quiet. I could hear Shay moving around when everyone had left, but she never came to check in on me. As far as I could tell, she and James did a bit of tidying up before she retired to bed.

That was fine.

She'd be back. I just needed to wait.

I won't pretend that I wasn't still afraid of what would happen when Shay returned for Alanna's body. I was terrified. More than that, I was already certain that I was going to die. I told myself that if I could just make her bleed, though, that would be worth it. I just needed to hurt her… just needed to remind her that she wasn't invincible.

Even though my heart was racing, even though I hadn't slept and had just lain in bed waiting for Shay to come, I knew I could do *that*.

And finally, I heard her.

I could hear the shower running in another room of the penthouse. I could hear her walking around, going downstairs and talking to James. I heard the phone ring a few times and vaguely heard James mention that a guest had arrived, but Shay simply said:

"Tell them I'm out right now. We can meet for lunch."

Before moving on.

The phone rang again after that, but this time Shay refused to answer it.

I just waited and listened. Waited for her to finally come for me… and eventually I heard her. I could hear those distinctive high heels clicking against the hardwood floor.

I closed my eyes.

I'd never felt so in the moment before. Never felt so centered in my own body… so alive. It felt wrong, especially since I knew I probably wouldn't be alive for much longer, but there was no time to dwell on it.

Shay stopped in front of the door and unlocked it. I rested my hand on my pillow and tried to steady my breathing as she opened the door for the last time.

She stared at me before scoffing through her nose.

"Enjoy your evening?" she asked. "I trust the company wasn't a bother?"

I didn't reply to her. I just watched as she lifted Alanna up over her shoulder.

"You know I really don't take any pleasure from this," she said. "I kind of liked this one and her sister. I don't know if this is more of a mess than you're worth yet... but either way, you're lucky I'm the forgiving type."

That familiar knowing grin flashed across her lips, before her eyes suddenly darted to the side... into the doorless bathroom.

I saw her entire body tense up.

She'd noticed the broken mirror.

Was it surprise or panic that she felt? I didn't have time to think about it. I just grabbed the shard of mirror from under my pillow, and with a manic scream, I lunged at her. The edge of the mirror cut into my hand, but the pain didn't slow me down. I'd been sitting there, waiting like a coiled spring for hours. I couldn't let anything stop me, not pain nor fear nor death.

Shay tried to position Alanna's body between us, and she spared herself from the first few stabs, but I could reach around the corpse, and I could feel the moment my makeshift knife dug into her flesh.

She stumbled back, frantically trying to get out of the room. I think she was hoping she could lock me in, but I was too close. Alanna was too unwieldy for her to carry, but protected her just enough that she couldn't risk tossing her aside. She tried to throw the body onto me, desperately hoping that the dead weight might push me back into my room, but I just pushed the body aside. Alanna's corpse thudded to the ground as I lunged directly at Shay, and this time, there was nothing to stop me from reaching her.

I wanted to bury my shard of mirror into her heart. Instead, it ended up in her bicep.

Shay threw her weight against me, knocking me off her and sending me tumbling to the ground.

"You little bitch!" she spat, and I could see the venom in her eyes as she glared at me. She gripped the shard of glass embedded in her right arm and ripped it free with a grunt of pain. Blood flowed freely from the wound. I could see it dripping from her fingertips.

I was right. She wasn't invincible.

But now she *was* furious, and more importantly, this time she'd been careless. The door to the hallway was open. She must have left it that way to make it easier to carry Alanna's body out.

That was my escape route.

I took off at a sprint, and Shay bolted after me.

"You're not going anywhere!"

I felt her fingers rake through my hair as I burst out into the hall. I only barely got past her. I had no idea where I was going, but running was better than dying. I could see the stairs up ahead. Maybe I could make it to the elevator? But was that a long shot? Maybe I'd be better off looking for a weapon, something else I could use to defend myself. The only thing I had in my pocket was my EpiPen and—

Before I could sift through my racing thoughts, I felt a hand grab my shoulder. Shay pulled me back toward her before slamming me into a wall.

"You think you can kill me?" she spat. *"I've been doing this for 400 years, Emily! You're not the first to try. You won't be the last!"*

Her hand closed around my throat. Her eyes burned hatefully into mine. I tried to suck in a breath… and on instinct, my hand dipped into my pocket, grasping at the only thing I could use.

"Shame to make an even bigger mess… but you're too much of a problem to keep alive."

My fingers struggled to open the case of my EpiPen, but I felt the lid pop open as her grip got tighter. She eyed my neck and began to lean closer for a final bite.

I almost dropped my EpiPen as I pulled it from my pocket, and with the last bit of strength I had, I pressed it hard into her neck until I heard it click.

Shay gasped. Her grip on my neck tightened as she pulled back, clutching at her own neck now.

"W-what the hell?" she stammered, hastily tearing the EpiPen out of her neck. Fresh blood gushed from the injection point. Her eyes settled on me, wide with panic.

"What did you do to me?"

I honestly wasn't sure what the injection was doing to her. I knew from experience that it was probably making her heart race, which couldn't have felt good… but I didn't know how long it would last on her. The effects only lasted around half an hour on me. I didn't know if they'd be longer or shorter for her, but I didn't want to take a risk.

Shay stumbled back a few steps, still clutching her neck. Her breathing had grown erratic. She braced herself against the railing, and I seized the opportunity. I threw myself at her, pushing her hard and sending her tumbling over with a scream of panic. I watched Shay hit the marble floor at the bottom, although I knew I'd only slowed her down. She writhed on the floor, smearing her blood along the white marble.

"*No...*" she rasped. "*No, no, no...*"

I paused, watching her for a moment. She was disoriented. Maybe this was my chance to finish her off? No... even if she was weak, I still didn't like my chances. I had to make it to the elevator. I had to get out of here! That was my top priority!

I started down the stairs, only to pause as Shay forced herself up to her feet again.

"*You...*"

She was unsteady on her feet, but through pure spite, she hauled herself over to the stairs, blocking my way.

I took a step back, watching as she shambled up them. She collapsed onto all fours to make it easier, looking at me like a wild animal as she climbed toward me, step by step.

"*I'll kill you slow, Emily...*" she panted, and I knew that was a promise.

I took another step back before taking off down the hall again. I needed to find a weapon, and fast. I knew she'd be back on her feet soon.

The sound of a phone ringing blared through the house, although neither of us was in a position to answer it.

I threw open the door of the first room I saw, desperately looking for something to use. This room looked to be Shay's bedroom. An elaborate king-sized bed with white satin sheets dominated the center of it. I scanned the room, looking for something I could use... and then I spotted it. A mostly empty wine bottle by what looked to be a reading chair. I grabbed it, then as I heard the telltale click of her high heels on the floor outside. Her gait was slower. She was struggling to walk now.

I spotted a closet nearby and, trying to think fast, closed myself inside. I didn't think it'd be much of a hiding spot, but I did hope she wouldn't realize I'd found something new to hit her with.

"*Where are you?*" she growled as she stepped into the bedroom. I could hear her sniffing the air.

"I can smell you in here, you know. Your fear... your adrenaline... your blood."

From my hiding spot, I could see her eyes settle on the closet.

"Such a waste of blood, too. Yours was decent enough. Nothing I'd want to spill needlessly. Maybe I'll bottle it? Make you watch as I extract every single drop from your veins, and let you feel yourself growing colder and weaker as death drags you into i—"

Her voice died in her throat as we heard a noise from the foyer—the telltale sound of the elevator arriving.

"Oh, for FUCK'S sake!" Shay snarled, tensing up again. "No, no, no... I said no visitors... not like this..."

She seemed to hesitate for a moment and shot one last glare at the closet before shambling out, slamming her bedroom door closed behind her. I heard her voice morph as she spoke. She was trying to put on that professional front again, but I could hear the strain behind it.

"I'm sorry, this really isn't a good time for company right now... can we meet up later to discuss—"

"I just need a moment, I promise!" another voice said.

A voice I knew I recognized. Ashley.

My heart skipped a beat.

Slowly, I stepped out of the closet and made my way back into the hall. There wasn't a doubt in my mind that the voice I was hearing was Ashley's.

"It's Alanna, she didn't come home last night," I heard her say.

"I told you, she left with someone else..." Shay panted. She was staying at the top of the stairs and looking down at Ashley. The moment I stepped out of the bedroom, she shot a glance over at me but didn't move. Her posture was tense. Panicked. Her breathing was heavy and labored.

"Look, I know this might be a lot to ask, but I didn't see who she left with last night. I just wanted to know if you got a look at them. Maybe it was someone you know? Or maybe I can just see the camera footage from the lobby?" Ashley asked before trailing off.

She must've just noticed the smeared blood on the marble floor.

"Oh my God... Shay, what happened? Are you all right?"

"I'm fine..." Shay insisted. "Just stay down there... don't come up the stairs! It's just a small accident with one of the volunteers. Nothing to worry about, I'm cleaning it up!"

"I can help if you need me to!" Ashley said. I could hear her on the stairs, although I heard her voice die in her throat. Had she noticed the state Shay was in?

Shay glanced back over at me. Her eyes were wide. Unsure.

Afraid.

"What the hell is going on here?" Ashley asked, her voice low and suspicious.

Shay opened her mouth to speak before grimacing. She hesitated. Tried to think of a lie. Tried to think of something to do... but I knew she had nothing.

"GOD FUCKING DAMN IT!"

She lunged for Ashley first, kicking her back down the stairs before turning to deal with me. I tried to rush her. Tried to swing the bottle at her head, but Shay caught me by the wrist.

"ENOUGH!"

With a cry of rage, she hurled me down the stairs as well. I caught myself screaming as I rolled down the steps into the foyer. I felt one of my ribs crack before landing in a painful heap beside Ashley Delaney.

Her short black hair was already matted with blood. She'd hit her head on the way down, but I watched her slowly pick herself up.

"W-what the hell?" she stammered. Her eyes settled on me, and I could see the confusion on her face.

"Emily?"

Before Ashley could say another word, Shay kicked her back to the ground.

"And the mess just gets bigger..." she spat. "Oh, you really are more trouble than you're worth..."

I tried to crawl away, but Shay grabbed me by the hair and dragged me back to the stairs.

"Just die already, you fucking—" Her final word was cut off by a pained scream. Shay's body contorted, and she frantically reached to try and pull something out of her back. She stumbled as she lost one of her high heels and almost collapsed before catching herself. The abandoned shoe lay discarded on the floor beside me.

From the corner of my eye, I saw James behind her, frantically backing away.

Shay gave him a look of utter disbelief before ripping a kitchen knife out of her back. James just tried to glare back at her and stopped after a few steps, defiant and waiting for her to come for him.

"No more..." was all he said.

Shay's lip quivered as if she wanted to scream at him. But when her lips parted, no words came out. Just a primal, animalistic scream as she lunged for him, grabbing him violently and hurling him against a wall. James tried to fight back. Tried to push her off, but Shay drove the knife into his chest.

"No more..." she spat before hurling him back to the ground. She wobbled unsteadily on her feet, and I could see Ashley starting to pick herself up again.

Shay looked back at us, but I could see the fight draining out of her. Her remaining heel was throwing her off balance, so she kicked it off. It didn't do much to keep her steady. She dragged her feet as she turned around. Blood dribbled out of her mouth. She looked like she was ready to collapse.

Ashley looked over at me, still confused but with a quiet understanding in her eyes.

"What did you do, Shay...?" was all she could ask.

Shay didn't respond, so Ashley asked a different question.

"Where is my sister?!"

"She killed her..." I said, my own exhaustion evident in my voice. "She found out she was feeding on me... so she murdered her... just to keep her quiet."

I saw a look of horror in Ashley's eyes.

"W-what? No..." she said under her breath. "No, no, no... that can't... no... she can't be..."

Shay braced herself against the wall.

"She just had to get involved..." she said. *"What a clusterfuck..."*

She tried to push off the wall and support herself on her own legs again but stumbled and collapsed back against the wall. Her knees threatened to buckle beneath her, and it took a few moments before she could try again.

She looked back over at us and seemed ready to speak... although the words seemed to get caught in her throat.

Ashley stared her down before finally drawing closer. Shay seemed to try to take a step back, but her legs finally gave out, and she slid down to the ground, still clutching the wall as she sank down beside James's body.

"You killed my sister..." Ashley said softly.

"Not the first time I've killed another vampire," Shay replied. *"Some just aren't cut out to be what we are... we're predators, my dear. She didn't understand that. Do you?"*

"You're about to find out," Ashley promised.

I saw an all too familiar knowing smile tug at Shay's lips.

"Oh, I'm sure..."

Something was wrong.

Shay lay slumped against the wall, watching as Ashley advanced on her. She almost looked helpless... but it felt wrong. It felt too easy.

"Wait!" I said, although my protest fell on deaf ears. Ashley only saw a dying vampire. She thought Shay was too weak to fight back.

When Shay kicked at her knee, she wasn't expecting it.

I heard Ashley's leg snap. It bent backward, and Ashley collapsed to the ground with a scream of pain.

Immediately, Shay was on top of her. She ripped James's kitchen knife out of his chest and buried it in Ashley's stomach, forcing another scream out of her. Shay's eyes lit up with a cruel triumph as she twisted the knife, and before I could even think about what I was doing, I was moving.

I grabbed the first thing I saw—Shay's lost stiletto heel—and scrambled toward her, swinging the heel toward her face.

Shay looked up at me as I rushed her, eyes widening in the moment before impact.

The heel went through her eye, sticking fast. Shay didn't even scream. She just let out a gasp as she rolled off Ashley, who was still writhing on the ground to try and pull the knife out of her.

"N-no..." I heard Shay rasp, before she let out a whimper of pain as she ripped the heel out of her eye. Blood dripped from her empty socket onto the marble floor, and Shay stared down at it in disbelief with her one remaining eye.

She pressed a shaking hand to her face as if it could stop the bleeding, while I checked on Ashley. She was alive, albeit in a lot of pain.

"Fuck... fuck she... oh God..." she panted.

"L-let's just get the hell out of here," I said and tried to help her up, but she pushed my hand away.

"No... no... no..." She glared over at Shay, who was still on her knees, clutching her eye. Ashley dragged herself closer to the wall, propping herself up beside James's body. She grabbed the knife, still buried in her stomach, and gritted her teeth before slowly pulling it free. I put a hand on her wrist, trying to stop her.

"Don't! You'll bleed out!"

"*Trust me... I'll be fine,*" she said under her breath. Her eyes locked with mine as, with a grunt of agony, she pulled the knife free and pushed the handle into my hand.

The message was clear.

I looked back over toward Shay. She was starting to move again, crawling along the floor on all fours to try and find something she could hold on to in order to pick herself back up.

My grip on the knife tightened as I shuffled over toward her. Shay noticed me coming from the corner of her good eye and tried to move faster, but it didn't change anything. I still caught up with her and rolled her onto her back.

"No..." she panted. "No, NO, NO, NO!"

I brought the knife down toward her chest, and she desperately grabbed my wrist, trying to save herself.

"*Wait... wait, wait... don't do this... you can go... you can go, I won't stop you... you win! O-okay? You win! You're free! We... we don't need to...*"

I threw my weight against her, pushing the knife a little closer to her heart. She still fought me as hard as she could, using the last of her strength to hold me back. I could see the terror in her one remaining eye.

She was scared of me.

Scared of dying.

"*NO!*" That one word almost sounded like a sob. "*Please... please don't... please don't... I don't want to... please no... no, no, no...*"

I grabbed her right arm. I could still feel the gash I'd left when I'd driven that shard of mirror into her earlier, and I pressed my thumb into it. Shay screamed as I tore my wrist from her grip. Her remaining eye widened as she let out one final plea... but she couldn't stop me this time.

I drove the knife into her throat. A wet, strangled wheeze escaped her. I felt her body twitch beneath me. Her legs kicked out frantically as she tried to get away, but it was already too late for her.

Blood gushed from Shay Blackburn's mouth. She tried to suck in air, but she couldn't. I kept my hands on the knife handle, pushing it into her neck as she struggled.

Her thrashing was getting weaker. I could see the light fading from her eye. Slowly, her strength left her, and with a few final twitches, she was gone.

I still kept the knife buried in her throat until my heart stopped racing, the adrenaline wore off, and I finally collapsed beside her.

Everything that followed happened in a blur.

I remember seeing Ashley taking out her phone and calling someone. I thought it might be the police, but the people who showed up didn't seem like cops or paramedics.

There was an ambulance there that took both Ashley and me away, but I couldn't shake the feeling that the people who were taking us weren't entirely human. Alanna had mentioned some kind of vampire organization? Was this it?

Whatever it was, I still ended up in a hospital... so there was that, at least. I spent a few days there recovering. A few people came in to talk to me about what had happened, but none of them gave me a whole lot of details. What they did give me was a payout for my 'pain and suffering' before politely but firmly requesting that I not go to any news outlets about what had happened. It didn't sound like they were threatening me, but after all that had happened, it was hard to tell for sure.

I read an article a few days later about how Shay Blackburn and Alanna Delaney had both been killed in a car accident in Upstate New York. Ashley was mentioned as having survived... so there was that.

I did reach out to her a few days later, and I saw her again at the funeral. She was looking a lot better, but I could see a newfound emptiness in her eyes. I can't pretend that I didn't understand. I knew she'd lost a lot.

For all intents and purposes, the funeral was the end of it.

I haven't heard anything from anyone since that incident. I've seen Ashley a few times, but that's just because she's probably the only one who knows what I've been through.

I don't know why I'm writing this down. Just to get it out, maybe? I haven't really been myself since what happened with Shay. I haven't had it in me to work. I've been turning down clients. I don't go out. I keep expecting I'll see her waiting for me if I do.

I'm scared... and I'm so, so tired of it.

So I guess I'm hoping that maybe if I put it down somewhere, I can put it away and start to move forward. Put my life back together and figure out where to go from here. I guess I'm being my own life coach now? I don't know. Maybe I'm done with that gig. Maybe there's more I could be doing with my life.

Maybe it's time to find out?

DON'T USE THE GLORY HOLE AT ROXY'S ROADHOUSE

My ex-wife once told me that nobody decent ever goes to Roxy's Roadhouse. On that, I beg to differ. Sure, it's a bit run-down, but I'll bet dollars to donuts that Roxy's is the best goddamn club in America! Hell, I could hit up all the nudie bars in the world and still not find a better place than Roxy's, and I mean that. Sure, it doesn't look like much. It's old and a bit run-down, sitting off the side of a quiet highway between towns. But it's got charm in spades. The girls there aren't afraid to be a little friendlier with you if you're a regular. Hell, every now and then, some of the girls are even inclined to give me a little something for free. Sometimes it comes to my table in a cold pitcher, sometimes I get it out back in my truck.

But the one thing I'd say that sets Roxy's apart from any other nudie bar in the world is that it ain't always just the girls working the floor who are available to you. No sir. Roxy's particular reputation draws all sorts. Older gentlemen such as myself who are just looking for a good time, boys who just want to say they touched a pair of tits, and, every now and then, a local girl looking for a ride.

They're more common than you might think. Some ladies might not show it, but they're just looking to fuck and they don't much care who they end up with. I've always been more than happy to oblige those sorts. I decided a long time ago that living with just one pussy to fuck wasn't exactly for me. I'm a man who likes variety, and Roxy's hasn't let me down once.

At least once or twice a night at Roxy's, you might see a girl headed off toward the washrooms. Usually, it's a dancer, looking to make a few extra bucks. But sometimes it's not, and those times are always something special.

See, there's only one washroom at Roxy's, and in it, there are two stalls. Now, some people do their business as usual in there and try not to notice the little hole in the little wall between those stalls, smoothed out with a fuckton of duct tape. Others are just there for the hole, if you catch my drift.

If you see a girl go into the washroom, chances are she's there to fool around, and I just love it when that happens.

Now, if it's one of the working girls, she'll probably want cash before she even does anything. But the walk-ins? They'll do it just for the hell of it, and sometimes, they're even better at it than the girls who work there!

I have made some genuine, sweet memories in that washroom, and I don't regret a single one of them. What could be better than cold beer and a blowjob from some pretty young thing, after all? If there's a better way to spend your evening, I haven't heard of it yet, and if you'd told me a few weeks back that a visit to the glory hole down at Roxy's could ever go wrong, I'd have laughed in your face.

I ain't laughing now though. No sir. Not one bit.

Ever since my ex-wife left me, I have spent a lot of my nights at Roxy's. It was for the best. The only reason I'd ever married her was because the goddamn rubber broke and she'd gotten herself pregnant. I'd figured that marriage wouldn't be too bad and took to some of my husbandly duties with enthusiasm. However, my ex-wife and I had different priorities. She wanted a family. I wanted to fuck, and it was only so long before we no longer shared a common interest. Leaving me was the best thing she could've done for both of us. And the kids, well, I can't say I missed any of them. I was happy to work through the day and spend my nights down at Roxy's.

Friday nights were usually some of the busiest, and the Friday that I got the last blowjob I'd ever have was no exception. Samantha was working that night, and while her tits were a little too plastic, she still had legs for days. I was halfway through a pitcher and had a wad of cash in my wallet, just in case one of the girls wanted to score an extra fifty dollars out in my truck. I was already feeling lucky that night, and when I saw that blonde come in, I was certain there was only one way my night was going to end.

She had messy blonde hair that went down to about her shoulders and a body to die for. Her crop top hugged her body tightly in all the right places, and you could see her nipples against the fabric. The shorts she wore were cut low enough that they might as well have just been denim panties. Just one look at her and I knew that she wouldn't be happy until she was getting plowed six ways from Sunday. She was exactly my kind of girl.

I kept an eye on her as I nursed my beer in my little booth. She sat at one of the tables, ordered herself a drink, and watched Samantha up on the stage. I knew I wasn't the only one with my eyes on her. I could see a couple of other regulars had noticed her as well, and no doubt they were thinking the exact same thing I was.

Our girl seemed to study the place around her, her eyes wandering over some of the regulars. I couldn't help but crack a grin when I caught her looking at me, and to my surprise, she actually smiled back.

Oh yes. I liked her, alright.

She raised her glass toward me, a playful little toast, and I returned the gesture in kind. I half expected her to come over and say hello, but she was either a lot shier than she looked or waiting on me to make the first move.

On the stage, Samantha switched out with a different woman. A new song played, and our sexy visitor kept her eyes on the stage, content to sit and watch for the time being.

I emptied my glass and mulled things over for a moment before getting up out of my booth.

I knew the girl was following me from the corner of her eye as I headed for the washroom, and I was sure I saw a tiny, knowing smile cross her lips.

Oh yes. We both knew what she was there for. I'd just given her an invitation to come and get it.

I stepped into the washroom and picked one of the stalls. I locked the door behind me and waited. I didn't have to wait long.

I heard the door to the washroom open and close. Through the cracks in the stall door, I saw that girl pass by my stall and head straight for the next one.

My heart was racing with a familiar anticipation as I heard her door lock with a click, and I waited until she was good and ready.

A small hand with pink-painted nails reached through the glory hole. Her fingers moved in a 'come hither' motion, and I finally undid my pants.

I could see part of her mouth through the hole as she sank down to her knees, and I gave her what she wanted.

I put my meat through that hole and waited for heaven… and at first, she didn't disappoint.

I closed my eyes and grunted in satisfaction as I felt her warm, wet mouth around me. Clearly, this bitch knew what she was doing. I pressed my whole body up against the wall, letting her have all of it and savoring the sensations I knew she'd give me as she used her hands and mouth to take good care of me, like a good slut.

"Fuck yes…" I grunted under my breath. With the way she was going, I wasn't gonna last long before I shot my load down her throat.

"That's it, girl. Keep going…"

Oh, she didn't disappoint. Not by a long shot, and I was quite vocal in letting her know just how satisfied I was. I could feel her tongue working on me as she took it deep, and then…

Pain.

It came on suddenly. A sharp, crushing sensation, like getting your hand caught in a car door. I felt her jerk me forward, and I swear I almost crashed through the wall.

I think I might've tried to say, "W-wait!" before that pain got a million times worse. It burned! It sank right through my manhood, and I could hear something ripping before that pain became way too much.

I screamed and on instinct, I pushed away from the wall. I'd expected to see blood when I looked down. But I didn't expect to see nothing *but* blood.

Well... that, and one hell of a messy stump where my dick used to be.

"FUCK!" I caught myself screaming before trying to scramble away. I collapsed against the door, and my weight was too much for it. I broke it off its hinges and spilled out onto the washroom floor, shrieking like a child as I desperately tried to stop the bleeding.

"JESUS FUCK! H-HELP ME!"

The stall the girl was in remained closed, although I could see movement on the wall inside. I watched, wide-eyed, as she climbed up it, moving like a fucking lizard! She fixed me in her sleepy eyes, her bloodstained lips curled into a mocking grin, and I looked back up at her in horror before I heard the washroom door behind me swing open.

Then came the screaming of the man who'd found me. I don't think he saw the girl on the wall before he was at my side, desperately trying to stop the bleeding.

"Somebody call an ambulance!" I heard him yell, but it sounded far away. My focus was still on that fucking girl... that fucking girl and that creepy, bloodstained smile of hers.

My vision was getting fuzzy. It was impossible to focus on her.

"T-there..." I tried to say, but I was choking on my own words. "THERE!" I tried to raise a hand to point at her. As soon as I did, she was gone.

Just one blink and the wall was empty. No girl. Nothing at all.

I don't know how much longer I remained conscious. Seconds. Minutes. More. Time hardly seemed to have any meaning at that point, and I barely registered the panicked folks around me, trying to figure out what had just happened.

I don't remember the paramedics getting there. The world around me just faded away and went blank.

When I woke up, I was in the hospital. The doctors had done what they could to keep me from bleeding out, but there wasn't a damn thing they could do about what had happened to me.

I never got a straight answer on exactly what went down that night. The best I could get was that there was an 'accident' and the girl had run off in a panic afterward, and I didn't believe that for a second.

I knew what I'd felt. That bitch hadn't just bitten me deliberately. I'd seen her scale the fucking wall like a goddamn spider afterward! I knew that for a goddamn fact, though whenever I tried to bring it up, I got ignored. I suppose I shouldn't have been surprised by that. Looking back over the next few weeks, it did sound insane, and more than once I doubted what I'd seen... but it had looked real, and that never quite left me.

It was a while before I could go home again, although I can't say I really healed.

What the hell kind of life can a man live without the most important part of his goddamn anatomy?

Of course, I returned to Roxy's, but it really wasn't the same. Beyond a slight rush, the girls really didn't do anything for me anymore, and even if I'd wanted to go into the washrooms, I couldn't. I couldn't drink with the painkillers I was on, I couldn't enjoy the simple pleasures of life I was so accustomed to...

My joints ached every day, and every single day, my beer gut looked larger and larger, to the point where I was sure something in me was swollen and infected. I felt sick to my stomach all the time, and I blamed that on the meds. Nothing felt right with me. Not a goddamn thing, and I hated it. I hated it so fucking much!

Every single day, I thought about what that bitch had taken from me... whatever she was. Part of me honestly hoped I'd see her again. If I did, I'm not sure what I would have done. Once or twice, I imagined her coming in like nothing had happened, then I'd get the revolver from my truck and blow her fucking brains out. I doubt that even if she did show, I'd have it in me to do anything like that. But God, it felt good to imagine it...

It was about a month after I came home that I decided there wasn't much in life to bother with anymore. My ex-wife had taken our kids when she'd left. At the time, I'd been happy to see them all go. Now, part of me wished they hadn't, and the rest of me wasn't so pathetic as to come groveling at their feet in my hour of need.

I was pushing fifty and staring down the barrel of life as an old man, deprived of the rush of endorphins that once kept him going, and frankly, that all just seemed a bit too much for me.

Deciding to end it all on my own terms was an easy decision. After all, it was better than the alternative, and once I'd made the decision, I figured I might as well not delay the inevitable.

It was dark when I waddled out to my truck and got in. I wasn't technically cleared to drive yet, but I figured that, given my situation, an exception could be made.

I knew of a bridge a few miles south, just past Roxy's. If I gained enough speed, I could probably break through the barrier and end up in the river. Even if I didn't, the crash by itself might well kill me. Either way, it would get the job done.

I had my last beer as I sped toward the bridge, more focused than I had been in a very long time. I did wonder a little bit about death, who doesn't every now and then, right? But in that moment, I saw it more as a fun little day trip than the ending of my life.

I picked up speed as I got closer and closer to the bridge. I could see it up ahead and took a final swig of my beer before pressing my foot down on the gas to go out in a blaze of glory.

What happened next was not exactly what I'd been anticipating.

The air in front of me seemed to shimmer. In my headlights, I saw a shape, although exactly what it was I really can't say. At a glance, I could've sworn it was a person. The closer I got, the less human they seemed.

On instinct, I swerved, and the figure just seemed to get closer. My truck fishtailed, and the bed struck the figure in the road head-on. The vehicle lurched to a violent and sudden stop, leaving me with whiplash on top of my regular pain.

My windshield had cracked, my driver's-side windows had shattered, and looking back, I was sure that my truck was bent damn near in two.

Panting heavily, I grabbed the revolver from my glove box and threw open the door to my truck, not knowing what the hell to expect but fearing it all the same.

My legs didn't support my weight, and I wound up collapsing just about as soon as I stepped out onto the pavement.

Through my blurred vision, I saw a shape standing over me. Not a shape I immediately recognized as a person, though. Not a shape I recognized as anything at all.

I saw eyes and teeth… far too many of them in all the wrong places, and they seemed to shift constantly. Those eyes seemed to look right at me before my vision began to even out and I saw *her*.

She was dressed in the exact same crop top and shorts she'd worn on the night I'd seen her come into Roxy's, and she looked down at me with cold eyes, ringed with red irises that seemed to shimmer like sunlight through water.

"You…" I rasped before I raised my gun and fired. I'm sure I should've blown her fucking head clean off, but aside from a slight blur to her face, she hardly even seemed to notice.

"What are you doing, Hank?" she asked, her voice a seething, bitter sound. With a shaking hand, I fired again, but it still did nothing, and she ripped the gun out of my hand before tossing it aside.

Her other hand grabbed me by the throat, and she forced me up off the ground and pinned me against the ruins of my truck.

"You bitch…" I spat. "Ruined my fucking life…"

"Please. I don't think you've realized that I've finally given you a purpose," she replied. "And here you are trying to throw it away…"

She pressed a hand up against my stomach, her brow furrowing in concern.

"Well… at least it's not dead."

"The fuck are you on about?" I growled, and her eyes returned to meet mine.

"You'll find out," she said. "In due time. Then you can die. But until then, you volunteered for this. So you're gonna tough it out…"

She patted me on the cheek and flashed me that same smile that had sucked me in back at Roxy's. Now, though, all it did was fill me with dread.

"What did you do to me?" I asked, my voice starting to quake as she locked her eyes with mine. "What the hell did you do to me?!"

"I gave you the opportunity to contribute to something more than yourself," she replied. "Now be a good Daddy, and get some rest…"

I woke up in my own bed that morning, with no recollection of how I'd gotten back there.

The police showed up at my doorstep a few hours later to let me know my totaled truck had been found in the river under the bridge, but I genuinely couldn't tell them how it had gotten there.

The last thing I remember was that woman had been clutching me by the throat and smiling, and after that... nothing.

I haven't tried to leave my house since the accident, but I have thought a lot about what she said to me.

Every day, I still feel sick. Every day, my joints still ache, and every day, I pop those painkillers, hoping that maybe the pain might stop. I did consider trying to OD once, but I'm afraid that if I did, she might come back.

In my dreams, I sometimes see countless eyes watching me, and when I wake up, I get the feeling that I'm not quite alone in my own bedroom.

Every day, my body seems to bloat. I wasn't sure what to chalk it up to before, but now I think I've got an idea.

She told me to be a good Daddy. She used those exact words. My ex-wife left me fifteen years back, and while I haven't seen or heard from our kids since then, I imagine they're old enough not to give a shit about me, nor need me. Even if I knew where to find them, I doubt they'd give me the time of day. I couldn't be a father to them even if I tried.

But I think I'm about to get my second chance, whether I like it or not...

Whatever is growing inside of me, I think it's gonna be coming out soon, and I don't know if I'm going to survive it when it does.

I've spent the past month or so being angry over what that bitch took from me at the glory hole... I never once thought that maybe she'd given me something in exchange, and now that the thought is in my head, I'm afraid to see just what it is.

I CAN NEVER RETURN TO THE OCEAN

I've been a fisherman for a very long time. It's what I know. All I know.

I'll confess, it's probably not the most glamorous job that a man can have. But if you know what you're doing, you can earn a living. I always figured I'd use my youth to make as much money as possible, save up a substantial nest egg, and then retire early. Find myself a wife, maybe have a few kids, and find some other work. As plans go, mine wasn't bad, and it wasn't anything that I hadn't seen other guys like me pull off before.

The difference between me and them, though, was Ash Bay.

If you've never heard of it, I'm not surprised. Ash Bay is something of a hidden gem along a quiet stretch of coastline in eastern Canada. I won't say exactly where for reasons that will become clear later, but if you're really that determined, it's not hard to find.

Not a lot of people seem to fish the waters around there, though. They generally go out much further, and as a result, you'll usually only see local ships in the thirty- to fifty-mile stretch between Ash Bay and the deeper parts of the Atlantic. It's always easy to tell which ships are local too. They're usually smaller fishing trawlers, but that's not what makes them distinct. No, what makes them stand out is the markings on the bottom hull. White painted swirls and patterns. You can always see the tops of them extending just over the water. I never quite understood why they did that... I also never understood why I only ever saw the Ash Bay ships out in that stretch of water. Everyone else just seemed to avoid that particular area. I always figured that there was just nothing to catch.

Then, of course, I started hearing the stories of the hauls of fish that the people in that area were bringing in.

I think the first person who told me about it was a guy I'd hired a couple of years back. He'd worked in Ash Bay for a few years and only recently left to be closer to his family, but the way he told it, those waters were absolutely teeming with fish, and the ships out that way only needed to head out for a week or so before coming back with a full hold. Anywhere else, you would've been out at sea for at least a month or so.

I vaguely recall thinking that he was bullshitting me at the time, but it wasn't long before he convinced me to visit the area.

Any doubts I had were gone by the end of the day. The waters were teeming with fish. I filled my hold in no time at all, and when I went out again, I wasted no time in heading back out there. The waters of Ash Bay didn't disappoint. They never have.

I thought I was being smart by packing up and moving out to Ash Bay. By the time I made the move, I'd already been fishing around those waters for the better part of a year and figured that I might as well save myself the fuel I'd been wasting by sailing out that way for so long. I'd been turning a pretty profit ever since I'd started fishing in the area, so cutting out the fuel expense just made sense.

Even before I made the move, I was aware of the... peculiarities of the locals. But I didn't think much of them. What town doesn't have a few odd quirks? Peculiarities were to be expected, especially in a place where most of the population consisted of sailors and fishermen. Anyone who's spent enough time on the water can tell you that we're a superstitious lot, and Ash Bay was a little more superstitious than most, especially when it came to the Stone Lady.

During one of my early visits, before I'd decided to move there, I'd seen the Stone Lady down by the harbor. She was a weathered statue depicting the torso of a nude woman that had been eroded by decades, if not centuries, of exposure to the elements. Moss had grown over much of the stone, covering her arms and most of her hair. She reminded me a little bit of that old painting, *The Birth of Venus*, or an old ship's figurehead.

Though it was hard to make out any of her worn features clearly, she had clearly once been a beautiful woman with a crown of reeds around her head. Delicately carved waves seemed to rise up around her legs, and as far as I could tell, her eyes were closed. The look carved onto her face was one of peace and serenity. At a glance, I might've thought that she belonged in a museum as opposed to being exposed to the elements by the coast. But just looking at her, it was clear that she was a source of reverence to the locals and didn't belong anywhere else but where she was.

There were countless flowers laid at the base of the statue and countless beaded necklaces adorned its neck, each of them lovingly handcrafted.

The statue sat within its own stone circle, not touched by anything else. It presented itself like an altar, although the significance of it all was lost on me at the time.

It wasn't until after the move that I ever got the chance to ask anyone about it.

David Scriver had lived in Ash Bay his entire life. Just by looking at the man, I knew that he knew his way around a trawler, and we hit it off quickly.

Most of my old crew wasn't interested in following me to a new town, so I'd started looking for help before I finished moving in. Scriver had been one of the first men who'd answered my job posting, and we'd agreed to meet for a beer at a local pub. One beer quickly turned into three or four, and we'd gotten to talking when I'd asked him about the statue down by the harbor.

"What? The Goddess of the Sea?" he'd asked. "It's something of a local superstition. I'm not sure if you've noticed, but the folks around here put a lot of stock in that kind of thing. Generally, the tradition is that before you go out, you give an offering to the statue of the Goddess to ensure your safe return. Beads or flowers, usually. Mostly it's the wives and the children who do it, but I've known a few men who will make their own beaded necklaces while they're ashore and bring them to the statue the morning before they cast off."

"I take it you don't put much stock in it?" I asked. Scriver was quiet for a moment before he answered. He took a thoughtful swig of his beer.

"Never been entirely sure what I thought of it, honestly. But it never hurts to feel like you've stacked the odds in your favor, does it?"

"I suppose not... What about those markings on the hulls of the boats? Does that have anything to do with the Goddess?"

The smile he'd been wearing a few moments back faded and was replaced by a more serious look.

"Yes and no," he said. "I've heard a few different answers from a few different people. My dad believed that the markings were there so that if the Goddess ever looks up, she knows that we're a friend. Otherwise, she might take offense to someone trespassing in her waters and sink the ship. Someone else said it was to help the boat stay afloat. Most versions I've heard are variations of the first one. Which reminds me, we should see about getting your hull painted."

I hadn't expected him to bring up painting the hull, so it caught me a little by surprise.

"What for?" I asked.

"Well, like I said, never hurts to stack the odds in your favor." Scriver took a pull on his beer.

"I suppose, but I don't really see the point. I've been fishing in these waters for about a year or so now. I've done just fine without using whatever pattern you folks have on your hulls."

"So far," Scriver replied. "I can't force you. But you'll have an easier time getting men on your boat if it's painted. Maybe it is just superstition. Maybe not. Either way. What've you got to lose?"

I let myself think it over for a moment. It's not like it would have impacted the performance of the boat or anything. Although having it hauled out of the water and painted to satisfy some superstition that wasn't my own seemed like a bit more hassle than I wanted to put up with.

"We'd have a hell of a time getting that done before we head out," I said. "Don't get me wrong. I don't mind if you're the superstitious sort. That'd be a hell of an expense, though."

"I'd just think of it as a safety precaution," Scriver said. His tone was blunt and matter-of-fact.

I shook my head and took another swig of my beer.

"Maybe when we come back to port, we've got some more money to spend," I said. "Right now, it seems like a bit more trouble than it's worth."

I could tell that Scriver didn't like that answer. But he wasn't about to get in my face over a fairy tale. Still, it only felt right to cut him a bit of slack. Sailors and fishermen are a superstitious lot. This wasn't the strangest thing I'd heard them do to stack the odds of coming home alive in their favor.

"I'll make an offering to the statue if it'll set your mind at ease," I said. "And when we come back, we'll talk about painting the hull some more."

Scriver nodded.

"It'll do," he said, although he didn't sound quite so sure about that. He took a reluctant sip of his beer and that was the last we said on the subject.

He wasn't wrong about having some trouble hiring hands for the boat. A few men I spoke to turned me down outright when they saw my hull wasn't painted. Superstition. It was almost enough to make me delay heading out to just get that stupid paint job over with. But moving isn't cheap. I had expenses that took priority, and putting my boat out of commission for a few days to get that job done would've put me in a tighter spot than I was comfortable with.

I was grateful that Scriver never pressed the issue, and he thankfully knew where to find some young men who didn't think too hard about superstition. I had my crew within a few days, and it wasn't long before we were ready to head out.

I honored my word for our first trip out, of course. As I made my way down to the harbor at dawn, I approached that moss-covered statue and laid some flowers at its base.

The weathered face regarded me indifferently, its features almost invisible in the shadows of the dawn.

Maybe it's silly, but I couldn't help but feel there was something slightly... off, as I laid the flowers at its feet. It was probably just in my head. I was letting Scriver's superstition get to me. Rationally, I knew there was no reason to feel anything towards that statue. It didn't change the fact that, looking at it, I couldn't help but feel this deep, uneasy pit in my stomach as if my guts were all tied up in knots. I stared back at that statue, then I backed away. Even with its eyes closed, I could've sworn that it was still watching me... It had to be my imagination, my own superstition taking charge. I tried not to dwell on it as I headed down to the docks to make the final preparations for our launch.

We made it out to open water with no issues. The sun was just rising as we sailed eastward into it, and I felt that familiar peace that always comes to me when I'm out on the water. It wasn't long before I forgot about the superstitions of Ash Bay. I had a good crew of men who were eager to work, and despite his superstitions, I trusted Scriver as a reliable second-in-command. He already wasn't letting me down. From the bridge, I could see him getting the men prepared to drop the nets once we were in deep enough water.

Our first day out went about as well as it could have. When we pulled up our nets, they were absolutely teeming with fish. The crew spent the better part of the afternoon processing and packing our catch in ice.

Rinse and repeat for the second day.

I was anticipating being back home by the end of the week, and admittedly, the color of my hull was the furthest thing from my mind.

I'd had no problems on these waters before. Why would I start having them now?

Then came the third day...

I knew something was wrong when we pulled in the nets. A full net has a heft to it. The sheer volume of fish is obvious once you start reeling it in. Likewise, an empty net comes in differently. There's no resistance. No weight to it.

Considering how rich the waters had been before, I knew something was off.

Both Scriver and I were on deck when the net got pulled in. Two of the boys he'd hired were standing by it, watching as the rope pulled it back aboard.

Even before it had returned to the boat, I could see the problem.

The net... what was left of it, trailed through the water, floating on the surface like a dead thing.

"It must've snapped," I heard one of the boys say as we pulled it aboard. "Maybe it caught on something underwater? A rock or something?"

Scriver stood beside me, dead silent. His brow furrowed. I didn't need to ask to know that he knew better. So did I.

"Could be," I said, although as I looked at the torn ends of the net, I couldn't help but feel that this had been no accident. The net appeared to have been cut open with a blade.

Sure. Maybe it could've been an accident.

But my gut told me otherwise.

I looked out at the water. It was a gray day out, and the surface seemed almost black against the dreary sky. But for a moment, in the distance, I swore I saw something moving. A splash as something large dove back down beneath the waves.

I knew that Scriver saw it too. I looked over at him to see his eyes narrowed at the horizon, the tension in his posture almost palpable.

He'd seen what I'd seen and something told me that he knew what it was.

Scriver came to me after supper to talk. I'd been up in the wheelhouse, enjoying a cigarette and bringing us a little further eastward. I'd had good luck in that area before. I expected to do so again.

"You got a moment?" he asked, after knocking on the doorframe.

"Course," I replied. "What's on your mind?"

"I think it might be best to head back to Ash Bay," he said. "We've pulled in a decent haul. It should be enough for wages and bills. We can come back out once the hull is painted."

"Go back?" I asked. "Now? We're barely half full!"

"And we're down a net. Look. I haven't pressed this issue. You're not a superstitious man, Wright. I can respect that. I'm not really one for superstition myself. But I also don't ignore it when something clearly isn't right. I've been fishing these waters for twenty years now. I've seen things. I know when a trip is about to turn bad. I'm asking you as a friend. Let's go home and paint the hull. Then we can come back out. If it's money you're worried about, I'll even forgo my wages for this trip."

This sort of plea sounded... odd, coming from the likes of him. Looking into his eyes, I could see an all-too-sincere concern.

Part of me wanted to humor him. But the rest of me didn't understand his cause for concern.

"We can fix the net and cast it again tomorrow," I said. "But I don't see any point in going all the way back home."

He didn't like that answer. I knew he wouldn't.

"At the very least, can we go no further out?" he asked, almost pleading with me. "Call me crazy if you'd like, but I believe that if we venture too far from the land, we won't be seeing it again."

I bit my lip, but having already dismissed his concerns, I didn't have it in me to do so again.

"I'll bring us closer to home," I promised him. "But I won't head back. At least not until after we've cast our nets tomorrow!"

That answer seemed to satisfy him, even if not completely. I saw him exhale a breath he'd been holding before he nodded.

"All right... I suppose that's enough..."

He hardly seemed satisfied, but he wasn't going to argue with me.

"Just stay close to home and don't keep us out much longer. I can't shake the feeling that we've worn out our welcome here."

He left without a further word, heading below deck to see to the crew. I almost asked him to stay, so I could ask him what he meant.

I wish I had.

My eyes returned to the darkened horizon. The lights of the boat illuminated the black waters, and I almost thought I saw something bobbing among the waves.

For a moment... It was gone when I tried to focus on it.

We cast our nets again the next day.

I'd held true to my promise to set a course closer to home. Ash Bay was visible in the distance. We weren't more than a few hours from home. I wasn't happy to be that close to land, but it seemed like an ideal compromise, given Scriver's concerns.

Regardless, the day carried on without incident. We brought in the first net after a few hours with no issues and received a generous haul for our troubles.

We started hauling in the second net. Judging by the resistance, I knew it was probably full, and my high spirits almost made me forget about all that strangeness from yesterday. Maybe I would have forgotten them completely if it all didn't come rushing back mere moments later.

As the net was pulled in, I could see the writhing of live fish inside it. It wasn't until we brought it around to empty it onto the deck that I noticed there was something else in there.

The sight of what looked to be a human arm jutting out of the side of the net made my heart skip a beat. My breath caught in my throat as, for a moment, I feared that we'd just found a body.

Maybe if I'd been faster, I could've stopped them from emptying the net. Then again... what good would that have done?

The net was emptied and its contents spilled all over the deck. Among the falling bodies of fish, I saw something large and man-shaped tumble onto the deck among them. It hit the metal with a heavy thud, followed by an even heavier silence.

Neither I nor Scriver nor the other men spoke as we looked at what lay among the mass of flopping, dying fish, although we could all see it clearly.

I, for one, certainly didn't believe what I was seeing. But that did not make it any less real.

From the waist up, she looked more or less like an ordinary woman. Her hair was long and tangled. Her skin was smooth and seemed as if it would have been soft to the touch, although it was riddled with deep cuts from the net. No doubt she'd gotten them struggling to escape it. She had an athletic physique and small, bare breasts, although those were not what any of us were looking at. No. The eyes of every man on that boat were trained below her breasts. On her sides, beneath her arms, and between her ribs were several slits in her skin. They reminded me of the gills of a shark and I imagine that's exactly what they were. Gills.

Beneath her waist was a strong, finned tail with silver scales that ended in a fluke, not unlike that of a whale but far more delicate. She had no legs—only that tail.

Never in all my years had I imagined I'd ever see a mermaid. I'd always thought they were nothing more than fairy tales.

But what else could I have called that which sat before me other than a mermaid? A mermaid who was still alive, if only barely.

Her eyes opened and she seemed to look around at us. Her arms moved, although her motions were sluggish. Weak. She seemed to gasp as she struggled to move.

We just watched her. Too in awe of her to think to help. Most of us were, anyway...

One of the boys that Scriver had hired took a step towards her, and as he did, Scriver himself put out an arm to stop him.

"No!" he cried. "No... leave it... let it die..."

Those words snapped me out of my daze.

"Let it die?" I repeated. "We should help it!"

"Believe me, if the stories I've heard about these things are true, then it would not care to do the same for us. Let it die!" he said, although I could see him doubting his own words.

The mermaid let out a growl of exertion before rolling herself onto her stomach. She looked up at us, teeth clenched in pain. Her teeth looked razor-sharp. Like a predator's teeth, not a human's.

But if she meant to attack us, she didn't have the strength. Her body seemed to collapse again as she struggled to breathe. I could see fresh blood pooling underneath her. She was bleeding out.

"We should throw her overboard," I said. "Come on. Let's just get rid of her, then! Before she dies!"

Scriver remained still as I ran to help the mermaid. The crewmen joined me.

Between us, we were able to pick the wheezing, dying mermaid up. She seemed to recoil from us at first, but didn't have the strength to fight us off even if she wanted to.

We picked her up and aside from a weak hiss of protest, she could do nothing but cling to one of the men for support. We brought her to the edge of the boat, and as we did, I saw the faces bobbing among the waves.

Other mermaids. More than I could count. All of them were watching us. Judging us for what we'd do next.

The sight of them made me freeze for a moment before I remembered just what it was that we'd set out to do.

The mermaid we'd caught was dying, and maybe they could save her...

I wish we could have been more gentle with how we sent her back to her people. With bloody hands, we tossed her overboard and let her fall back into the water, which turned red as she sank beneath it.

I saw several other mermaids dive down after her and after a few moments, they resurfaced, clutching their fallen comrade close. They looked at us before taking her back beneath the waves.

It was the last time I saw her.

The others lingered, though. They watched us intently, and I'd be lying if I said that their cold, inhuman stares did not send a chill through me.

Behind me, I could hear Scriver approaching. He stared out into the sea of unforgiving faces and I could sense the dread radiating off of him.

"I do not think that was the right call," he said softly. "Although… I don't know what would have been."

One by one, the faces began to disappear beneath the waves until only one remained. It looked to be a young woman with long brown hair that bobbed around her head. She wore a wreath of reeds around her head, and her green eyes burned into me with an intensity that turned my stomach.

From beneath the surface of the water, she raised an arm and in her pale hand, she held an ornate weapon. An axe with a wide, fanlike blade.

She pointed it directly at me, almost as if uttering a threat, before she turned and sank down beneath the waves with her sisters.

We were silent, with only the sounds of the ocean filling the air in the wake of what had just happened.

It was Scriver who spoke first.

"We need to get back to shore. Now… before they come back!"

He didn't wait for my permission. He didn't need to. Scriver made for the wheelhouse to steer us home and I was grateful that he did. My hands were shaking. It took me a few moments to gather my thoughts enough to register what needed to be done.

We didn't bother packing the bounty from the nets. If anything, we let the fish die and rot in the sun. We were a few hours from shore, and suddenly that seemed too far away.

We kept a lookout on the water, but it didn't do us much good. When the attack came, it came from beneath us and so suddenly that I'm not even sure we could have prepared for it.

As the boat sped homeward, it rocked suddenly as something struck the hull beneath us.

I sent one of the men down to check on it. He came up a moment later, running as if the devil itself was on his tail.

"We're taking on water!" he cried. "Something tore a hole in us!"

No sooner had the words left his mouth than the boat was hit again. This time, it rocked hard enough to throw me off my feet.

The engine seemed to sputter. In the wheelhouse, I could see a look of utter terror on Scriver's face.

I wasted no time in running up to check on him.

"What's our condition?" I asked.

"Not good. I think something just damaged the engine. We're losing speed!" he said. "In our current state, we might be able to limp home. *Might*! But when our state gets worse…"

"Damnit…"

I knew at that moment that the ship was going down. There wasn't a damn thing I could do to stop it.

But maybe we didn't have to go down with it.

"Let's get the dinghies ready. Raise flares to signal for help. We're close enough to shore, someone will see us."

Scriver nodded solemnly before I left him. I took the crewmen to get the dinghies. Small, inflatable things that wouldn't get us far. But given our circumstances, they were exactly what we needed.

We hauled them to the front of the deck and got them inflated. As we did that, I felt another impact rock the boat.

Scriver left the wheelhouse. I could see a flare gun in his hand and he aimed it at the sky and fired. The flare arced upward, and as it did, I told myself that we'd be okay.

After that, everything was a blur.

I remember the final impact that struck the boat. I remember that it threw me off my feet. I remember feeling the deck tilt beneath me as the boat began to tilt.

But I never saw what tilted it. It couldn't have been the mermaids, could it?

All I know is that one minute, I was sure that we were going home and the next, the boat was tilting. I was falling and when I landed, I was enveloped by the cold black waters of the ocean.

I remember seeing some of the men in the water around me. I think Scriver was among them… I think he was the first one they grabbed.

It was hard to see underwater. In the chaos, it was hard to be sure what was happening. But I'm sure that I saw Scriver just a few feet away from me the moment before a figure swam up from beneath him, grabbed him around the waist, and pulled him deeper under the water.

Maybe it's just a trick of my memory, but I could almost swear I heard him screaming the entire time...

I could see more of them coming, rising out of the blackness of the depths. I remember the panic in my chest as I tried to swim away.

Looking up, I could see one of the dinghies we'd inflated. I could see the white pattern on the bottom of it. Almost identical to the one the larger ships had.

I didn't think about the mermaids. I didn't think about the crew. I just thought about the dinghy and swam upward until I felt my hand against the bottom of it. I pulled myself aboard and tried not to imagine the cold hands reaching out of the depths to pull me down...

The flare was still in the sky when I broke the surface. It had reached its highest point and was coming down slowly... someone had to have seen it. Ash Bay was close. They definitely would have seen it, right?

God... God, I hoped I was right.

I looked back at my boat, which had now capsized. From the dinghy, I could see deep gashes in the hull. Deeper gashes than could have been caused by weapons...

But despite that, the waters around me were calm.

Too calm.

None of the crew surfaced around me. Neither did any of the mermaids, although I was still certain that I could see shapes moving beneath the surface of the water.

Figures circled my dinghy, deciding whether or not to sink it. I prayed to whatever God would listen that they wouldn't do it.

Maybe I got lucky that day. Maybe it was the markings on the bottom of the dinghy that dissuaded them.

I can't say for sure.

I was picked up by another boat about an hour later. By then, my boat had almost completely disappeared beneath the waves.

They looked for my crew, but they never found them. I can't say I'm surprised...

As they brought me back to Ash Bay, I couldn't help but look out at the waters behind us. Where my boat was sinking, I know I saw a single head rise above the water. I know that a pair of bitter green eyes watched me as I left.

I still see those green eyes in my dreams every night.

I left Ash Bay a few weeks later. I put the house I'd bought up for sale and cut my losses. It seemed the only sensible thing to do.

I remember that as I drove out of town that last time, I passed by the harbor and took one final look at the statue they kept there. Just the sight of it sent a chill through me.

Were I a braver man, maybe I would have taken a hammer to it in defiance of what it stood for. But I can only imagine that would have ended badly in one way or another, and I had no interest in continuing to tempt fate.

I've been a fisherman for a very long time. It's what I know. All I know.

I came to Ash Bay for that purpose, and I've left with nothing.

I don't know what I'll do now. I don't know where I'll go next. But I know that my days as a fisherman are over.

I can never return to the ocean now. I've worn out my welcome. I know that they'll be waiting for me. She'll be waiting for me.

Maybe I deserve whatever fate they'd bestow upon me. Maybe I'm a coward for avoiding it.

Maybe…

Maybe…

PREMATURE DECAY

This letter was found in the home of Jacob Bronson, on a table close to his remains.

Mr. Bronson was estimated to have been dead for approximately six months; however, the last confirmed sighting of him had been less than a week prior. His body was discovered by a friend who had gone to check on him, and who called the police upon discovering his remains.

The letter reads as follows.

Hey Jake.

If you're reading this, that means you've opened the box. You know, that large cardboard box that was in my car. My car, in my driveway... which was locked.

Now, I'm sure that you *"Didn't touch muh fuckin' car"* just like last time. This box just magically appeared in your hands, already opened. Or perhaps you just *"found"* it on your porch and opened it because, since it was on your property, it belongs to you.

It's okay. You really don't need to justify your actions to me anymore. I don't even want you to try. I learned my lesson the hard way after you whipped out your dick and started pissing on my shoes when I spoke to you last time about the unknown assailant who just so happened to look like you, who broke into my car last month and has been stealing my packages ever since I moved in.

Clearly, it was a case of mistaken identity, and the police will never figure out who that scrawny, blond man who comes out of your front door, walks over to my house, and takes things off my porch is.

I'm not really sure why I'm bothering to write this. I'm not entirely sure if you can actually read, and if you can, I doubt you'd actually care enough to read through this whole thing I've typed up just for you. Chances are, you're going to throw it away immediately and try to figure out what that thing in the box is, so you can hawk it and get your tweak on.

Sorry to burst your bubble, but you probably won't be able to sell it for very much. I'm sure you were hoping for another game console, like the one that disappeared off of Mr. Jackson's porch, down the street. That must've netted you some decent money. I imagine that scalpers turn a somewhat decent profit. Then again, I don't know if other scalpers use all of their earnings to get high off their ass. I don't really hang out with those kinds of people.

Anyway, about the contents of the box: I'm sure you're wondering just what the fuck is in there, and I'm thinking that I might as well tell you. It's not like anyone will believe you if you tell them, after all.

You see, I'd like to consider myself an educated man. I've been to school, I've gotten a diploma, I've traveled to different parts of the world, experienced other cultures and yadda, yadda, yadda. But there are some things about the world you really can't see for yourself unless you know where to find a good book, and with certain books, the more you read and the more you learn, the more you change.

I don't expect you to know what a "grimoire" is, but that's where I learned the little recipe for the bundle of straw and rags you've probably removed from the box by now. I put this note underneath it, so you'll at the very least have touched it if you're reading this.

That little straw effigy of you is a little bit crude, and it took me some time to construct. But I got one of your shirts after you got into a brawl with your friend in the street the other day, and you ripped it off for some stupid reason. I cut off a little bit of your hair when I noticed you sleeping in that lawn chair you have out front about a month back, and I got your blood from my smashed car window. You probably should have been a little smarter when you reached through my broken window to unlock my car door.

There was only one missing ingredient left to activate the effigy. It needed to be touched, and I'll assume that you've done just that.

You see, effigies like this are really quite simple. They can be used for a lot of different things. You can create one to make someone fall in love with you, you can create one to make someone behave in a certain way for your benefit, or you can use one to inflict a curse upon someone.

Guess what the purpose of yours is.

I spent a very long time thinking of what I wanted to happen to you, Jake. Having you just drop dead would be too anticlimactic, and I probably wouldn't be able to enjoy the show.

Anything too bloody would also be off the table. A tragic accident, a summoned demon, or something else like that would probably risk raising a few too many questions, and I don't think I'd be quite as satisfied with your suffering in those cases.

You've made the past year and a half of living on this street hell. At least once a week, there's a screaming match on your front lawn between two high strangers. I've seen the police out front so many times and watched so many drug- and alcohol-induced brawls in your driveway that they didn't break up. Every other day, I look outside and see you or one of your doped-up friends out front or in the backyard, doing the Crackhead Funky Chicken dance, and all I really feel for you is disgust.

Not even pity... Disgust... See, I truly believe that a lot of your friends are people who are desperately in need of help. They've lived fucked up lives, but they aren't inherently bad.

You, on the other hand? I think that you're way beyond saving.

I don't doubt for a second that they only tolerate you because you're the one supplying them. You buy as much as you can, you sell and smoke it away, and then you buy more.

You're like a human millstone, dragging everyone around you down in some way or another. I'd say that your death would be a service to mankind, but the way I see it, you're really already dead. Your whole life revolves around existing in a state of mindlessness. When I see you outside, you're nothing but a shambling zombie who is premature in his decay. But for some reason... your body is too stubborn to give up the ghost. So, this is my remedy for that.

It will probably be a few days before you waste away to nothing... but I'm going to enjoy it. From what I understand about this curse, it devours you from the inside out. Food no longer nourishes or satisfies. Drink no longer quenches. Substances do nothing to sustain you. It's the slowest, cruelest death I can grant, and you deserve every slow, agonizing second of it.

My guess is that you'll be sober by the end. You might be going into withdrawal, but you'll be sober. Hopefully, when you finally can't survive any longer, you'll be aware enough to understand just how much of a waste you are... well... were...

Goodbye, Jake.

Have a nice death.

The letter was not signed, making it unclear who had sent it. Various opened boxes with various names were found in Mr. Bronson's home, and there were approximately three different complaints about him breaking into, or attempting to break into, a vehicle from the past several months. These factors make it difficult, if not impossible, to determine who sent the letter.

No evidence of the effigy mentioned in this letter was found on the premises; however, some burned straw was found in a makeshift fire pit in Mr. Bronson's backyard. It is inconclusive if this is related to the letter he received.

At this time, there has been no conclusive evidence of foul play in Mr. Bronson's death, and his passing has been attributed to heart failure.

SPACEGIRL

PART 1: JANE'S STORY

We called her Spacegirl.

Her real name was Megan Daniels, but nobody actually called her that. Since second grade, she'd always been Spacegirl. She was the kind of kid who stuck out in the crowd with her long red hair, ghostly pale skin, and Coke-bottle glasses that hid the coldest blue eyes I'd ever seen. For as long as I'd known her, Spacegirl had been quiet. She didn't like to be around us. She didn't play with us when we were kids; she didn't even talk much.

Most of the time, she'd find somewhere to sit, far away from everyone else. Then she'd open up her little notebook and scribble inside of it. Sometimes she wrote poems, sometimes she drew. But she was always off in her own little world. Nowadays, I understand why we targeted her. She was different and she was alone. That doesn't justify any of it, but kids can be cruel.

I remember it was Sasha Brown who told me that Spacegirl was retarded because her mother was on drugs. Thinking back on it, Sasha had probably just made that up. But we all believed it anyway. She had always been the worst toward Spacegirl, and she kept that up until the end. I can't pinpoint one particular moment where everything started to go downhill. But the moment I remember best is when Sasha took her notebook.

It had been sometime in fifth grade. It had been raining that day, so we had an indoor recess. Spacegirl sat in the corner at her desk, eyes focused on her notebook as she methodically worked on a drawing.

Sasha and I had been sitting nearby at our desks, and we simply watched her do her thing.

"I can't believe they let that retard sit in with us," Sasha murmured. "Look at her... Why do they even let them in schools? They aren't gonna learn anything."

"Better than leaving her at home with her crackhead mother," said Tanya Evrett. She and I weren't exactly friends, but she sat close to Sasha and me. "My dad says he sees a different car in front of her house every day. He says that she lets boys come and they pay her so they can have S-E-X."

None of us could actually say the dreaded S-word at the time. Sex was still a terrible unknown thing, and we all had been raised to believe that nobody decent would ever do it.

Spacegirl paused, and her eyes darted away from her book to look at us. I can only imagine she'd heard us. Sasha just stared right back at her.

"What? Do you have a problem, Spacegirl?" she asked. The teacher was out of earshot, and that gave her carte blanche to say whatever she wanted.

Spacegirl didn't respond. She just looked back down at her notebook, but Sasha had been challenged (or at least she thought she'd been).

She looked over to the teacher's desk to make sure she was busy, then she got up and moved closer to Spacegirl.

"What are you even doing in there, retard?"

She'd reached out to snatch the book before Spacegirl could stop her.

"What even is this? A unicorn? What are you, five?"

She handed the book to me, and I took it on instinct. There was a brightly colored drawing of a unicorn inside. The artwork was actually pretty nice, but I would never have said so. The book was passed on to Tanya next, and Spacegirl could only look at us helplessly.

"Wow. You can't even draw. Look at this!"

She tore the page out of the notebook. Spacegirl let out a whimper of protest, as if she'd just been struck.

The picture was crumpled up and the book was thrown on the floor by her desk.

"Draw something that isn't trash next time," Tanya said, and Sasha just giggled as if it was anything other than being mean-spirited just for the sake of it.

Spacegirl slowly picked her book up off the floor, avoiding eye contact as Tanya and Sasha turned away from her. I continued to stare. I remember that the way she moved was so defeated, as if she were shrinking in on herself. She looked up at me, but only for a moment, and I felt bad for her. I really did. But I didn't do anything about it. I just left her to rejoin the others.

After that, Spacegirl became an easy target for Sasha and Tanya. Every chance they got, they'd harass her, and I regret to admit that I was usually right there with them.

During the days where we could go outside for recess, Spacegirl would always sit beneath the same tree, and she'd always work in her notebook.

Sometimes Sasha, Tanya, and I would just go and stand by her tree to hang out. Sasha would always lean on the trunk and look down over Spacegirl's shoulder.

"Wow, that's really good, Spacegirl." That was how most of her comments would start. "Did you mean to draw it like it got hit by a truck, or is that just your style?"

There was never a compliment. She would always find something to needle, and she would do it over and over again until finally, Spacegirl moved. Then we'd follow her, harassing her about her work. Most of her art was fantastical. She liked unicorns, detailed kingdoms in the clouds, fairies, mermaids, and things like that. She didn't deserve the treatment we gave her... but she got it anyway.

"Can you draw me?" Tanya asked once. "I heard that retards were always like art geniuses or something. Maybe it'll even look like a person!"

Spacegirl didn't look up at her. She seemed to be trying not to acknowledge the insults. Usually, Sasha and Tanya didn't care, although every now and then they'd steal her book just to thumb through it, make fun of everything she'd drawn, or just tear out the pages.

I won't pretend like I was blameless either. I never stopped them, and there were plenty of times where I was right there, making fun of her, because that was what we did. We made fun of Spacegirl, and we weren't the only ones. More or less, everyone hurt her in some way or another. But she never complained. I think she was too scared to.

It was late December in seventh grade when things got even worse. I don't know all the details, and I don't know just how long things had been boiling over, but I'd heard a rumor that James Hardy had it out for Spacegirl.

James had only been in my class a few times, and he wasn't in my class that year. He was a small, mousy-looking kid who was convinced he was the world's toughest gangster. By the time we were twelve, he dressed in loose basketball jerseys and jeans that sagged. He was as white as they came, but he listened to censored Eminem, so that made him a gangster.

The rumors said that someone had seen his dad going into Spacegirl's house. Naturally, there had been speculation that his dad was sleeping with her mom. Someone told me that James's parents had been divorcing because of it. Somehow, all of these rumors had mutated into claims that James and Spacegirl were dating, and I think that was what had rubbed him the wrong way.

We were coming in from recess when some boys decided to pull a little prank on James. The whole prank had been set up by Brian Jordan and his brother Mike. They had some mistletoe for the holiday season and had set it up in the hall leading back to our classroom. Mike had grabbed Spacegirl during recess and was holding her behind the door where the mistletoe was. When James walked through, they pushed her at him and snapped a picture.

I'd been just behind James when it happened. I watched as Spacegirl came flying out of seemingly nowhere, eyes wide and afraid as she crashed into James.

They both hit the ground, and I could hear the other boys laughing.

"LOOK! She wanted to give you a kiss!" one of the boys said. Spacegirl was trying to crawl away from James and pick up her notebook, but somebody had kicked it out of sight. I remember that she looked back toward James and there were tears in her eyes. She must have been terrified by everything that was going on. She clearly hadn't wanted any part in this, but there she was at the center of it.

"You fucking assholes!" James yelled as he picked himself up, along with some other slurs I won't repeat.

"Hey, she just wanted to give you a smooch," laughed Brian. "Come on, give her a kiss!"

Someone pushed Spacegirl toward James and he glared at her, as if all of this was her fault. She tried to stand and run, but he was angry and wasn't thinking straight. He lashed out at her with a square punch to the jaw. Then he tossed her to the ground and went after Brian next. A teacher had to get in to pull James off of him. He, Spacegirl, and the Jordan brothers ended up getting suspended right before the Christmas holiday. We didn't see Spacegirl until January, and we didn't see James or his friends ever again.

On Christmas Eve, there was a car accident on the highway outside of my town. Supposedly, it had swerved off the road to avoid an animal of some kind and gone into a ditch. Mike, Brian, and their parents didn't survive.

On December 27, James was killed while shoveling his driveway. My parents told me that he'd been attacked by an animal, probably a deer or something. But that seemed so unusual... I'd never heard anything about deer attacking people before, especially not in my area.

I went over to Sasha's house on the day before New Year's. We'd both gotten some gift cards for Christmas, and we were planning to walk to the mall together to use them.

Sasha's parents weren't home; they both had to work. So it was just us when I got there.

"Hey! Kept me waiting!" she said when I knocked on the door.

"Sorry."

"It's fine. I'll be ready in a bit. Come on upstairs, I wanna show you something!"

I didn't question what it was. I figured it was just something else she'd gotten for Christmas, so I went upstairs with her.

"You're gonna love it," she promised me. "It's gonna be so funny..."

She led me to her bedroom, and as soon as she opened the door, I spotted a familiar notebook on her desk.

"Where did you get this?" I asked, walking closer to it.

"Spacegirl dropped it when Brian and his brother pulled that prank the other day. I saw it, so I grabbed it. Y'know, just for safekeeping."

She cracked a wry grin before opening the notebook.

"Look at this. She's been drawing the same damn unicorns forever. She didn't even finish this one!"

She paused at one small picture that was labeled 'The Unicorn Prince'. It depicted an empty field with a blank space where the titular prince should have been. Sasha flipped through the pages a little more until she got to the newer ones.

"I figured since they kicked Spacegirl out for a little while and her mom is too poor to get her anything for the holidays, I'd step up! What do you think?"

Sasha wasn't anywhere near as good an artist as Spacegirl was, but the simple detail in what she had drawn turned my stomach.

In her first picture, Spacegirl was hanging from a rope. Her tongue was hanging out, and her eyes were closed.

In the second one, Spacegirl had a gun in her mouth.

In the third one, she was standing on the edge of a building.

Sasha giggled as I flipped through her crude depictions of suicide. A bottle of pills, getting hit by a car, and slitting her wrists.

"What do you think?" she asked with a grin. "I'll bet she'll lose her shit!"

I closed the notebook and looked over at Sasha. Why was she so happy with this?

How did she not realize what she was doing?

"A-are you out of your mind?" I asked. Sasha's grin faded.

"What do you mean?"

"You stole her notebook, just so you could draw these? Sasha, that's really messed up!"

"It's Spacegirl. Who the hell cares about Spacegirl, Jane?"

"You just... drew her killing herself over and over again!" I took the book off her desk. "How don't you understand what's wrong with that?"

Sasha just stared at me like I was crazy. Maybe I was crazy, but not for drawing the line there. I was crazy for not drawing it sooner.

"Fine. Sue me for trying to be funny," Sasha said. "Just give it here..." She stretched out her hand to take the notebook, but I pulled back from her.

"No. You're just going to put something else in there."

Anger flared in Sasha's eyes.

"Jane, just give me the book."

"No! I don't trust you!"

I opened the book and I started to tear out those pages of Spacegirl's suicide. Sasha lunged for me, trying to grab at the book and stop me, and I pushed her back. I didn't mean to push so hard, but I did and she fell, landing hard on the ground.

Sasha looked up at me, wide-eyed and shocked. I don't think anyone had laid a hand on her like that before.

Then I saw something in her eyes... not just anger. Something worse. It was the same thing that had prompted her to draw those horrible pictures of Spacegirl. Slowly, she got to her feet, her eyes trained on me. I could hear her breathing getting heavier, and I took a step back. It wasn't the first time I'd seen the really ugly side of Sasha. But it was the first time it was ever directed at me, and now that I looked into her eyes, what I saw scared me.

I turned and ran, bolting down her stairs, out her front door, and back into the snow. I clutched Spacegirl's notebook to my chest the entire time, and I didn't let it go until I got home.

I spent the rest of the Christmas break terrified that my parents would get a call from Sasha's. I'd pushed her, and that seemed like such a big deal at the time. In hindsight, I doubt Sasha would have told her parents what had happened. They would have asked why I'd pushed her, and I would have told them about the notebook. On some level, she must have known that what she'd done was wrong. She was a cruel person, but there had to be a point where even she would recognize that she'd gone too far. Part of me hoped that she'd realize that I was right and we could patch things up when school started again, but honestly, I wasn't so sure.

I remember looking through Spacegirl's drawings. The ones that she'd done. I remembered the ones I'd made fun of the most. There was one with a mermaid on a rock, combing her hair. Her eyes were closed in a relaxed bliss. I remembered saying how stupid her facial expression had looked. Honestly, I kinda liked it.

I flipped through the pages some more, through unicorns, fairies, and castles. But I paused at the page depicting the Unicorn Prince.

Back at Sasha's place, it had been blank, but at my house, it was finished. The Unicorn Prince stood proudly in his field, looking skyward with his horn proudly displayed.

Maybe I had been thinking of a different picture?

I brushed it off and flipped to the back, where Sasha's pictures were. One by one, I started tearing them out of the notebook and tossing them in the trash. It was a waste of paper, but I refused to give it back to Spacegirl with those images still in it.

On the first day back to school, I was up early. I made sure the notebook was packed into my bag and was out the door as early as I could be.

The snow on the ground was almost pristine as I walked to school, but I remember seeing some tracks on my lawn, headed down the side of my house. Deep, U-shaped indents that looked like they'd been made by hooves. A deer, perhaps?

I didn't dwell on them and made my way down the freshly shoveled sidewalk and back to school.

I wasn't entirely sure if Spacegirl would be back yet, but she was. She was alone in the classroom, sitting at her desk and drawing in a brand-new notebook. She paused briefly when I walked in to join her and could see her side-eyeing me. She didn't say a word as I drew nearer, but I thought I saw her shoulders tense up ever so slightly.

"Hey," I said. "I'm... I hope you had a nice holiday."

She didn't respond. She just watched me from behind her Coke-bottle glasses, and I could sense the distrust radiating off of her.

"I'm sorry about what happened the other day. I didn't know anything about it, but it just seemed really mean-spirited."

Still no answer. I reached into my backpack, taking out her old notebook. I put it on her desk in front of her. She stared at it, still silent, then back at me.

"Sasha took it. I was over at her house the other day and she showed it to me. I'm sorry that I had to take some pages out. She drew some really awful things in there. I didn't think it would be right to give it back with those things still in there..." I paused, feeling smaller as Spacegirl stared at me. She didn't seem angry or thankful. She didn't seem anything at all. Just stoic.

"I'm sorry if I wasn't all that great to you before," I said, and then shuffled off to my desk. Spacegirl waited until I sat down before she opened her notebook and inspected it. Then she closed her new book and started something new on a fresh page in her old one.

It wasn't much. But it made me feel at least a little good for what I'd done.

When Sasha got in, she didn't talk to me. She didn't even look at me. Neither did Tanya nor any of our other mutual friends. I knew from the moment they walked in that I'd burned my bridges with them. But I still wanted to try.

The teacher hadn't come in yet, so I figured it might be worth it to try and talk to Sasha. I got up to move closer to her, and she gave me a look of utter disgust.

"What do you want?" she spat.

Now it was my turn to be silent.

"Fuck off and leave us alone," Tanya said. "You'd obviously rather hang out with the fucking retard than us. I really don't want you spreading your retard germs to us. It's a quarantine issue."

I stared at both of them, and I could've sworn I knew how Spacegirl felt. What was I supposed to say to any of that? Instead, I just returned to my desk without a word. Spacegirl stared at me the entire time. Her pencil rested over her notebook, but she didn't write anything. She set it down, tore out the page she'd been writing on, and jammed it into her pocket. I later saw her toss it into the trash during lunch.

I didn't really have anyone left, so I thought that maybe it might be a good idea to pull it out. Maybe it was something she wasn't happy with? I'd never seen her throw a drawing out before. I was thinking that maybe I could use it as a peace offering of sorts or something along those lines. Looking back on it, I'm not entirely sure what I was expecting to do with it. When I saw what she'd written on it, though, I almost threw it back into the trash.

Your Words
There is a land where your sorry may go.
A sickening land where it always snows
The snow is putrid in color and smell
Its substance—filth and things I won't tell.
Only your father has been there before.
One day your boyfriend will visit once more.
This place in your carcass, this humanoid hell.

Your sorry can go there to this hole in your shell.
My unsubtle message, this subtextual jazz.
Is to take your apology and stuff it up your ass.

This was unlike anything I'd ever seen her write. It was so crass and spiteful. This was as close to hatred as she could have gotten.

I understood why she'd thrown it out. It didn't fit with everything else she'd done. Those things had been beautiful, despite what people had said and done to her; she still tried to make beautiful things. This was angry and ugly. This was something she'd written for *me*.

I put it in my pocket. I wasn't going to give it back to her, but I wanted to keep it. Even if she'd thrown it away, she'd written it about me. She'd written it about the way I'd treated her, and I wanted to remember that.

There was a service for James, Brian, and Mike a few days into the first week back. No one mentioned what had happened to them, but there were a few whispers that Spacegirl had somehow been responsible. Of course, nobody actually believed it. It was more of a joke than anything else. Their deaths had been tragic accidents... supposedly. But kids would always gossip.

Those three boys were more or less forgotten after seventh grade, and their prank was forgotten too. People instead chose to paint them as bright young spirits who'd been lost before their time instead of the pieces of shit they really were.

Eighth grade wasn't fun for me.

I had very few friends left, and Sasha never forgave me for turning on her. Her version of the story was slowly warped as time went on.

First, I'd punched her and stolen the book. Then I tried to kiss her, punched her when she'd refused, then stole the book to try and get her in trouble. Rumors of me being a dyke spread pretty quickly, and hot on their heels came the rumors that I was dating Spacegirl.

I tried not to let them bother me too much. I knew the truth, and at the end of the day, I'd done the right thing.

By the time high school rolled around, I was hoping for a fresh start. There were new faces, and I figured I could make friends with them before Sasha's rumors spread. I had a bit of success in that department. I fell in with a better crowd, at least.

Sasha stuck with her same old clique. It grew ever so slightly, but she was determined to live out the movie *Mean Girls*, and most people didn't pay her any mind.

Spacegirl barely changed at all. I didn't see her much when high school started. She was in a few of my classes, but I rarely saw her outside of them. Whenever she had a moment, she'd be in the library, usually working on her drawings in one of the corner cubicles.

Sometimes, I thought about talking to her and trying to strike up a friendship… but it never felt right. Years had quietly passed, and I'd never forgotten the way I'd treated her, or that angry little poem she'd written.

Sasha's bullying never let up, of course. Of course, she stalked Spacegirl to the library, where she'd pull the same old shit she'd been pulling since the fifth grade. She'd leer over her cubicle and comment on her drawings, picking them apart just like she always had. I stopped her whenever I saw it… but I didn't always see it.

"Coming to her rescue again, huh, Jane?" Sasha asked once when I'd interrupted her. Tanya leered at me from behind her, chewing gum with her mouth open.

"What's she ever done to you anyway?" I asked. "She's just minding her own business."

"Oh? What's she done to you, dyke?" Sasha hissed. She leaned down over her cubicle and looked at the notebook.

"Unicorns… unicorns, unicorns, fucking unicorns. When are you going to grow up, Spacegirl?"

"Hey! I told you to stop." I rounded the cubicle, and I saw Sasha recoil. For a moment, I saw a bit of fear in her eyes. It vanished quickly and was replaced with a familiar rage.

"Fine," she said. "Let's leave the happy couple to their alone time then."

She pulled away from the cubicle and disappeared with Tanya nipping at her heels like a faithful terrier.

Spacegirl remained hunched over her notebook, her long red hair spilling over her shoulders. She seemed impossibly still.

I turned to leave her when I heard:

"Thanks."

I looked back at her and saw that she was looking at me.

"Um... you're welcome," I said. "Let me know if she bothers you again, all right?"

"I will. But... you're usually there anyway."

Her voice was soft and low. I'd heard it before, but I don't remember her ever speaking directly to me.

"Yeah, well. It's just not right. She's such a child. One of these days, she's going to have to grow up."

Spacegirl just nodded, looking over toward the library door, then back down at her notebook again.

For a moment, I thought about asking her about what she was drawing. I thought about saying something else but... no. I didn't want to make her uncomfortable. I left her alone again.

In tenth grade, I took art as an elective. I wasn't much of an artist, but I figured it would be an easy course. To the surprise of no one, Spacegirl was there. She'd grown into her red hair as she got older and had otherwise barely changed since the day I'd met her. She was as quiet as ever, although I couldn't help but notice that in art class, she seemed just a little bit happier.

I actually asked her to work with me on the first group project of the semester. I think the prospect of being asked to work together was foreign to her. She looked at me suspiciously when I did it, but when she realized that this wasn't just another sick prank or attempt to harass her, she actually smiled. It was a slowly spreading smile that seemed just a little bit goofy, and it was the cutest thing I'd ever seen.

"I'd like that," she said, and the modest tone in her voice just cemented my own decision.

I ended up going to her house that weekend to work on the project. We were supposed to take turns drawing portraits of each other, and I'd volunteered to let her draw me first.

Rumors of her mother's sexuality had always surrounded Spacegirl, so I wasn't entirely sure what to expect when I got there. I certainly wasn't expecting the quiet and neatly kept house that I found.

Her mother was the one who answered the door, and she looked like an older version of her daughter, sans the Coke-bottle glasses.

"You must be Jane," she said. She wasn't smiling, but she didn't sound upset either.

"Yes, ma'am..."

"Come on in. Megan's upstairs. She was just getting ready for you."

The house was warm and cozy with plenty of knickknacks on the walls—plates and porcelain dolls, mostly. The living room looked more like a waiting room, and I spotted a few framed degrees on some of the walls. I'd later end up learning that her home was actually her office. Her mother was a psychiatrist who worked out of her home.

"I was just about to bring some snacks upstairs," her mom said, "but Megan gets very focused when she's working. She doesn't like being bothered. Would you mind running them up for me?"

"Sure thing," I said, and her mother handed me a plate full of peanut butter cookies.

"Thanks. I'll be down here if you or Megan need anything."

That sounded almost like a warning, and I wondered if her mom knew about the way I'd treated her daughter in the past. I didn't ask about it and just quietly took the cookies upstairs.

On the landing leading up to Spacegirl's room, I could see a mural of family photos and paused to look at them.

I could recognize Spacegirl and her mother in most of them. Spacegirl never seemed to be smiling, although her mother usually had a wide grin. I only saw her father in a few of the very early pictures. He was a gruff-looking man with glasses and a beard. Spacegirl looked like she was only a young child in the few pictures I saw him in, though.

I didn't dwell for long and headed toward what I assumed was her room. The cardboard stars and planets on the door gave it away.

Sure enough, she was inside waiting for me. She sat facing the door behind an easel in the center of her room. Her bed was neatly made and tucked away in the corner. She had a clean little desk that she'd clearly been working on and had set a chair out for me to sit on. I hadn't expected something so overwhelmingly formal, and I almost started laughing. But then I noticed her walls.

They weren't just covered in drawings. The art pieces on them were full-on paintings. They were the same fantasy depictions she usually did, but the colors were so vivid. The clouds looked like fluffy pillows, and the castles seemed great and infinite. There was something lonely about them, though. The subjects were always in the center, surrounded by a vast, colorful world that seemed so beautiful and yet so empty.

"Hey..." I said, but I was clearly distracted. "Holy shit, are these yours?"

"They are," Spacegirl said softly. She stood up and took the plate of cookies from me, then moved it to her desk.

"It... it's soothing," she said after a while. "Painting, I mean. I pick the drawings I like the most and I finish them."

She spoke slowly, like she was carefully choosing her words. I almost felt like there was something that she was trying to avoid.

I spotted a painting on the floor that looked like her father. The style was similar, although a little less refined. This looked like an older piece. I would have figured she'd done it as a child if not for the way her father looked in it. The look on his face was one of absolute terror. Even in that cruder format, it was impossible to mistake it for anything else. His eyes were wide. His mouth was open, and he looked like he was screaming. Spacegirl looked down at it, and her brow furrowed in disapproval. She turned it around so I wouldn't have to look at it.

"We should get started," she said. "Sorry... I shouldn't have been talking."

"No, it's all right!" I said. I sat in the chair for her. "I'd like to hear about it."

Spacegirl watched me from the corner of her eye for a moment as if she doubted I was being serious. But eventually, she sat down behind the easel and started to draw. Soon after that, she was talking too.

I stayed long after she'd gotten what she needed for her sketch. I made her tell me about her art.

She told me that she'd always liked fantasy and how she liked unicorns because they were simple but pretty. I hung on to every word, and I could've sworn I saw her smiling shyly as she talked.

The portrait she'd done of me was something else entirely.

Her work had always been beautiful... but this made me look transcendent. I wasn't entirely sure that I was looking at myself at first. There was something about the look on my face. There was a small, almost content smile there. The warmth it conveyed was almost Disney-esque.

"I love it!" I told her. "That's incredible, Spa—Megan. That's really great!"

"You can call me Spacegirl if you want," she said. "I don't mind the nickname. Not as much as I mind the people, at least."

My awe quickly turned to shame, but Spacegirl didn't look upset. She just stared at me blankly like she so often did. No... not blankly. Her face might not have conveyed much, but there was definitely something there.

"I wish... I wish I'd been nicer to you when we were younger," I said.

"Is that why you're here right now?" Spacegirl asked.

"No! I... I'm here for the assignment. I mean... the art assignment. The portraits..."

She continued to stare.

"Did you pick me because you felt bad for me?" she asked.

"No! I just thought it would be cool to work with you."

Spacegirl didn't react for a moment, but then she just nodded.

"Okay." Her flat tone made it hard to know what she meant by that. She stood up and started cleaning up her supplies.

"Mom can drive you home if you need a ride," she said. She didn't look at me. I opened my mouth to say something else. I wanted to apologize, but I didn't know what to say.

Had I offended her? Had I said something wrong?

"All right. Thanks." It was the only thing I could think of. "See you tomorrow."

With that, I left her.

I was almost afraid to see Spacegirl the next morning. I drifted through my classes that day until I reached art... and when I did, I wasn't expecting what I saw.

Spacegirl had clearly been up late... but what she'd brought in stole my breath away.

It was my portrait, but she'd done more with it than I thought possible. She'd painted over the sketch, turning me into something beautiful. Flowers bloomed around my brown hair, and a crown of daisies, lilies, and chrysanthemums adorned my head. The colors were so vivid, and I looked so at peace in it. Spacegirl was looking right at me as I came in, as if she was gauging my reaction. But I simply didn't know how to react!

All I could do was stare wide-eyed and in awe. When I looked back at Spacegirl, I saw that smile I'd come to love. Small and subdued, but so much bigger than it seemed.

My portrait of her didn't turn out nearly as good, but Spacegirl's had not only netted us an A on the project but also got the privilege of being hung up outside of the art classroom.

Of course, I told her how much I loved it, although I don't remember what words I used, nor if they were coherent. Whatever I said, Spacegirl only listened with a small, knowing smile as her cheeks flushed red, and I remember thinking how pretty she looked when her blush matched her hair.

My portrait was up for barely a day before Sasha had to make a comment.

I'd been at lunch and had just gotten some fries from the cafeteria when she and Tanya ambushed me.

"Where's your flower crown, dyke?" Sasha sneered. "Did she draw you like one of her French girls too?"

Tanya snickered at that, even though it wasn't even funny.

"Leave me alone," I said, brushing past them, but Sasha was out for blood.

"I always knew you were a little dyke. But now you've posted solid proof of it! We've gone and cracked the case, haven't we? So what happened? Did you go to her house and lick her retarded little snatch? You must be a real good dyke because she went and drew that for you!"

I tried to walk away from her, but Sasha and Tanya just kept following me.

"What's wrong? Am I not pretty enough for you, dyke?" she snapped at me.

"Maybe she only fucks retarded girls," Tanya said. "I'll bet Spacegirl squealed like a pig when she came."

I stopped dead in my tracks, and I heard Sasha stop behind me. I don't know what it was about what she'd said that pissed me off so much. But those two had finally struck a nerve. I spun around, swinging my lunch tray as hard as I could. Fries were scattered everywhere, but although I was aiming for Tanya, I hit Sasha.

She went down hard, and I'm not sure if she was even still conscious when she hit the ground. Tanya was on me in an instant. She slammed me back against a wall and kept me pinned. She had size and strength on me. There wasn't a thing I could do to stop her.

"WHAT THE FUCK?" I heard her shout as several other students grabbed at us. A teacher finally got involved, and all three of us got escorted to see the principal.

As we left the cafeteria, I saw Spacegirl in one of the halls, just staring at me.

Naturally, I got a three-day suspension, but Tanya and Sasha were fine. Both of them said they'd just been walking and I'd attacked unprovoked. It was their word against mine.

Sasha had a familiar shit-eating grin on as she left the office with only a bruise on her forehead to show for her troubles, but there was a familiar look in her eyes. That same anger I'd seen last time I'd laid a hand on her, and it scared me just as much as it had the last time I'd seen it.

When I came back to school, I realized that I had every reason to be afraid. My portrait was missing. I wondered if they'd taken it down because I'd attacked Sasha, but the truth was a lot worse.

"Someone took it," Spacegirl said. She was sitting in her usual spot in the library when I found her, sketching flowers in her notebook.

"When?"

"The day after you hit Sasha... I don't think anyone's found it yet."

She didn't look up at me, just stayed focused on her art. She didn't need to say it for me to know who she blamed. Who else would it be? Though she didn't show it, I could tell from the thick, aggressive lines in her sketch that the theft had gotten to her. She'd been proud of that portrait. She'd put so much work into it, and now Sasha had taken that too, just like she'd taken and ruined everything else.

I had half a mind to confront Sasha about it, but I didn't know if that would be a good idea or not. Sasha could easily just cry wolf. I wouldn't put it past her. I would probably just leave it alone. But Sasha wasn't done yet. No, she'd been good and pissed off at me for years, and she finally was ready to do something about it. I should have known she would.

About an hour later, when I was headed to art class, the painting was back. But there had been some modifications made to it. The words *Retard Fucking Dyke* had been crudely painted across my portrait in bright red. I saw it from down the hall and could see some other students whispering among themselves beneath it. I didn't know what to say or do. But this felt like too much.

The picture was taken down quickly... but the damage was done. Sasha had gotten her revenge, and it didn't stop with just the painting.

Spacegirl looked different than when I'd seen her in the library. She seemed uneasy, and her eyes were red like she'd been crying.

"I'm sorry about the painting..." I said softly. She looked at me before sighing.

"I knew she'd do something like that..." she said. "I'm so used to it by now that it doesn't bother me anymore. I'm sorry she wrote those things about you, though."

"But you worked hard on that," I said. "I'd be upset too."

She just shook her head.

"That's not it," she said. She reached into her pocket, pulling out a crumpled-up piece of paper, then slid it over to me.

Slowly, I uncrumpled the paper, and my eyes widened as I recognized what was on it.

It wasn't the same drawing... but it was close enough. It was a depiction of Spacegirl hanging herself, and this time, I was there beside her. A caption read '*Retard Dyke Wedding.*'

"There were so many in my locker..." Spacegirl said. "She slid them through the cracks... I don't know how many..."

"I know..." I said softly. "This is what she drew in your notebook when I returned it to you. This is what I had to take out."

Spacegirl looked down at the picture again before averting her eyes. As class started, I jammed the drawing into my pocket so I could throw it away later.

Spacegirl didn't pay much attention during class. Instead of taking notes, she sketched in her notebook. I looked over a few times to see her drawing another unicorn. This one seemed so similar to the prince I'd seen before. She must not have been quite happy with it, though. When I looked back at her notebook, the unicorn wasn't there anymore. She must have just erased it... but it seemed so clean, like it hadn't been there in the first place.

I remember seeing Tanya give me a shit-eating smirk in the hall near the end of the day, and when I started my walk home, I noticed that Tanya was following me.

It was hard to say for sure at first, but as I got further away from the school, I realized that she was doing it deliberately.

I didn't know what she had in mind, but I didn't want to put up with it.

When I was in the middle of a small walking path that cut behind some of the houses on my street, I stopped and looked at Tanya as she kept approaching.

"What do you want?" I asked.

"Just seeing where you go," Tanya replied. "I was wondering if you were just fucking Spacegirl, or if you did a whole tour of all the retarded girls in town."

She was avoiding the question.

"Very funny. What are you really up to?" I asked. Tanya just continued to smile at me.

"It's a surprise," she said. "Sasha and I just want you to know how much we love dykes in this town. Oops, I've said too much."

I wanted to hit her. Dear God, I just wanted to hit her, but we both knew she could overpower me. I didn't want to go home either.

Whatever Tanya had in mind... it wasn't anything good. She drew closer to me, unafraid of anything I'd do.

"Come on, dyke. Go home," she said. "Let's go check out your surprise."

In a sudden, horrible moment, I realized that Tanya was threatening me. I also realized that I couldn't outrun her... I couldn't fight her off. I didn't really have much of a choice but to do as she asked.

Slowly, I turned and walked toward my house, with Tanya at my heels. It wasn't far, and up ahead, I could see Sasha sitting on a park bench. From a distance, I recognized the red gas can beside her, and I stopped dead in my tracks.

"What the fuck are you..."

Tanya seized me by the arm and dragged me toward the bench. Sasha just watched with a wide, manic grin.

"Heya, Jane," she said. "How's it going?"

"What the fuck is this?!"

"Just wanted to chat," Sasha said with a cold chuckle. "You think you can get away with pulling the shit you did the other day? No. You've been treating me like garbage for years, and for what? Because of Spacegirl? You know who you're fucking choosing, right? Right?"

She sighed in frustration.

"God... I hate that retard girl. But you know what? I hate you even more. Acting like you're better than me just because you feel bad for her."

"You're crazy."

Sasha just laughed.

"I'm not the one who clocked someone with a fucking tray just for a little teasing. You're absolutely fucking psycho!"

On the bench behind her, I saw the portrait that Spacegirl had painted of me. Sasha picked it up and tossed it in front of me, then picked up the gas can and dumped it onto the canvas.

"You wanna be a dyke, I don't care. But I'm not letting you and your retarded whore put your shit up! So say goodbye to your little project, slut!"

Sasha reached into her pocket and took out a book of matches. Her grin widened before vanishing as she looked at something behind us.

"Holy shit..." Tanya said, and I craned my neck to try and see what they were seeing.

As for believing it... that was another story entirely.

Standing on the path behind us was a unicorn, although there was something very wrong with it. This looked nothing like a regular horse. Its body was plain white and almost textureless save for the many thin, blue lines that ran along its body. It looked like it had been cut out from a sheet of lined paper, but... that was impossible. It had to be impossible! Neatly done gray lines defined the shape of the horse. In fact, it looked exactly like one of the unicorns Spacegirl drew. It almost looked as if it had walked out of one of her notebooks!

Tanya let me go and stumbled back a few steps, wide-eyed as she stared at the advancing unicorn. Its tail swished violently back and forth. Its ears seemed to be pressed to its head.

It let out an angry noise before charging straight for her.

She panicked and tried to run. In her desperation to escape, she bolted down the path. But she couldn't outrun the paper unicorn.

It lowered its head as it drew nearer to her. In one swift movement, the horn pierced Tanya's back, impaling her straight through the chest. She screamed as she was hoisted off the ground, and the unicorn circled back to fix Sasha in a murderous glare.

Tanya looked down at the massive spike sticking out of her, eyes wide with horror and her body twitching its last spasms as life quickly drained from her. The unicorn lowered its head to let her slide off its horn, and she hit the ground in a bundle of limbs.

Sasha and I stared in silent terror as the unicorn reared up on its hind legs and brought its hooves down upon Tanya's body. She didn't scream. She didn't fight. She simply lay there as she was trampled again and again. I can only hope she died quickly.

Sasha dropped the unlit match and took a slow, terrified step back before toppling over.

I stumbled back and looked down to see the portrait of me at her feet. But it had changed.

That beautifully painted version of me was now leaning out of the canvas, invading the real world and clutching Sasha's leg tightly.

Still with that look of contentment on her face, I watched as the painted version of me slowly slipped back into her painting and took Sasha's leg with her.

"FUCK, FUCK, FUCK!"

Sasha desperately swatted at the painted me, but she couldn't overpower it. She couldn't escape. Her nails tried to dig into the pavement as she was slowly dragged into the canvas. She looked at me in horror, silently begging for help, but all I could do was stare back at her in silence.

"JANE! JANE HELP! PLEASE! OH GOD! JANE! JAAAAANE!!!"

The hands of the painted version of me reached up, seizing Sasha by the hair and forcing her down into the canvas. It was like watching something pull her underwater. One minute she was there, the next she was gone.

I stood silent in the park, staring at the painting, then at the paper unicorn.

The unicorn huffed before retreating off into the woods. Then, I was alone.

Slowly, I approached the painting and looked down at it. It had changed. The writing was gone, the art style was the same, but I was no longer the subject. Now, it only depicted Sasha as she reached out for help with her mouth open in an eternal scream of terror.

After some hesitation, I picked up the painting.

I could return it to Spacegirl in the morning.

They chalked Tanya's death up to an animal attack, and nobody ever found Sasha. Rumors of her being kidnapped or getting knocked up and running away were the most popular ones. They were whispered between students for the rest of tenth grade, but in the end, they petered out. There was a simple memorial service, and a picture in the yearbook before Sasha and Tanya were cast into the back of everyone's memories, just like Mike, Brian, and James had been all those years before.

I never asked Spacegirl about what I saw that day. I don't know if she even would have been able to explain it, although she certainly knew much more than I did. Whatever she'd done, whatever she had the ability to do, it wasn't my place to ask about it.

High school was ten years ago, though, and I've chosen not to remember much of it. I'm a different person now, and so much has changed. I've got my own life to live now. I try not to question the things that I shouldn't. Sometimes I see paintings move, but when they do, I don't bother with a second glance, and I never ask my wife about them. She doesn't like to talk about it, and I won't ever force her. She has her secrets, but that doesn't change how much I love her.

The painting of Sasha hangs in her studio at home, right beside the painting of her father. Sometimes I look at it and I wonder if maybe things could have been different... but I don't feel too guilty about it. I wouldn't feel too guilty if I heard another story about a suspicious trampling or animal attack either, but to my knowledge, there's been nothing of the sort. Megan is calmer when she's with me. I think that's part of why we ended up together. I guess I shouldn't be too surprised. I do what I can to make sure that nobody ever hurts my beautiful Spacegirl.

Part 2: Megan's Story

I need you to understand that I never wanted anybody to get hurt. I don't know what's wrong with me, but I can't stop myself from doing it. My mom once told me that what I can do is a gift, but some days I'm not so sure. What exactly do you call it when everything you draw or paint comes to life?

My name is Megan Daniels, but people have been calling me Spacegirl for years, and I've had my 'ability' for as long as I can remember. I never really questioned it when I was a child. On the contrary, I remember that I couldn't have been happier. I was by myself so often that it was nice to be able to literally make my own friends.

Mom was never a bad parent, but she had a career to focus on as well. I know she made some sacrifices while juggling motherhood and her practice as a psychiatrist. She'd set up a home office while I was still fairly young and spent a lot of her time there with her patients. While she was working, I would usually play in my room.

Dad, on the other hand, was a bit of a different story. He wasn't home very often, so I didn't see much of him. I barely even remember what he looked like. If it weren't for the few photographs my mom kept, I would have forgotten everything except his intense blue eyes and the smell of alcohol that often hung like a cloud around him. I could smell it on his breath every time he was close to me, and even now, years later, I can't help but think of him every time I catch a whiff of alcohol.

He worked a nine-to-five office job, but usually wasn't home until long after I'd gone to bed. When I was young, I never understood why. Mom never talked about it in front of me, but I knew from the arguments that sometimes kept me awake that she was mad at him for it.

Since Dad was never around and Mom was always busy, I was often left to my own devices more often than not, and that was just fine by me. As I said before, I made my own friends.

Some of my earliest memories involve watching the sea creatures I'd drawn float off the paper and swim around my bedroom. Crude fish and an octopus with only four tentacles swam around, dancing out of my grip as I chased them around the room, laughing all the while.

I remember a portrait of my family, consisting of three stick figures moving around on the page, all together and smiling in a way that my own family never did. I remember them standing around my room, content to play with me since I had no one else.

Whatever I wanted, I could create with nothing more than some crayons and paper. My work was crude back then. I was just a child after all, but the quality didn't matter. Just as I'd drawn them, my work would come to life just for me.

Of course, everything would return to its place the moment I heard footsteps in the hall. I'd learned quickly that the things I'd created were shy. They were just for me and didn't want to be seen by anybody else. While I'd told my parents everything, they just dismissed it as my imagination. One can't possibly keep a secret that big for long, though.

When I was four, I'd gotten it into my head that I wanted a pony, and I did what any little girl with my ability would have done. I drew my own.

I remember laying out a sheet of lined paper and grabbing some of my crayons before I started on the landscape. As I drew, I imagined what my pony would be like. He would be noble, just, and kind. He would be brave and strong... He would be a Knight—no, a Prince! A Unicorn Prince, in fact!

I remember gleefully drawing his limbs and his horn, giving him shape and making him real.

I remember setting my crayon down and watching expectantly as my Prince began to move. He shook his head. If he'd had a mane at that point, it would have tossed about majestically. Instead, all he had were two dot eyes and a dopey smile. It didn't seem to matter, though. He moved all the same, and just like everything else, he emerged from the paper. He wasn't quite as big as a real horse. At that age, I had no idea how big a horse really was. But he was still taller than I was.

I remember reaching out to pet him for the very first time. His hide felt like paper, although it held a warmth in it.

He remained still and even lowered himself a bit so I could ride on his back. His paper hooves thudded against the hardwood floor as he let out a bold whinny, and I suppose that was a little *too* much noise.

As my Unicorn Prince circled my room, I didn't hear the footsteps in the hall over the clop of my impromptu pony ride. I didn't hear my mom coming in to check on me, not until I saw the door open from the corner of my eye, and even then, all I could do was grin at my mother and wave.

"Hi, Mom!"

She didn't smile back at me, nor did she wave. Instead, her eyes went wide. Her hand went to her mouth to stifle a scream.

The Unicorn Prince froze. I remember feeling his body tense up before he rushed toward the piece of paper sitting on the floor. In an instant, it was gone, and I was on the floor. Mom raced toward me and scooped me up, pulling me away from the drawing on the ground.

I couldn't understand why she was so afraid. She frisked me, checking me for injuries, and when she found none, she looked me dead in the eye.

"What was that?" she demanded. "Megan, what was that?"

"He's my pet unicorn, Mommy! I drew him!"

"Where did it come from?!"

"I drew him! I really did!"

I looked back at the picture on the floor. The Unicorn Prince didn't move, but I knew he was staring at me. Even in those simple dot eyes, I could see some sign of life.

My mother fixated on the picture, studying it in silence but keeping her distance as she processed what she'd just seen. She didn't speak for a few moments. She just held me protectively close.

"Can you make him come out again?" she finally asked. Her voice had a notable tremble in it. Slowly, she set me down again, and I went to kneel beside my drawing.

"It's okay. She's not going to hurt you," I whispered to my Prince. "It's just Mommy."

The drawing remained still for a moment before finally starting to move. He didn't leave the paper, not again. He was either scared or trying not to scare my mom. Even without stepping out again, though, just moving was enough.

Mom stared down at him, eyes wide in disbelief.

"Can I take him outside and ride him in the park?" I asked eagerly.

"No." The response was curt and automatic. "No! No... Just... Just leave him for now. Okay, honey?"

Mom brushed her hair back and looked at me. She still looked as if she couldn't quite believe her eyes before shaking her head and forcing an uneasy smile.

"How about some lunch?" she said, hiding the stammer in her voice. "I'll make Alphagetti."

"Can my unicorn have Alphagetti too?"

"Maybe later, baby. Let's just talk about this first..."

She offered me a hand, and I took it as she led me downstairs.

"Did I ever tell you about Great-Grandma Ruth?" she asked as I sat over my bowl of hot alphabet soup.

"Who's Great-Grandma Ruth?" I asked. Mom managed a sad smile as she sat down across from me.

"Well, she was my grandmother," she replied. "When I was very young, Grandma and Grandpa sometimes let me stay over at her place. I always loved it there. She had a cottage in the woods, way up past London. It was quiet; there was a big forest to play in. It was beautiful."

"Can we go and see Great-Grandma Ruth?"

"Unfortunately, no. She's been dead a very long time. She liked to draw too, though, just like you, and when I was a little girl, I used to like to pretend that some of her drawings would come out and play with me."

She paused, watching me carefully. I stared back at her, my eyes lighting up a little bit.

"Did they really come out? Just like my drawings do?" I asked.

"I... I don't really know, baby," she said with a sigh. "I used to think it was all my imagination. She died when I was young, and Grandma's gone too, so... I guess I'll never know for sure. What you can do, though, not everyone can do. Maybe Great-Grandma Ruth could, but you have to understand that this isn't... most people can't do it, and they might not understand it if they see the things you drew coming out of their drawings..."

"What do you mean?" I asked. Mom tried to put on a reassuring smile.

"People aren't always nice, honey, and when they see something they don't understand, sometimes they get scared. I need you to be careful with your drawings. You're going to be starting school soon, and people can't see them move..."

"They don't like it when people see them," I said.

"And that's good! We just need to make sure it stays that way."

"Are you mad at me?"

Mom's eyes widened.

"No! No, sweetie. Absolutely not! Why would I be mad at you?" She left her chair to crouch down beside me and wrapped me in a tight hug. "I'm not mad at you. I promise. I just want you to be safe, that's all... It's best we don't tell Daddy about this, though. It'll be our secret. You and me," she said.

"Why can't we tell Daddy?" I asked, and she hesitated for a moment before giving me an answer.

"Daddy... sometimes he doesn't think and says things he shouldn't. We can show him one day. Just not right now, okay?"

"Okay," I said and gave a slight nod. Even now, I'm still not sure I fully trusted her tone. *'Mad'* might not be the right word to describe how I think she felt. *Afraid* might be more fitting, and I suppose if it were me in her position, I would've been afraid too. At the time, though, I hardly knew any better. I was so sure that she was angry with me, and I wasn't quite sure what to do about it.

For the next little while, I didn't play with the things I had created. Even if my mom hadn't intended it, the idea that my ability was somehow wrong had entered my mind, and it wouldn't go away.

But just because I wasn't playing with them didn't mean they stopped being alive. When I was in my room, I could see them moving around on the paper, watching me. I'd hung the Unicorn Prince up on my wall and could see him pacing about restlessly. His simple facial features betrayed a look of unease that was impossible to mistake and, beyond that, a look of concern.

My own emotional state must have rubbed off on them. They knew that something wasn't quite right, and so they stayed in place, moving less often and rarely coming out.

I remember that part of me felt relieved that they could be normal... and yet part of me missed them. It's not easy for a child to go from having something so magical in their life to having nothing at all, and without the things I'd drawn, I had nothing.

I think it was obvious that it wasn't going to last. Maybe my artwork knew it too, I can't say for sure. But it wasn't long before I couldn't help myself.

When I told my mom I wanted to go outside and play, I only took one drawing outside with me. It was carefully folded up in my pocket, and the choice was an obvious one.

I'd never had a chance to properly ride the pony I'd drawn. Since it was an overcast day, I thought I could slip out and do it while Mom was busy.

Our yard backed onto a small park. There was only a chain-link fence and a small gate separating us from the park itself, and I remember that the day was gloomy and foggy. No one else was out and about, and there were enough trees that I probably wouldn't be seen. Mom had told me to stay in the backyard, but I knew she had a patient and wouldn't check on me. I knew I had time.

As soon as I knew she wasn't looking, I opened the gate and stepped out into the park. I remember that giddy feeling of doing something I knew I wasn't supposed to be doing. Tasting a forbidden fruit, as it were. I didn't understand just how dangerous it was for a four-year-old to be running around unsupervised, and being a four-year-old myself, I simply didn't care.

I took the folded drawing from my pocket and opened it, smiling as I looked down at my Unicorn Prince.

"You can come out now," I whispered to it and watched with a familiar excitement as he bounded off the paper.

I remember thinking that he looked happy to see me as I petted his neck. The light rain didn't seem to have much of an effect on his paper hide, and after examining his surroundings, he knelt down before me, offering me a place on his back. I felt like the Queen of the world as I climbed on.

"Go!" I said as I held on to him. "Run!" and he did exactly that. The park was abandoned, and we were lucky for that. My Prince might not have been as fast as a real pony, but I didn't care. For a little while, I was completely free, and I will never forget that wonderful feeling.

Mom never caught on to my little adventures with the Unicorn Prince, which very quickly became my go-to activity. In a sense, he became one of my best friends.

When we weren't outside, I spent my time drawing newer and better versions of him. My art style began to get better with practice as my Prince slowly began to resemble a real horse.

It was always *him* who came out of the newest drawing. No matter how he'd changed, *he* was always the same. When we were together, he and I would linger by the edge of the park in a small spot covered by trees and away from prying eyes. That small patch of 'woods' wasn't much, but for me it might as well have been my very own fantasy land.

I only got caught outside of the backyard once, and even then, Mom had no idea that I'd had one of my drawings out with me.

Once, I remember that I'd brought out two pictures of the Unicorn Prince. I'd been hoping that maybe I could create two of him, although he only came out of the newer drawing. I suspect that was only because it was the better one, and he seemed to prefer looking good. He was a vain one, but I suppose I made him that way. When I looked at the paper, both of them only showed the background. The Prince himself was absent. It's how I knew that no matter how many times I drew him, so long as it was meant to be him, he was the one who'd come out.

That didn't mean I couldn't draw other unicorns, though. I only tried it once before deciding that if I had too many unicorns out at once, I'd probably get caught and Mom would get mad.

It was on one of those overcast days when I saw the coyote. I'd finished my newest drawing of the Unicorn Prince and wanted to see how he'd turned out. As soon as I knew Mom wasn't watching, I slipped out the back gate and ran for the trees, hiding my drawing under my raincoat.

When I made it to the safety of the trees, I took it out and watched as the Prince stepped off the paper. He was still a little cartoonish, but I was sure that he looked better than he had before.

The Prince lowered his head to me, a gesture of respect, and I bowed in response before moving to climb on his back. Before I could, though, I saw something moving through the trees out of the corner of my eye.

It looked like a dog, although I couldn't quite identify the breed. I remember thinking that it might have been a husky, only it had a gray coat with spots of brown. Its ears were triangular and folded back as it crept toward me. I got the impression that it looked a little shy. Nowadays, I'd recognize it as a coyote, but at that age, I doubt I even knew what a coyote was.

"Hello puppy!" I said and took a step toward it. It shrank back, baring its teeth at me as it did. I didn't take the hint, though. Behind me, the Prince protectively moved to my side. From the corner of my eye, I saw him watching the coyote carefully. It never occurred to me that the animal could've been dangerous. I just saw a dog and wanted to pet it, not understanding that it didn't want to be petted.

When I reached out for it, the coyote snapped at me before darting to the side. It didn't bite me, but I leapt back as if it had all the same, and that seemed to be the only provocation the Unicorn Prince needed.

When he moved, the coyote tried to get out of the way, but the Prince was faster. I remember hearing the crack of its bones under the Prince's hooves. I remember seeing its body distort as it was pulverized. It died instantly, and I suppose that was for the best. I'm not sure how I would've handled watching it suffer. But the sight of the thing that I'd drawn trampling the life out of another living thing was hardly much of an improvement.

As the Prince rammed its horn into the broken corpse, goring it in a show of violence that was like nothing I'd seen before, I screamed and stumbled backward. I lost my footing and fell as I stared in horror up at my unicorn. He looked at me with big, colorful eyes, soft and kind, and yet his hide was spattered with blood.

I stared up at my Prince, looking at him and shaking as he stood over the corpse. He shook his head, shaking some of the blood off before he advanced on me.

I tried to crawl away, tears streaming down my cheeks.

"No…" I stammered. "D-don't hurt me! P-please."

The Prince stopped and looked down at me, studying me. I could see in his eyes that he knew I was upset. I could tell that he was thinking about what to do, and after a moment, he just bowed his head and knelt down in a gesture of submission.

For a few moments, neither of us moved. I was still shaking and crying. The Prince waited for me to make the first move, and when I did, all I could manage was to quietly take out the paper I'd drawn him on so he could go back.

He stood up and approached me slowly. He didn't go back to the paper, though, not at first. Instead, he lowered his head toward me and gave me an affectionate nudge, silently asking if I was okay.

I looked over at the pulverized carcass of the coyote, and I remembered the way it had snapped at me. I think I realized that it would have hurt me if it had gotten the chance… and if that was the case, then my Prince had done nothing but defend me.

I looked over at him and finally reached out to pet the side of his face. He nuzzled into my hand before returning to his drawing.

I went straight back into the backyard. Mom didn't know I'd been gone; I had no intention of telling her either. I didn't go on any more adventures after that.

I think it goes without saying that I didn't spend much time around other children when I was young. Mom had a few friends who'd bring their kids over every now and then, but that was it. Mom had told me that she'd wanted me to go to preschool, but my dad was adamant that it was a waste of money. I'm sure they argued about it more than once during the occasional fights I'd overhear as I lay awake in my bedroom at night.

That lack of socialization, though, made it so much more difficult when I started school. I won't pretend to remember every single detail, but I remember the fear.

I could handle being on my own. I'd been alone for more of my life than I probably should have. It was being around other people that was hard. I preferred to simply avoid the other kids. During playtime, I'd sit on my own and draw. I'd bring a notepad to school and fill it with crayon drawings of fantasy lands, mermaids, and the like. That isolation made it difficult for me to make friends, and I suppose it made me an easy target.

People can be cruel, but children have a special kind of cruelty to them. I know that the bullying started early. If it wasn't my Coke-bottle glasses they made fun of, it was my frizzy red hair. But more than any of those, they teased me because I wanted to be by myself with nothing but my notepads and sketchbooks.

I think it was around second grade when someone first came up with the name 'Spacegirl', because I was *always spaced out*, but I don't remember exactly who used it first. Either way, it caught on to the point that people called me that more often than they called me by my actual name, and it wasn't long before some people started taking it further.

It was a few months into second grade that Chris Burton took my sketchbook. I usually spent my recesses out in the field behind the school. If the weather was good, I'd sit down beneath one of the trees and draw. Sometimes people bothered me, but my mom had told me to ignore them, and that's what I tried to do.

Chris was a couple of grades above me, and I was one of his favorite targets. He just loved trying to get a reaction, however he could. Sometimes he would pull grass out of the ground and sprinkle it in my hair, trying to get a reaction. I usually just brushed it out and moved to a different tree.

On that day, though, I guess he wasn't going to accept being ignored.

I could see him from the corner of my eye as he came toward me, flanked by a few other boys.

"Whatcha drawing today, Spacegirl?" he asked as he reached me. He leaned against the tree and tried to peer over my shoulder. I didn't give him an answer. Mom had said not to dignify him with an answer. He gave me a light push, trying to get my attention.

"Hey, Spacegirl. *Spaaaacegirl...*"

I still didn't reply, even when the questions started.

"Are you ignoring me? Don't you talk? Do you know how to talk?"

No answer. I just continued working in my sketchbook. I was nearly done with a drawing of the Unicorn Prince.

"You know that unicorns are for babies, right?"

I kept my head down, trying to at least finish my sketch before moving. I never got that chance. Before I could react, Chris had snatched my sketchbook from my hands, and with a manic grin on his face, he took off.

"Give it back!" I yelled after him before scrambling to my feet. Chris already had a head start on me, and I was barely on my feet before someone else had pushed me over. As I hit the ground, all I could do was watch as Chris took off toward the school. I scrambled to pick myself up again and give chase. I wasn't as fast as him. There was no way I'd catch up in time.

He was already inside the school by the time I got to the doors. I had no idea where he'd gone. He couldn't have been in one of the classrooms, could he? Maybe he'd gone to hide in one of the bathrooms? I knew that technically I wasn't supposed to be in the boys' bathroom, but where else could he have gone?

"Hey! Spacegirl!" I heard him call from just down the hall. I turned and sure enough, I saw him standing in the doorway to one of the bathrooms. My heart skipped a beat as I began to dread what he'd done. I took off after him. I didn't see my sketchbook in his hands, and I tore past him toward the boys' bathroom.

The smell was the first thing I noticed, and I could see one of the stall doors hanging open. I came to a stop in front of it, already knowing what I'd see.

Chris had thrown my sketchbook in the toilet. The pages were soaked, and it stank like piss. Behind me, I could hear Chris laughing as if he'd just played the greatest prank in the world.

I gagged as I took my sketchbook out of the toilet. The pages were soaking wet when I pried the book open. Most of my drawings were ruined. The things that had been on them didn't move. They were still and lifeless, and that sent an unfamiliar stab of panic through my chest.

I flipped over to the incomplete sketch of the Unicorn Prince, expecting it to be damaged as well. That page had been spared the worst of the damage, but I could only see the background I'd drawn—no sign of the Prince himself.

"See? I made some improvements?" Chris teased. From the corner of my eye, I could see him hovering over my shoulder. My heart raced, and I felt a flash of rage.

Before I knew it, I could feel my fist against his face.

"You ruined them!" I cried. "You ruined all of them!"

Chris stumbled back a step, no longer smiling. I could see a thin trail of blood running from his nose before he hit back. We were both on the ground, hitting each other, when a teacher found us and broke us up a few minutes later.

Chris and I were both sent home that day, and I never got my sketchbook back. I imagine that one of the teachers threw it out. It was ruined anyway.

It was Dad who picked me up from school that day, not Mom. If I hadn't known better, I would've thought that was punishment enough. It was something of a blessing that I barely saw him. I never felt comfortable when I was around him.

As we left, he seemed quiet. Not angry, just quiet. It wasn't until we got in the car that he said anything.

"So... you hit that boy back, huh?" His tone was gruff and made me a bit uneasy.

"He took my sketchbook," I replied. Dad just chuckled.

"Well, boys will be boys. I guess he had a crush, huh? When should I expect you to bring home your new boyfriend?"

I shifted uneasily in my seat. I'd expected him to be angry, but something about the way he was talking seemed... off. I could smell the familiar smell of alcohol on him as he keyed the engine and pulled out of the parking lot.

"Chris is a jerk," I said quietly.

"Most boys are, kiddo. You'll learn to like it eventually. You'll notice it more when you get older. You're probably gonna look a little like your mother. Legs for days."

He lit up a cigarette as we drove, and I looked out the window, quietly shrinking away from him. I could feel him looking at me, and I hated it.

Mom was waiting for me when we got home, and as soon as I got through the door, she had me wrapped up in her arms, already fussing over me.

"Megan, what were you thinking? Did he hurt you? What happened?"

"Chris threw my sketchbook in the toilet," I said quietly. "I'm sorry. I got mad and I hit him..."

"Relax, Annie. It's just kids being kids," Dad said, brushing past her to head to the kitchen and get a beer. "There's no point in making a big fuss over it. Sounds to me like it's just a little boy with a crush."

Mom looked over in his direction, glaring daggers at him. She watched as he took two beers out of the fridge.

"Kids being kids?" she repeated. "Did you look at her? She's got bruises all over her arms!"

"It's a bit of roughhousing. Nothing to worry about," Dad said with a shrug. He opened one of the beers and took a sip.

"Did you even ask what happened? How many times has she told us that the other children were bothering her? We need to set up a meeting with the school."

"Don't you think that's overreacting?" Dad stood in the doorway of the kitchen. "This kind of thing is normal. The school will tell you the same thing. Stop worrying. It'll toughen her up a little, make her socialize. God knows she could use a kick in the ass."

"Excuse me?" Mom snapped. Her tone of voice made me flinch, but my dad hardly seemed to notice it. He just took another sip of his beer.

I could see the rage in Mom's eyes as she tried to figure out just what to say to him. Her attention shifted to me for a moment.

"Megan, why don't you go upstairs to your room? Daddy and I need to talk."

"Why are you coddling her? She's a big girl, she can take it," Dad said as I headed for the stairs. The argument had already begun before I even made it to the top.

"She's six years old, James. Do you really think she deserves to be harassed?"

"They're kids! This is what they do. It's natural. It'll help her grow a thicker skin. Just relax, will you?"

I took off toward my room and closed the door behind me. My hands were shaking. Even through the door, I could hear the muffled sounds of my parents screaming at each other.

From the corner of my eye, I could see the drawings I'd put up on my walls shifting around, sharing in my discomfort. I could feel them watching me.

I pulled away from my bedroom door and went toward a recent piece I'd done of the Unicorn Prince. I needed him, if for no other reason than to have something I knew I could call a friend close by.

But as soon as I approached the picture, I saw that it was empty. The Prince was nowhere in sight. He'd left his drawing, and the sight of that gave me pause.

He'd never left his drawing without me before.

I looked around, and none of the other subjects from my artwork were missing. It was just him...

As my parents argued downstairs, I felt alone and sick to my stomach. Somehow in my gut, I knew something was wrong. Something bad was happening. I didn't know just what. Not yet... But I could sense it, and that alone was enough to scare me.

The Unicorn Prince was back in his drawing the next morning. I remember seeing him standing just as I'd drawn him in the picture. He didn't move when I looked at him, and I didn't have the time to bring him out. Remembering his absence left me with a lingering sense of unease, and it wouldn't go away.

I went back to school the next day and didn't see Chris in the recess yard at all. Later that morning, we were told that recess would be indoors for the next few days in spite of the lovely weather.

The teachers didn't tell us why. That much I overheard from a few of the students.

During the first indoor recess, I could hear one of the other girls, Sasha, talking to some of her friends about how Chris Burton hadn't quite made it home the other night.

"My dad works at the hospital and he said that he'd heard that Chris and his mom got attacked by an animal yesterday! He said that they're probably gonna die." There was a glee in her voice that didn't quite fit in with what she was describing.

I didn't listen in for long. I couldn't even if I wanted to. A hollow feeling in my stomach overtook me, and I suddenly felt sick. I was a child, but that didn't mean I couldn't put two and two together. The Prince had been out of his drawing the other day... and it just so happened that Chris and his mom had been attacked by 'an animal.'

A vivid memory of the coyote lying dead on the ground flashed through my mind. I remembered its vacant eyes and caught myself wondering if Chris would look the same if he were to die.

I sat still, the color draining from my skin. I couldn't even bring myself to look at the fresh sketchbook I'd brought. How could I, knowing that one of my drawings had just put another person in the hospital?

The other kids in the classroom around me paid me no mind. The teacher didn't even seem to notice my trembling hands as I tried to comprehend the truth that I couldn't avoid.

My drawings had nearly killed someone. That sat on me like a weight, and I didn't know how to handle it. I felt like I could barely breathe. The next thing I knew, I was crying, and I couldn't tell a single person the truth as to why.

I didn't know what to do about what had happened. When I got home after school, the thought of ripping every drawing off my wall and tearing them to shreds had crossed my mind, but when I tried to make myself do it, I couldn't.

I could only stare at them as they watched me, waiting for me to do something. These were my creations. I had given them life. Could I really bring myself to take it away from them?

I remember looking at the newest drawing of the Unicorn Prince I'd made. I could see myself tearing the paper, but even if that didn't kill him, I'd have felt guilty for even trying to hurt him. The Prince just stared back at me, a quiet resolve on his face. I knew that even if I could destroy him, it wouldn't be what I wanted. I knew I'd need to do something else, and I wasn't quite sure just what else I could do... aside from draw.

Maybe in hindsight, it was likely a bad idea. My art had put Chris and his mother in the hospital in the first place. Sending him a drawing probably would have seemed more like a threat than an apology, but I still convinced myself it was a good idea. If nothing else, maybe it would make me feel better.

I looked up at the drawing of the Prince again, my brow furrowed.

"Why'd you do it?" I asked. "Why'd you have to hurt them?"

He just looked back at me before stepping off the paper. I took a step back as he stared me down.

"You can't just hurt people whenever you feel like it! You can't!"

The Prince just huffed. I'd never imagined a fake unicorn could sound dismissive, but he somehow pulled it off. He tossed his mane before nudging me with his head. I pulled away from him.

"You're never going to hurt anyone else again!" I said, my voice shaking. "Do you understand me? Never again!"

My eyes darted around to the rest of my drawings. I could feel them all watching me.

"None of you is going to hurt anyone!"

I got no replies... no sign of agreement from them—just uneasy silence.

The Prince quietly turned away from me and stepped back into his drawing. What he meant by that, I wasn't quite sure.

I got myself some fresh paper and started on a handmade card. I can't say I ever knew Chris particularly well. Aside from harassing me, I didn't know what he liked, so I stuck with something simple. I drew a picture of him. People liked seeing portraits of themselves, right?

I spent almost an hour working on it, drawing him from memory. Out of the corner of my eye, I could see my other drawings moving around on my wall. On the inside of the card, I wrote a simple message.

I'm sorry that you got hurt. I hope you get well soon.

Just writing that made me feel a little better. I looked at the drawing I'd made of the Prince. He was still watching me intently, as if he had a problem with what I was doing.

"I'm apologizing," I said defensively. "You hurt him. I have to do something!"

The Prince just huffed. That same dismissive sound as before.

"I'll take the card to the hospital, and when he's better, maybe he'll leave me alone. It's better than just... just attacking him!"

I checked my clock. Maybe I could get Mom to drive me before it got too late. I knew she'd been in her office when I got home. I imagined she was probably still there. I held the card I'd made for Chris close as I went downstairs.

Mom would understand. She'd probably be happy to help me make amends!

As I reached the bottom of the stairs, I heard the TV blaring from the living room. Maybe Mom wasn't busy? Even better.

I wasn't greeted by the sight of Mom sitting and watching the television, though. She was nowhere to be seen.

Instead, it was my dad on the couch. He'd taken off his tie, and I saw a half-empty bottle of scotch on the table in front of him. He was in the midst of nursing another glass.

"Hey there, kiddo," he said. He didn't even look away from the TV.

"Hi, Dad. Where's Mom?"

"She went out for a bit. Shrink work, you know." He finally looked over at me. "What do you want, kiddo?"

"Could you drive me to the hospital?" I asked timidly. "I wanted to visit someone."

"Oh, so you've got a friend now?" he asked playfully. "C'mon. Sit down. Why don't you tell me about them?"

I hesitated for a moment before I sat beside him.

"What did you draw?" Dad asked, noticing the card I was holding. He snatched it from me before I could stop him. "A boy, huh? Your friend from the other day? What was his name? Chris?"

"Y-yeah. It's for Chris..." I murmured as I sat down beside him. Dad studied the card, a smile on his face, before he chuckled.

"Isn't that cute. I guess you've got yourself a boyfriend then, huh?"

"I feel bad cuz we got in a fight yesterday and now he's sick."

"Yeah, yeah. I get it," he said. "Hey, he's a lucky guy. You're gonna grow up just like your mom. I can already see it."

I could feel his eyes on me, and it made me uncomfortable.

"Can you drive me to the hospital?" I asked again.

"It's too late for that. I'll take you on the weekend," he said and downed his drink. "I'd like to meet the young man who's got my little girl all worked up. Hell, you look all shy now. Isn't that cute…"

He pulled me closer to him, and the stink of alcohol was almost overpowering. I didn't want to get closer, but I didn't know what else to do. The card was tossed onto the coffee table.

"So did you steal any kisses from your new boyfriend, yet?" he asked, grinning as he fixed me in that hateful stare of his.

"No! He's not my friend!"

"It's all right. I get it. You're growing up. You're getting to be a big girl, and you're beautiful just like your mom," he said. He gently ran his fingers through my hair, and for a moment, he looked thoughtful. "Just like your mom…"

The next thing I knew, he'd leaned in to kiss me. Not in the way a parent should ever kiss a child. The stink of alcohol was overpowering and made me sick. Every nerve in my body wanted to pull back, but I couldn't. Even if he had let me, I was too scared of what he'd do if I did.

"It's all right, baby. You can trust Daddy…" he whispered, but I knew he was lying. I knew something was wrong, but for all the fear that I felt, I couldn't fight back. I didn't know how.

I could feel his hands on me as he tried to pull me onto his lap, and it was then that I resisted.

"S-stop…" I stammered as I finally tried to pull away, but his grip on me tightened. I saw a flash of rage in his eyes that was enough to break whatever terrified defiance I had in me.

However, what he might have done to me was nothing compared to what was about to be done to him.

From the corner of my eye, I saw movement on the coffee table. Fresh panic kicked in as I struggled to get away.

I saw hands reaching out of the card and pressing onto the table. I could see the drawing I'd made of Chris beginning to pull itself out, and I knew what was about to happen.

In a panic, I pulled away from my dad. I kicked at him and scrambled off the couch. There was confusion on his face, followed by a look of realization... or perhaps remorse. Then came the terror when he at last noticed the living illustration of Chris that now reared out of the card on the coffee table.

He screamed and froze, eyes wide as he looked at the drawing. But he didn't run. He didn't fight. As the impossible loomed over him, all he could do was scream.

I covered my eyes as the hands of my drawing gripped his throat. I couldn't watch it. I didn't want to.

I could hear it, though. The screams. I could hear a terror deeper than anything I'd heard before, and that was enough...

There were screams, and then there was silence.

It was a while before I allowed myself to look and see what had happened.

The picture of Chris was gone, and in its place, I saw one of my dad. The style of art was mine, that much I knew, but I hadn't drawn this. His mouth was open in a silent scream. His eyes were wide with terror... and he was completely immobile. He didn't move like in my other pictures. He didn't shift. He just remained there, still and silent. Lifeless.

My heart was racing. As afraid of my own father as I'd been a moment ago, I wanted him to move! I wanted to see some sign of life!

I held the card, silently begging for something to happen, but nothing did. I remember the quiet, creeping realization that he wasn't going to move again. He was gone.

I never wanted anybody to get hurt. The coyote, Chris, my dad, or any of the people who have fallen victim to my ability in the years since. But the choice isn't mine. I learned that the hard way.

Perhaps they deserved what they got. The things they did were not by accident, after all. Chris chose to bully me. My dad chose to try to hurt me, and so many others have hurt me since then. But that doesn't mean I wanted the same for them.

Over the years, I've done what I can to keep myself in check... They react to my rage and my fear. As long as I control those, I can keep them at bay. But every now and then, I slip. Someone pushes me too hard, and I can't bury the rage or the fear. It gets out, and when it does, *they* react to it, and people die.

I thought I could do it forever. I really did. But I have my limits. Well... *had*. Not anymore. You'll see what I mean. Soon.

I WAS AWAKE

God, I never should have married Heidi...

Back in the day, she was something special. Blonde hair, blue eyes, and fresh out of high school with a cunt that sucked you in with every thrust.

She had a thing for older men... a thing I was willing to oblige. The sex was fantastic. She moaned like a porn star and made me feel twenty years younger...

But as good as it was, I should've kicked her to the curb while I still had the chance.

When she started talking about marriage, that should've been my sign to leave. I'd made it to forty without some needy bitch tying me down. But I guess with age come regrets. I started wondering if maybe it was time to settle down... and Heidi was a good girl. She was smart, but not too smart. Confident, but obedient. She listened when I spoke, and she knew I was the man in charge.

I figured, what the hell? Why not?

Stupidest fucking mistake of my life...

The first couple of years were great. But eventually, she started changing. I should've known. She was twenty-one when we got hitched. By twenty-five, nobody's really the same person they were a few years ago.

She started questioning me more often. Trying to tell me to do shit her way. She got argumentative, telling me I never listened.

So I set her right. It shut her up for a little while.

I didn't like hitting her or anything. But she needed to understand that I was the one in control. Not her. I was the man of the house, the man of the relationship! Not her!

And until she realized her place and decided to stay in line, I was happy to put her there every now and again. Sometimes she threatened to leave me... but we both knew she wouldn't. Where the fuck was she going to go? Her parents wouldn't take her back. She barely had any friends. No. She wasn't going to leave me, and she knew it. She belonged to me until the day I died.

And if it weren't for my fucking heart, that day would be a long way off.

I suppose I should've seen the heart problems coming. I haven't exactly lived the healthiest life. Lotta fast food, long hours at a desk, lotta nights drinking with the boys. The best workout I got was when I plowed Heidi. That girl had energy for days, and even then, she'd been slowing down as she inched into her late twenties.

The doctor said I needed surgery to get a pacemaker.

If it were up to me, I wouldn't have bothered with that shit. But no, Heidi told me to get it, and it was one of the few fights she won.

Not because she convinced me. But because at one point, she just folded her arms and said:

"Fine! Die then. See if I give a shit!"

At the time, I'd just laughed and told her I wasn't going to die.

I wasn't laughing so much that night...

What she said got in my head, made me start thinking... worrying.

Shit, what if she was right? What if this did kill me?

I didn't want to die! Fuck no!

After a few days of dwelling on it, I caved. I called the doctor, said I was open to surgery, and got put on a list.

I was told the operation wouldn't be so bad.

The doctor said they'd put me out, do their thing, stitch me up, and in about a month, I'd be better than ever. It would suck for a bit, but in the long term, I'd be better off.

A few hours before the surgery, while I was waiting in the hospital room with Heidi, I had a coffee with her and we talked for a bit. The coffee was shit. Way too bitter... she should've put more sugar in it, but I didn't complain about it much.

I remember she seemed in better spirits than usual, at least. She smiled more... almost reminded me why I'd wanted her in the first place, and if we'd had a little more time, I would've fucked her in the bathroom for good luck.

I did suggest it, but she just said:

"You'll be going in any minute now. Let's not."

She'd squeezed my hand as if to say that once I was good to go, her legs would be open for business. Or at least that's the impression I got...

About a half hour later, the doctor came in to wheel me away. The anesthesiologists did their thing and I was out, just like they promised.

I just wasn't out for as long as they might've expected...

I don't remember much about waking up.

I just remember feeling groggy... not quite there. My head was woozy, and my thoughts were scattered and disorganized. I remember thinking something like: *'We need to get the hamster off the roof. She's not an owl, even though she has wings.'* And that thought seemed so important for a few moments before I realized that it made zero sense.

I opened my eyes a little and was blinded by the light above me.

I could see shadows moving around me and hear voices... words...

"He's stable. He's doing fine..." A woman's voice with a heavy Jamaican accent. It was the anesthesiologist.

"All right. Anyway... so, do you get out to see your family often?" another voice asked. I recognized it as the surgeon my doctor had introduced me to.

"I'd like to go more. My mom likes to call, yeah? Keeps asking when I'm going to bring the kids down."

"Why not tell her to come up?"

"I do."

I blinked. I could see the surgeon and the anesthesiologist standing over me. The anesthesiologist was looking at something, but I wasn't sure what. My mind wasn't all there. She seemed more focused on her work than on the surgeon.

"All the time, I do. But no. She doesn't want to come out here. Says it's too cold."

"Well, can't argue with that," my surgeon said with a shrug. "You ever miss it back home?"

"Sometimes yes, sometimes no. It's a very different lifestyle in Jamaica, you know? Here you work and live. In Jamaica, you live and work."

"Poetic."

"You like it? My husband thought of that..." The anesthesiologist laughed before changing the subject. "Speaking of... how's your wife?"

"Oh, you know. Same old. She's taking up crochet. Might be good for the grandkids..."

The two carried on their mundane discussion about their lives, oblivious to the fact that I could hear them. Maybe I would've kept listening for lack of anything better to do, but a sharp pain ignited in my chest. I would've screamed, but I couldn't make a sound. I couldn't move. My body just lay there as it was cut into. The surgeon paused for a moment, narrowing his eyes as he fixated on something.

"How's he doing?" he asked.

"Vitals look good. Seems like he's still under."

"Okay... heart's beating a little fast."

"I'll give him another dose."

I felt my head swim. But I didn't pass out again. I was awake... *wide* awake as they did their surgery.

I tried to blink. No luck. My eyes closed but didn't open again. I could still hear everything... and still feel everything.

The hands inside my body, where I was never meant to be touched. The pain of my skin being pulled apart and cut...

Oh God... I felt all of it, and each new sensation made me want to scream.

The anesthesiologist started talking again. I didn't hear what she had to say. The pain dominated every thought. It made me want to squirm and thrash, but my body stayed still...

"Almost done..." I heard the surgeon say, and I almost felt grateful for that...

But *almost* felt as if it took hours... days even.

Each new sensation sent waves of agony through my body. I could feel it as he put the pacemaker inside of me... I could feel it when he started to close me up. The needle entering and sewing my flesh...

I could feel everything, and when it was done, the pain radiated, leaving me wanting to sob in agony in the horrible aftermath of it.

"Let's get him back to his room," I heard the surgeon say. "I could use a bite. Should we order something?"

He spoke so casually... as if he hadn't just cut me open. I think that part disturbed me the most. The lack of concern in his voice. The utter detachment from what he'd just done to me.

I was awake when they took the tubes out of me...

I was awake when they wheeled me back into my room, and as the drugs wore off, the pain kept radiating...

At least it was more manageable in the hours that followed. But the memory was still fresh in my mind. The indescribable sensation of hands reaching into my chest...

Oh God...

I was still unable to move when I heard Heidi come in to check on me. I recognized her by her footsteps.

I smelled her perfume as she sat by the bed and I was almost relieved...

Almost...

She leaned down to kiss me on the forehead and run her fingers through my hair and then I heard her whisper quietly in my ear.

"How was it, Chris? Did it hurt?"

If my blood could have frozen at that moment, it would have...

I felt my heart starting to beat faster as Heidi leaned closer to me. I could envision the smile on her face.

I wanted to yell at her. To scream at her and demand to know why she'd done this to me! If I'd had the strength, I would've put her in her place... I would've beaten her fucking bloody... I would've...

I would've...

I *would have...*

If I had the strength.

"It's okay, baby. You're with me now," she crooned. *"I'll take good care of you for the next few weeks. The doctor said you'll be weak. But he said you'll probably survive... probably..."*

She chuckled. It was a low, dark sound that I'd never heard her make before.

"Oh, I'm going to put you in your place, Chris... I'm going to put you right where you belong..."

I could feel my heart rate suddenly spiking as new terror welled up in my stomach and took hold of me. The machines hooked up to me were beeping. I wanted to scream and cry but I still couldn't move... not yet.

Heidi pulled away from me as the nurses came to check on me. I could hear her speaking. Playing the innocent wife to them, while they sedated me more.

I finally drifted off into darkness.

Although there was no solace to be found in sleep.

Heidi will be back in a few hours. I don't have much time... I'm still out of it. I need someone to call the police. Still not fully awake yet. Just typing this on my phone has been an effort. I can't speak well. I've tried... the nurses don't listen to me when I speak. They just smile and walk away.

I need help...

She's going to kill me. I know it. She's going to kill me...

I'm not ready to die yet...

Not yet...

MY ORGANIZATION MONITORS POTENTIAL APOCALYPTIC SCENARIOS

You know how every morning, you wake up in a nice, warm, cozy bed and not in an alien slave camp, where they're going to work you to death until it's time to chop you up for meat?

Yeah. You're welcome.

My name's Bill and I've probably got the most thankless fucking job in the world.

Sure, on paper it doesn't sound like much. I sit at a desk all day and look at data on a computer. But I'm the one who keeps the world turning, and I am damn good at my job.

Whenever the dreaded End of Days draws near, I'm the one who sees it coming and makes sure it doesn't. Maybe I'm not the guy they send out into the field to do the dirty work. But those guys only do what I tell them to do. Without me, society as you know it would not exist, and I am trying to remain as humble as humanly possible when I say that.

Now, I'll give credit where it's due. I'm not the one who invented the Future Probe technology. That was done by a guy named Dr. Johann Pinter back in the '70s. I won't get into the technical details of it, but simply put, Pinter figured out time travel.

He also figured out that time travel was a goddamn mess. Sci-fi nerds will understand.

Through his experiments, Pinter figured out that you can't really alter the past. You can go back in time, sure, and you can create a NEW future. But your original future will still exist. Let's say that you had a bad day, got drunk, and ran over a pedestrian, then decided to go back in time to steal your keys that night to prevent it. When you went back to the future, the pedestrian would still be dead and you'd still be a murderer. However, you would have created an alternate timeline where you didn't run over a pedestrian.

Theoretically, you can go and live in the timeline where you didn't murder a pedestrian; it would be weird, and you'd have to figure out how to handle the other version of you. But you wouldn't have technically changed anything.

Furthermore, Pinter determined that the present has multiple branching possible futures. Some of which are messier than others.

So, with all this in mind, Pinter figured that the best thing to do was, instead of going back and trying to fix some great injustices in the world (especially since he'd concluded that an alternative version of him almost certainly decided to do exactly that anyways), he instead decided to focus on improving the future. That is why he founded *Foresight*.

Now, officially, *Foresight* is classified as a research company, and we legitimately do offer some of that. I'm not really involved in that end of things, but I know that some large companies and even some arms of the US Government consult with us, looking for data to help them predict shit like economic growth and depressions, effects from certain actions on the world stage, and other shit like that.

As a rule, we don't really do the time travel thing for them unless we have to. We don't really advertise that because it's best not to leave time travel in careless hands. We don't actually know what happens if you fuck with time too much, and we really don't want to find out.

The research is just the front, though. The real goal behind Foresight was always the Future Probe program.

See, Pinter figured out pretty early on that sending people into the future was not a good idea. First off, people can die. Second off, people can be intrusive and fuck things up. So he decided a less invasive approach was necessary.

So he started using probes. They're less impressive than they sound. The probes are just mobile cameras, not that different from the Mars rover. The design has changed a bit over the years. The first ones looked more like RC cars, then they went with a sorta metal spider look, now they're drones. They record what they see and bring it back to us. Back when the program started, we literally needed to watch through whatever they'd recorded, but nowadays we can get it broadcast back to us in what's more or less real time, so to speak.

Now, obviously the logistics of sending drones into every possible future is a little over the top. So Pinter developed a machine that basically analyzes possible futures. Do not ask me how it works. That's above my pay grade. Anyways, potential apocalyptic scenarios show up as data that gets transmitted to us. Or, more specifically, to me.

My job is to filter out the less likely scenarios (There are a lot of them) and only really focus on the ones that have a real, almost certain risk of causing the end of the world. The more potential futures feature that apocalypse, the more severe the risk.

Thankfully, if we know that the world is ending, and we know why, we can also figure out how to prevent it. I can use the probes to look at futures where the world *didn't* end, and figure out why and how to make sure we steer ourselves towards that future.

Usually, we get a few years' fair warning before an apocalyptic event, so there's plenty of time to make adjustments, and so far, I'd say that we've done a pretty damn good job.

Pinter died back in the '90s, a few years before I joined up with the organization, but I'd like to think he'd be happy with the fact that most of the world's population isn't either dead or worse. I'm gonna be honest, I'm pretty proud of the work I've done with *Foresight*! Which leads me to why I'm sharing this...

You can probably guess that we're not supposed to openly talk about the Future Probe program. I'm technically violating my contract and opening myself up to a whole host of legal hot water just by sharing this. But hey, I figure it's not going to matter soon, so what the hell, right?

You guys just dodged a fucking bullet.

I don't think there's a single person on this planet who knows how lucky they are right now, and they've all got me to thank. Now, obviously, this isn't my first time saving the world. But I'd say it is the most noteworthy. I'll explain why in a little bit.

See, it all started a couple of weeks ago.

I mentioned before that when an apocalyptic scenario pops up, we've usually got a few years' notice. The circumstances that will lead to the end of civilization as we know it don't just pop up overnight. There are usually years of buildup.

But every now and then, we get an exception, and exceptions scare the living shit out of me.

Needless to say, when I got an alert telling me that 65% of the possible futures that our program surveyed involved an apocalyptic scenario within the next four days, I couldn't help but panic a little.

Naturally, I flagged it as DEFCON 1 and immediately sent it off to the higher-ups, as protocol dictates. Then, I started sending out the probes.

Now, usually when we get a high-priority scenario like this, it's because some group of nutjobs is about to do something drastic in service of whatever fucked up agenda they believe in. You may not think that a bunch of lunatics could bring about the end of the world, but if there's one lesson that history has shown again and again, it is that you should never underestimate the power of very stupid people left unattended in a large group.

Needless to say, as scary as these scenarios are, these idiots are usually not that hard to deal with. Once we've got the alert, we can either notify the proper people that some assholes are trying to make a move or get our own guys to handle it. Usually, said assholes aren't smart enough to bumble their way into the apocalypse in most future timelines, thus reducing the likelihood of our world ending to a much lower, more acceptable percentage.

With that in mind, when I sent out the probes and started reviewing the footage, I was expecting to find the usual suspects of an apocalyptic future. I wasn't entirely disappointed.

A lot of what the probes sent back was footage of empty streets and signs of carnage. Smears of blood on the pavement, mangled corpses in the streets...

I'd seen things like this before. In timelines where a sudden event caused the rapid collapse of society, you'd usually see signs of violence in the streets, but this wasn't really like that...

See, that kind of violence tends to be caused by sudden riots. People go crazy once society breaks down. You'll see shit on fire, storefronts smashed, vehicles tipped over, shit like that.

Well, storefronts were indeed smashed. Vehicles were tipped over. There was clearly some violence. But this didn't look like it had been caused by a riot.

For starters, rioters don't pry cars open like tin cans...

Rioters don't rip into people the way the bodies in the streets had been torn into.

Rioters also don't seem to only be going in one direction.

There was something about the way the bodies were spaced out. They weren't scattered around. They looked like they'd been moving... running. From what exactly? I didn't know.

With no obvious signs of what had caused the carnage, I decided to try something new. I tuned the probes to start scanning the local radio stations. Usually, in an emergency event, there's some sort of broadcast. One thing that's just about constant is that they're usually on the same frequencies, so it didn't take me long to find.

Through the static, I could clearly make out a voice I recognized as the President of the United States. It took a little bit of work to make the message come through clearly, but this is what it said:

"My fellow Americans. To those of you who are left...

We are fighting as hard as we can. The situation on the West Coast has continued to deteriorate. The incident in Reno a few days ago has spread throughout Nevada, into California, Oregon, Washington, Arizona, Texas, Utah, Idaho, Colorado, Wyoming, Montana, and Oklahoma. The Bugs have also been confirmed to have crossed the borders into Canada and Mexico, and reports indicate that the situation is dire. To those of you still alive in the affected states, I urge you to remain in your homes. Remain indoors, away from the outside. We will send help if we can. But until then, you must survive as long as you can.

To those of you in the east, where this infestation continues to spread—do not panic. But do not assume that this infestation will not continue its advance. We have continued our efforts to evacuate the areas that will inevitably be hit by the Bugs. If you live in one of these areas, we ask that you do not fight to remain in your home. It will be overrun and you and your loved ones will be in danger. The only promise of safety lies further east. If your community has not yet been evacuated, then I urge you to begin preparing to leave now. Take only what you need to survive. Food, water, and medicine. As we evacuate, we are actively looking into strategies to repel this threat. Your soldiers continue to fight valiantly for your protection against the oncoming horde, and they will triumph. But victory will come at a cost..."

The speech went on for some time, even after that. But by that point, I'd stopped listening.

Reno. That was where this had originated. Naturally, the next step was to study Reno and start looking for a potential source of the problem.

The President had said something about bugs... I'd seen some things involving bugs before, sure. But never anything on this scale. I supposed I'd find out for sure soon enough.

The higher-ups had sent me an email asking for a status update, so I sent them the radio transmission I'd gotten along with the footage. I noted that I'd be looking into Reno next.

I recalled all previous probes and requested that 28 probes be sent into different times in the next week.

Each probe would appear within the city of Reno over the next 168 hours, one appearing every six hours.

This was a fairly standard procedure. The basic idea is that once you've found Ground Zero for the apocalypse, you monitor it as heavily as possible until you find the moment it starts. Then, you go back and study that moment from every possible angle and trace it back to its source.

It's basically just the process of elimination, only using time travel.

Now, the nice thing about the six-hour model is that it makes it relatively easy to figure out an overall timeline of events. For example, most of the probes from the tail end of that 168-hour window all picked up a bloodstained disaster that used to be the city of Reno. And it wasn't pretty.

There were bodies in the streets, cars torn open, the same shit I'd seen before. Only now, I was getting a better look at just what was behind it.

Some of the probes recorded footage of massive flies. They didn't seem to hurt people; at least, they mostly just seemed to be feeding on the remains.

Looking back further though, I could see video footage of massive creatures that sort of resembled a praying mantis, only they had a physical texture more like tree bark.

A couple of those mantis things took out the goddamn drones. But at least I got a good look at them.

The drones I had left kept sending me more footage of the violence following the apocalypse. Giant, spider-like creatures crawled through Reno, stalking fleeing prey. Spiky things like grasshoppers leapt around, feeding on whoever they could catch.

There were so many, all of them flooding out of Reno as if someone had opened up the gates to an insectophobe's personal Hell. Crabs, pill bugs, centipedes, dragonflies, moths... Some of them didn't seem dangerous. Others were more than happy to kill.

I must've spent an hour or so reviewing the footage of the bugs, perplexed, before I started going back further.

These things were fascinating. I'd never seen them in any potential future before. Where the hell had they even come from? Some sort of genetic experiment gone wrong, maybe? But we would've had more warning if that were the case, wouldn't we? Sabotage perhaps?

I looked at the footage from the drones earlier in the timeline. Looking at the dates, the inciting incident in question seemed to happen in four days' time from when I was currently. The drones stopped picking up footage of the bugs around Thursday morning. It had to be sometime around then.

I spent the better part of my day analyzing the footage I got from my drones. I redirected several of them to focus on what took place during Wednesday and Thursday. I listened to radio broadcasts, swept the sewers, and looked for evidence of what was to come.

Sometime early in the afternoon on Thursday, I picked up radio chatter on some police channels about a car being found torn open by a water treatment plant outside of town. So I directed the drones there.

Sure enough, I got some decent footage of the attack. One of those spider things came out of the woods and tore into the car. It was a little fascinating to watch. It moved so fast, grabbing it and wrapping its legs around it. The goddamn thing was massive!

I watched as it used its fangs to tear through the metal before digesting the poor fuckers inside alive and slurping up the gooey mess...

Ugly way to die.

I sent some drones back about a half hour before the attack to keep an eye out for the spider. It took a bit of searching, but I eventually found it moving through the woods, coming from the water treatment plant.

Interesting...

I left one drone to keep an eye on it, while I sent some of the others back again. This time, to explore the plant itself, an hour before the attack.

I sent two of them in through a pipe that I figured the spider had come out of. Sure enough, I found the spider there, chilling in a giant web. I made sure to keep the drones away from it.

Moving through the interior of the plant, I wasn't that surprised to find more of the bugs waiting there.

From the looks of it, they'd been causing one hell of a mess. I could see the bodies of dead men, mostly eaten, along with evidence of the bugs preying on each other.

But no obvious indicator as to where they were coming from. Not at first, anyway.

I sent the drones back in time again. One went back to the day before, one only went back two hours.

One day ago, the water treatment plant looked normal. No corpses. No horde of bug creatures ready to destroy America. Just a normal water treatment plant.

Two hours ago, on the other hand, the water treatment plant had been a lot less crowded...

Most of the staff looked to be dead, and those that weren't were in the middle of being eaten by all sorts of nasty things.

Where they were coming from still wasn't obvious, but I only needed to sit and wait to find out.

It didn't take that long.

I could see shapes bubbling up from some of the pools of treated water. The machines had been shut down, and all sorts of horrors pulled themselves out of the rotten depths.

Those mantis things, flies, mosquitoes... they all came to life, confused and hungry, shambling around looking for food.

They all came from the water.

I brought my drone closer, trying to see what was in there. That was a mistake. One of the mantis-things grabbed it, mistaking it for dinner.

Welp. Back to my other drone.

I used the one I'd sent back one day and sent it to a point in time three hours before I'd lost my other drone to the mantis. Five hours before first contact.

Already, I could see a few of the bugs there... I could see new ones, smaller ones, coming out of the stagnant water.

And I could see a man.

He was standing on a balcony, looking down at the pools of untreated water with a stony expression.

Yeah. This was the fucking guy behind all this. It had to be. Nobody stares at a giant mantis crawling out of a pool of wastewater without screaming and running away like a little bitch unless they *expect* a giant mantis to crawl out of that pool of wastewater.

This was the fucking guy!

I moved my drone towards him, ready to get a good look at this asshole's face...

And then.

Well.

I got exactly that.

Only the asshole wasn't just some asshole.

The asshole was me.

For a moment, I sat in my chair, looking at this man who looked exactly like me, calmly watching the fucking Bug Apocalypse crawl out of the city of Reno's collective wastewater. And as I sat there in utter disbelief, the man turned his head to look right at the drone. He fucking smiled.

Then, without missing a beat, he took a piece of paper out of his pocket and showed it to the camera. In big, bold writing, I could see what I recognized as a radio station.

He—I—was sending me a message...

My palms suddenly felt sweaty. My heart was racing a little too fast.

Should I even listen to what this guy had to say? Whatever it was, it was crazy, right?

Even if he was, I still should hear what he had to say... I still should document it, maybe it would explain why, right?

If it were anyone else, that's exactly what I would have done.

But it wasn't anyone else. It was me.

What would I have to say to myself? Something that would make me do this?

That was crazy, right? It had to be fucking crazy!

Right...?

I thought it over, sitting in silence for several minutes.

The man on the screen... me, just went back to studying the creatures coming out of the wastewater before walking away, towards the offices. I made the drone follow him for every step.

He didn't seem to mind. He kept looking back at the camera, smiling every now and then as he kept walking.

He walked through the door to the offices and locked it behind him, then sat in a chair in a cubicle. He took one last look at the camera, his smile fading slightly...

Then he took out a gun.

He set the paper on the desk before he put it to his head.

I watched him pull the trigger.

I watched myself die.

It was...

I don't know how to describe it...

For a moment, I just sat there in silence, my hand over my mouth as I tried to process what I'd just seen.

Then, inevitably, my eyes were drawn to the paper he'd set down... The radio station.

His last words.

My last words.

I had to know.

I tuned to the station and started cutting through the static... This was what I got.

"Hey, Bill. I know you're probably pretty confused by all this. Trust me, I was too. But you and I both know that I wouldn't be doing this if it didn't make sense. Use your drones. Take a good, hard look at the future of these timelines. Not the immediate future. Give it a hundred, two hundred years. Just look. That's all I'm asking you. Look."

The message paused there.

I opened the settings of the drone. I had nothing to lose by looking, right? So I sent it forward.

First by one hundred years.

Then by two hundred... then by three hundred...

And I saw it all...

A new world. A *united* world on the other side of the generations of hardship wrought by the bugs.

Technology is taking one step back, followed by one incredible leap forward. A new renaissance. One I can't even begin to describe.

I looked through the centuries with awe, wanting to explore the paradise I saw before me... God, I could've lost hours looking into the future. But what I saw was enough.

I tried looking for the same results in other futures. But they weren't there.

Humanity wouldn't thrive the way it would after the hardship of the bugs. Not under any other circumstance...

Nothing would change. We would remain the same miserable species for the rest of our tragic existence. Nothing would change unless we let it...

The more I looked, the more I understood...

And almost as if on cue, the message on the radio began again.

Of course, it was on cue. Future me would've known what past me would do...

"If you've seen what I've seen... Then there's a way forward. There's a man, Dr. Gene Pedri. You'll find what you need there. They grow best in water, so... You'll figure it out. You know what has to be done. If I'm right, most versions of you will do it. Some of you will even succeed... Others will, of course, fail. But that's okay. You and I both know we can't save every future... But we'll save enough of them. Isn't that worth it?"

It was.

It is.

That leaves me here.

Like I said before, you've all just dodged a bullet. I'm not going to prevent what's coming. Not this time. My job is to save the world, and that's just what I intend to do. I've found the path to a better future. I've found the world humanity *deserves*! I'm going to break us out of the endless stagnation of our existence. The road will be hard, but it *will* be worth it.

Nobody ever made an omelet without breaking a few eggs. I realize that my former employers aren't going to see it that way, though. I fabricated some updates and bogus reports to throw them off my trail for a little while. But chances are, they'll catch on soon, if they haven't already. I'm on borrowed time, as it were. But I'm not afraid. I already know how this is going to end.

So, if you're reading this, then one of two things is going to happen.

One: My former employers will kill me and stop me from doing what I have to do… and the world you know won't change. Life will just continue as it was, and if you're living in that world, I'm sorry. I can't save every future. You'll be fine, probably live a nice life and all that, but when the future comes, your grandchildren will never have it any better than you did. Life will stagnate until it finally ends.

Two: I'll succeed, and if I do, I'm sorry. You're probably going to die because of what I've done. But I don't regret it. Not one bit.

What's at stake here is worth it. The future is worth it. I can't pretend it isn't.

Some people are going to call me a monster. That's fine. I don't care.

But I've seen what's coming…

And it's worth the price we'll pay.

It's worth it.

THE HIGHWAY MAN GAME

Transcript of an interview with Terry Smith, regarding something known as "The Highway Man Game," dated September 26, 2021. Interview conducted by Jane Daniels for the benefit of the Spectre Archive.

Daniels: Alright... We're rolling.

Smith: You're recording?

Daniels: Yup. So. About the Highway Man Game, that's what it's called, correct?

Smith: Well, that's what I call it. A lotta people call it other things. Some folks call it the Candlewax Game, the Highway Game, or just the Backroads Game. Some people don't even call it a game at all. For them, it's just survival.

Daniels: I see... So what exactly can you tell me about the nature of this game?

Smith: A lot. But can you answer some questions for me first?

Daniels: Um... I can certainly try. Questions like what?

Smith: Why are you interested? No offense, but you don't seem like the sorta lady who'd be interested in this sort of thing. Y'know, rituals, other worlds, occult-type shit. I guess what I'm wondering is, what's your angle?

Daniels: I guess I've got a couple... I've got a friend. She asked me to keep an eye out for any information on something pretty similar to this, and the organization I work with has an interest in this sort of thing. I guess you could say I'm trying to kill two birds with one stone.

Smith: But that doesn't answer my question, though. Why are you interested in this?

[Silence]

Daniels: I... I suppose it's because I'd like to understand more about the parts of the world that we don't always see.

Smith: You ever actually seen anything?

Daniels: Yes... Yes, I have. More than you'd expect.

Smith: Shit... Well, now you've got me curious, then.

Daniels: Tell you what, you tell me about the game and I'll tell you about some of the things I've seen after the tape stops rolling. Deal?

Smith: Alright... Alright. Yeah. You've got yourself a deal, Mrs. Daniels.

Daniels: So. The Highway Man Game. What can you tell me about it? What's the point?

Smith: The point is to win. I guess part of it is the rush. When you're in the car, and the game is on... The danger is real. At the same time, though, it's not quite as risky as some of the other games out there. It's dangerous, sure. But it's a little more friendly for the inexperienced. So long as you remember the rules and keep your head on straight. I guess I'd say it's sort of like... You know how when you go to the CN Tower, you can pay to walk on the edge outside? They put you in a safety harness and everything and tie you to the side so you won't fall off. But if it weren't for that harness, well, you're basically just hanging on the very edge of the tower, past the point where you'd normally have fallen off completely. You've heard of that, right?

Daniels: Yeah. I've heard of it.

Smith: It's exactly like that, only you get something at the end of it! It's a rush, it's risky, and the reward you get is usually worth it. As long as you take the proper precautions, you should be completely fine. Granted, if you end up playing the game without planning on it and you're not prepared, well then you're S.O.L.

Daniels: How exactly does one end up playing the game without planning on it?

Smith: It's a lot easier than you think. The chances are slim. You need to be in the right place, at the right time, and even then, it's a long shot. A guy could drive the backroads all night, every night, and never run into the game while another guy can venture onto those backroads just once at the wrong time of night and never come back.

Daniels: How do you play the game if the chances of even starting it are so slim, then?

Smith: Well, you gotta stack the deck a little bit. If the Highway Man knows you've got an offering, you're more likely to end up in the game. Like, a lot more likely. But it's never a sure bet. I've gone out on the roads plenty of times with the right offering in the perfect conditions, drove until morning, and didn't see a single thing. Again, it's all up to chance if you ever actually start the game or not.

Daniels: I see... Alright. So tell me about these offerings. How can you increase your chances of playing the Highway Man Game?

Smith: What you need is a candle made of tallow. Some people swear by other offerings, but my friends and I have always had the most success with a tallow candle. You should also be on the road before it gets dark. You don't technically have to, but it's best to start in the late afternoon before dusk sets in. That way, you can get far away from anywhere too populated. The backroads are the best, especially the ones with heavy forest, although I ended up in the game while driving through farmland a couple of times too.

Once the sun starts going down and it starts getting dark out, pull over to the side of the road and light the candle. It should have a particular smell to it as it burns. It's not a great smell, but I'm pretty sure it's the scent of the offering that draws him in. Let the candle burn for a little bit, until it starts to look melted and the wax is running down the sides. Then you take some dirt from the side of the road and pour it over the fire until it goes out. Once it's snuffed, you light the candle again, put it in your car, and keep driving until it's either dawn, the candle burns out, or the Highway Man comes.

Daniels: And... that draws him?

Smith: It makes your chances of drawing him a whole hell of a lot higher. Maybe... I dunno, one in ten, maybe? As opposed to one in a million. Like I said before, it's never a sure thing. There's a good chance that he won't come at all. If morning comes or the candle burns out, then the game's basically over. Honestly, you'd probably best hope that morning comes first, cuz if your candle goes out and you're in the middle of nowhere at three in the morning, that can put you in some real shit. That's when the game is the most dangerous, because if he comes for you, you won't have anything to offer him. My advice, if that ever happens, haul ass to the nearest patch of civilization you can find and wait until the sun comes up. Gas station, hotel, a McDicks. Doesn't matter. Just get off the backroads and don't drive again until morning.

Daniels: I see... I take it, not having an offering is a bad thing, then.

Smith: It's a real bad thing, and I'll tell you why in a minute... See, if you're lucky and the Highway Man comes for you, then you'll know it. The first thing you'll probably notice is how your car goes all wonky. The radio, the clock, and the dials stop working right and start going all over the place. You might get some cell reception, but don't count on it. You might also notice that the road gets really dark, too. Heavy trees on either side of the road, streetlights are few and far between, and always on the left-hand side. Even if you turn around, they'll still be on the left-hand side and under those streetlights... That's where you'll see him.

Daniels: The Highway Man?

Smith: Yeah... He might be out in the darkness at first. But he'll be there. If you wait around, he'll probably show himself. Best not to wait around at the first streetlight, though, or the second. Just keep driving until he comes out on his own. He'll always be there. Under every streetlight you pass. Sooner or later, you'll see him.

Daniels: I see... So, I assume that you've seen the Highway Man, then, right? Could you tell me what he looks like?

Smith: Yeah... Yeah, I've seen him. He... He looks mostly like a man from a distance. The skin isn't quite the right color. He doesn't wear clothes, not that there's anything to see and... I dunno. Maybe he used to be a regular guy or something but his features, they look... warped. Like they're melting off his face. Everything's in the wrong place... I don't like looking at him for too long, honestly. Even the noises he makes. These tinny rasping sounds... Fuck... Usually, he stays by the side of the road, under the streetlight. Sometimes he'll just watch you. Usually, he'll wave, like he's saying hello.

Daniels: I see...

Smith: Anyway... Once you start seeing him under the streetlight, keep count. The road you're on sorta loops. It doesn't turn or anything. But it keeps going. It doesn't change much. Occasionally, you might find a wrecked car or something, but no matter what, you'll always come back to the streetlight and you'll always come back to the Highway Man.

Anyway, you have to keep going once you see him. When you see him the first time, you have to pass him. Same drill when you see him the second time. It's when you see him the third time that it's important. See, once you've passed him the third time, you've got to turn around. You never pass him a fourth time. Never.

Daniels: May I ask why?

Smith: I was told that he doesn't like it. I dunno if that's true. But it's what I heard. When you pass him the third time, you turn around and drive until you see the streetlight again. It'll still be on your left side, even though you turned around, and he'll be there. That's when you stop.

When you stop, he's probably going to approach the car. He's slow, but you've still gotta be quick. See, when you stop and see that he's coming, you've got to take the candle out of your car and place it in the middle of the road. Then you get back into your car and wait. If your candle burned out, then you're fucked and there's nothing you can really do but keep driving and hope to find a way out... Not that I think there is one. I've never heard of anyone who came back without giving him an offering... But I dunno... Maybe there's a way.

Anyway, he'll take the candle. Sometimes, he'll just pick it up, turn around, and walk back into the woods. But I've also just seen him swallow the thing whole, flame and all, before he leaves.

That's how you know that your offering was accepted, and that's how you know you're allowed to leave.

Daniels: And how do you leave?

Smith: You've got a window. See, the Highway Man is supposed to still be waiting for you the next time you pass the streetlight in either direction. So you've got to get off the road before you get there. My advice is to drive slowly. Sooner or later, you'll see a narrow path through the trees. There's no light. It's hard to see, and it might be blocked by a busted old car. But so long as your offering was accepted, it'll be there. That's your ticket out. You take the path and you keep driving until it ends. When it ends, you'll be on a different road. No Highway Man. No more glitches in your car, and it should be dawn, so you're safe to drive home. That's it. That's how you win the game.

Daniels: That seems like a hell of a lot of trouble to go through just for an adrenaline rush, if you ask me.

Smith: It's not just the rush! Like I said before, there's a reward for it. Every time you make it out alive, there's a reward. You'll find it when you get home, waiting right outside the door to wherever it is you live.

Daniels: What kind of reward?

Smith: It varies. But they say that it's always something that was lost. Sometimes, it's something of yours that was lost. Something valuable. A relic of your childhood, a keepsake, some sort of personal treasure. But other times, it's something that belongs to someone else. Sometimes it's valuable. One time, I got this stuffed dog I had when I was a baby, Rufus. Another time, I got a set of solid gold cufflinks. Those brought me a half-decent payday. Once, I just got a hat... Although I guess it was a hat that was important to somebody. It's hit and miss on what you get, but play it enough times and you'll make some decent money.

Daniels: Still seems like a lot of trouble to me...

Smith: Hey, it ain't for everyone. Like I said, if you're smart and you take precautions, everything should be just fine. My friends and I play all the time. We've all got stories!

Daniels: I'll bet... Have you ever lost anyone?

Smith: Have we... Well... Yeah... Yeah, there was Nick, a couple of years back... We... Uh... He went out one night. Didn't come back. We figured that something went wrong. Either his candle had gone out or he'd passed too many times... Something. I dunno...

Daniels: And that doesn't worry you?

Smith: When you deal with this kinda thing, there's always a risk. The world we can't see is not a safe place. There's no lifeguard on duty. There are just rules. People make mistakes. Nick fucked up and he... Look, I didn't wish anything bad on him. None of us did. It could've just as easily been me, and Nick would've said the exact same thing. You said you've seen some of this shit firsthand, so you know what I mean, right?

Daniels: Yeah... Yeah, I do. But I also don't take risks like that. I'm sorry. I'm not judging you. I'm really not. I suppose... I suppose I just don't think I'd be as calm about it as you are.

Smith: Yeah, well... Every few years, it's someone... Usually someone on the forums. Sometimes you see their cars out on the road, doors torn off, windshields smashed. I recognize some of them from the pictures they posted... I've stopped a couple of times. Picked through them, tried to see if there was anything they left behind... Letters, phones, something... Y'know. To get to the people they cared about. I don't usually find anything.

Daniels: Did you ever see Nick's car out there?

Smith: I... Y-yeah... Yeah, I've seen it... A couple of times... Never in the same place. The road shifts. Everything moves... I try to make sure it reminds me to play it smart. Remember the rules. Don't get cocky and stay focused... Yeah... Yeah, that's it...

Daniels: I see... That's all I had. Thanks for your time, Terry.

Smith: Yeah, yeah. No problem... Hey, you said that if I told you mine, you'd tell me yours. What exactly is it that you've seen, huh?

Daniels: Right. A deal's a deal. Here... Let me just turn this-

[End Recording]

THE PERFECT SIN

Rachael De Groote died last week.

She'd been one of my best friends ever since we were kids. We used to share almost everything with each other... and now she's gone.

I can't remember the last time I even saw her in person. We fell out of touch over the past few years. Nothing happened between us or anything; it's just that our lives were heading in different directions. I had my career to focus on and Rachael... well, she was Rachael.

Her family was from old money, and she was generally savvy with her investments, so it freed her up to follow whatever flights of fancy she was pursuing at the time. They changed pretty often, so it was hard to keep up with her current obsession.

Last I spoke to her, a few months back, she mentioned her latest fixation seemed to be old curiosities—antiques with bloody stories behind them. She talked my ear off for hours over the phone about an old journal she'd purchased at auction. Supposedly, it had belonged to some serial killer from the 1800s.

I won't pretend that I understood any of it... but I won't pretend I ever really understood Rachael either. She was always the kind of person who just marched to the beat of her own drum, never caring what anyone else thought or did. I always admired that about her... I don't think I ever could've been so devil-may-care. I kinda envied her for that.

I heard about her passing from a mutual friend. She was found hanging in her bedroom. Her death was ruled a suicide.

Suicide... I couldn't believe it when I heard it. It just sounded so out of character for her. Rachael had never struck me as the suicidal type. She was always too vibrant, too full of life. I suppose the people in the most pain tend to smile the brightest, but I couldn't honestly believe that she was in the sort of headspace where she'd just up and kill herself. She would have reached out to someone—if not me, then maybe to a professional. She sure as hell had the money for it. It just didn't make any sense.

She wouldn't do that.

And yet... she did.

I was at the funeral.

I saw her body.

I knew she was gone... and there wasn't really any other answer to the question of why.

She was just gone.

I think on some level, I knew that what I was feeling was just grief. Denial. I didn't want her to be gone, but that didn't change the fact that she was.

I've never lost anyone before... it figures that losing someone like her would hit me hard, right?

I told myself that I had to move on. Loss doesn't really leave you with much of a choice but to move on, and I'd already made as much peace with that as I could. I didn't know if I'd ever get any satisfying answers about what had happened to Rachael... but I sure as hell didn't expect her to give them to me herself.

Guess she had one last surprise for me after all.

I received this letter in the mail a few days after the funeral. The postmark indicates that she sent this before she died, and I can't shake the mental image of her coming back home after sending it, calmly going up to her bedroom and...

I... I can't complete that sentence.

I've included a copy of the letter here. I think Rachael explains things in her own words far better than I ever could.

I've read it over a few times now, trying to internalize every word, trying to understand what she felt in her final days that drove her to take her own life. I believe that it's the closest thing I'll get to closure, the closest thing I can get to being with her at the end.

It's not enough. But it is something.

My dearest Kimberly,

Let me preface this with: I'm sorry... I can't imagine what you must have heard about what happened to me. I suspect many will speculate about the cause of my death, but I don't think anyone will truly understand why. No one but you, at least.

As I write this, I imagine I have only days at most to live. Maybe less. I can hear the song growing louder by the minute. I know I won't be able to resist it for much longer, but I can't allow myself to go without at least telling you why.

You, above anyone else, deserve to know that much.

I found something special at a private auction a few weeks ago, an alleged copy of the original Domenico Cesari recording of 'The Perfect Sin.' It's something I've been looking for for a while. I thought it might be a good addition to my little collection of curiosities, although I'll be honest, I didn't have high hopes about its legitimacy.

There are a lot of people who will insist that there is no original recording of 'The Perfect Sin.' Not one sung by Domenico Cesari, at least. They chalk it up as just another urban legend, and I've personally never been sure if that was the case or not. I always figured that even if the recording did exist, the stories told about it were most likely just stories... but I'm getting ahead of myself, aren't I?

I suppose I should take a moment to explain what exactly I'm talking about when I mention 'The Perfect Sin,' shouldn't I? I can't imagine you're familiar with it. Most people aren't.

Honestly, most people probably wouldn't really care. As urban legends go, it's relatively obscure, and for the curious, there's a recording of the song floating around the internet that effectively puts the mystique to bed... for most, anyway. But that isn't the real song. By all accounts the lyrics are there, but it's not the right singer, and the melody isn't quite the same. It's not The Perfect Sin. Functionally, it's just a cover performed by someone who had enough secondhand knowledge about the original recording to fake it.

As far as I can tell, there is no publicly available recording of the original version of the song... and that's probably for the best.

According to the sources I've found, The Perfect Sin was authored by a man named Samuel Andress sometime around 1891.

Andress was a... controversial figure. A lot of the details I could find about his life are inconsistent and contradictory. It's hard to know what was fact and what he just made up to sound more interesting. There are verifiable records that indicate he started out as a Catholic priest in England back during the late 1800s (although he often claimed to have been either an Anglican or Protestant priest).

His time with the Church was... well, messy, to say the least. There are references to him hosting exclusive prayer circles in exchange for money and a few rumored scandals of him sleeping with members of his congregation.

In 1883, he was laicized and excommunicated after claims that he was practicing occultism surfaced... although if anything, that just seemed to let him off the leash. He leaned into the occultist label and made a modest career for himself in those circles. That's where the details of his life get a bit murkier—which is to say, he started lying his ass off about who he was. He made claims of having traveled to the Holy Land and learned 'secret truths' from sages in the desert. A few people state that Andress claimed he had even brought back the True Cross from an expedition and had it on display in his home. Others state that Andress often said he had personally been to Heaven and that he'd actually been excommunicated for growing closer to God in ways that he claims violated the—in his own words—'feeble restrictions of Dogma.'

The general consensus is that Andress was, for all intents and purposes, a pathological liar, and it's unclear just how much of his own bullshit he actually seemed to believe. That said, the details of his teachings have survived history relatively intact.

Andress believed that humans could achieve some form of spiritual enlightenment or even apotheosis through a combination of music and meditation. He believed that: "When one enters a Deep Meditative State while exposed to the correct auditory stimulation, one can experience a state of elevated consciousness and transcend the barrier between Earth and Heaven." To demonstrate, he would hold sermons where he would sit for hours on end listening to musical compositions and claiming his consciousness was astral projecting out of his body.

According to witnesses, knocking would be heard around the room where he was meditating. Things would seemingly move on their own, and he would sometimes speak in a low, monotone voice, disclosing things about his audience that he shouldn't have been able to know. Most of these tricks were confirmed to be hoaxes after his death... and aside from a few followers, Andress did not receive the same widespread popularity that a few others did. Most people (correctly) just figured he was either insane or a grifter.

The stories about him start to change around 1890, though. That was around the time when Andress came into contact with Edouard Gauthier.

Gauthier was a failed French composer who had his own unique set of beliefs about music. Specifically, he believed that it was the language of God. The songs that Gauthier wrote were more or less his idea of a prayer to a higher power.

I don't know if Andress actually believed that Gauthier was on to something or if he simply saw him as a way to add another layer of mystic bullshit to his grift, but according to his followers, he became adamant that Gauthier's music would be the key to ascending to a higher plane of existence. To that end, he asked Gauthier to compose a sonata for him.

I don't know for sure what happened after that. None of the records I was able to find went into any detail, and the rumors I've heard tell a few different stories. Some say that nothing ever came of the request. Others say that Gauthier did write a sonata—and that it serves as the instrumental portion of the original recording.

Aside from the alleged recording itself, nothing I was able to find gave any indication of what the truth was. All I knew was that the few sources I could find about the life of Samuel Andress indicated that he and Gauthier fell out of contact a few months after that request was made, and nobody was entirely sure what had happened. Gauthier abruptly returned to France and was committed to an asylum soon after... neither for the first nor the last time, and Andress quietly retreated from the public eye.

There are a few accounts I've read that claim he left England and traveled to Italy to meet with Domenico Cesari a few months later, although others question the credibility of that. Cesari was a singer in the Sistine Chapel Choir, a castrato. He wasn't the sort of man who one would expect to associate with an occultist grifter like Andress. If they did meet—Cesari never spoke about it, and there's so little documentation about Andress during those months that it's impossible to say for sure what did or did not happen, or how any such meeting might have gone. That said, according to the stories, Cesari consented to record the song, and that original version was recorded on two wax phonograph cylinders, with several other cylinders that contained the remainder of the sonata composed by Gauthier.

From what I've heard about the original recording... it is haunting. Cesari sings in a slow, trembling voice. He sounds ready to burst into tears. At one point, he can supposedly be heard hyperventilating before he continues. Gauthier's score has been described as... tumultuous. A heavy piano dirge that sounds like death itself. Slow, discordant, and at times painful to listen to.

It is not said to be a pleasant listening experience, and most who claimed to have heard the original recording mentioned that they were unable to finish it.

I always figured that was an exaggeration. People trying to make it sound more frightening than it is. The version that's available online isn't that bad to listen to, although the backing composition sounds more like Scriabin than Gauthier... but I digress.

Samuel Andress passed away in Rome in February of 1892. His body was found floating in the Tiber, and his pockets were filled with rocks. What is believed to be the original lyrics of The Perfect Sin were found in his private journals, and I have included them here.

The stars go out above us.
The Moon will cease to glow.
The Sun will fade to embers.
And with it all we know.
Thy flesh exists imperfect.
Destined to decay.
And echoes of thy kingdoms
Shalt slowly fade away.
Oh beast of endless darkness
Consume thine endless prey
For nameless piles of meat
Rot in thy gullet every day.
Upon the void of Heaven.
The truest peace awaits.
A refuge of divinity

Within the wings of fate.
Be all our sins forgotten.
Let good and evil fade.
For just and wicked both be humbled
By the Judgement Day.
Clasp not thy hands together,
or look to the sky and pray.
For in the face of what shall come
God's grace shan't keep thee safe.
And pray not for thy Savior.
Pray not for Heaven's Gate.
For in the wake of Perfect Sin
All Angels are erased.
Find refuge in thy slumber.
Within cold arms of stone.
Let thyself fall freely
And thou shalt find thy way home.

Domenico Cesari passed away in April that same year. Officially, his cause of death was heart failure. Supposedly, his health had been deteriorating for a few months before his death... although a few of the accounts I found mentioned that he had been suffering from extreme insomnia during those months. I've seen people speculate about any sort of connection to The Perfect Sin, but unfortunately, I really can't offer any more insight than that.

Right now, I'm sure you're probably thinking exactly what I was thinking.

It's a neat little story and probably nothing more. There are too many gaps, too much that can't be verified, too much to speculate on. None of the information I found came from particularly reliable sources either. It's all secondhand. Scans of old journals on forums run by people who want the story to be true. It's easy to fake, easy to lie about.

It would make more sense if it were just a story... and that's part of why I doubted the authenticity of the recording I purchased. It really didn't make sense for it to be true.

But I liked the story, and this looked legitimate enough that even if it wasn't true, who else was going to know? Just like in the story, it was contained on a set of fourteen wax phonograph cylinders. Those aren't *exactly easy to play. Real or not, it'd still be a hell of a story for my collection! Real cursed audio! What a rush!*

And despite my doubts, I still went through the trouble of obtaining a phonograph to find out for sure.

I figured that what I'd hear would be the same version of the song everyone seemed to know. Someone who thought they were smart probably just went through the trouble of creating a fake just to make something convincing. If nothing else, I would've respected the effort put into faking it!

But when the song began to play… it wasn't the one I recognized.

This was something different. Something I'd never heard before.

Something I haven't been able to stop hearing since.

Oh Kimmie…

I can't describe it… I truly don't have the words.

Beautiful… horrible… it was neither and both.

The bitter melancholy of the piano hurt my ears to listen to, but I could not make it stop… and Cesari's voice…

His voice was small, childlike, and afraid, yet stoic. It was unquestionably the voice of a castrato and was as hauntingly beautiful as one would expect, but that beauty felt… tortured… by this song.

Have you ever seen the footage of the Hindenburg explosion? If so, you'll remember the way Herbert Morrison spoke as he watched the disaster unfold before his very eyes. Measured. Professional… and yet the horror in his voice bleeds through every word until he can't stand to watch another moment. You can hear the deep pit in his stomach in the way he speaks, and you know that he will still see the fires whenever he closes his eyes for the rest of his life.

Domenico Cesari sang with that same measured horror. He sang as if he were describing what he was seeing, and as if he were moments away from breaking down into tears. He sounded like he so desperately wanted to stop, but he couldn't, as if the words were forcing their way out of his throat with the viscosity of cold honey. His voice was so angelic, and yet it made me sick… but I did not turn it off.

When the first cylinder finished, I put the next one in. The movement was almost mechanical on my part. My hand was shaking a little as I switched it over, and the silence did not feel like a break in the song. It felt like part of it. A deep breath before the next plunge.

Gauthier's sonata continued on the next cylinder... and the next... and the next. God... I've never heard anything so... wrong. The piano was slow and confusing. Sometimes it sounded like thunder. Sometimes it sounded like howling wolves, or crashing waves, or flapping wings. Sometimes it sounded like something else. Sometimes it sounded like sobbing or screaming. And yet every note radiated a deep, resonant despair.

Even when it ended, it didn't feel like it had stopped. It just felt like it had gone still... like an animal ending its death throes, and I kept waiting for it to start up again, even when I knew it wouldn't.

As soon as I rose to my feet, I felt dizzy. I tried to stumble to the bathroom to vomit, but I couldn't make it. I just felt so sick to my stomach.

I couldn't listen to it again. I put the cylinders back inside their box and set them aside. I didn't want to ever listen to that again.

And yet I still heard it...

It came to me in my sleep at first—dreams of a void filled with echoes and Gauthier's sonata, far away and mournful.

Looking up into the void, I knew in my knotted guts that what I saw was not simple darkness but something so vast I could only see a small fraction of it, like an ant standing in the palm of a person's hand.

I could feel it getting closer. I could feel the immensity of it, crushing me like deep-sea pressure, and I knew that this was not all of it. I could not comprehend all of it. Truthfully, I wasn't sure if it even understood me. I couldn't be sure if what this was was a thing of malice or if it just simply was. Oblivious to my presence before it and oblivious to the inevitable destruction it would bring me. In its palm, I was but the most insignificant little speck. A sandcastle storm wall in the face of a hurricane.

Oh God, Kimmie... I can't describe the deep helplessness I felt swallowing me whole. Knowing what was there, or at least as much as one could know... and knowing it could not be stopped.

When I'd wake, I'd still hear the song echoing through my memory. My hands would shake, and I struggled to focus on anything else.

Sometimes when I was alone, I swore I could hear the melody. The slow, dirgelike, despairing drone of the piano... I was sure I even heard the lyrics in the things people said to me. At first, I thought it might just be a coincidence, but now I'm certain it isn't.

I couldn't get it out of my head, no matter what I tried.

I've spoken to so many people, hoping that maybe I could find someone else who's come across a genuine recording of the song... but to my knowledge, no one has.

No one still alive, at least...

I did what I could to follow up on the more credible accounts I'd heard of the song, but just about all of them were literal dead ends.

Professor Umi Shahid, for instance.

His name had come up a few times in my search for the original recording. He was a musical theory professor at Upper Lake University. Supposedly, Shahid had come across a copy of the original recording—a claim I was able to back up from a few old forum posts from him.

Shahid had disappeared from the internet soon after that, though. Reaching out to Upper Lake University, I learned that he had left his position there two years ago. With a little persistence, I managed to reach out to his wife.

She told me that Professor Shahid had passed away soon after leaving the University. A car accident, she said.

She didn't give me any further details, but I still looked into it.

God, Kimmie...

The man drove off a fucking bridge!

Jodi Mountain—an antiques collector who was active in those same communities—mentioned that she believed she had an authentic copy. She died last year, an overdose of pills. No suicide note... her neighbor found her after a few days when she'd started to stink.

In some of her final forum posts, she described the original song, and her description sounded hauntingly similar to what I had heard. She described how sick it had made her feel and how she was hearing it in her dreams, just as I'd been hearing it!

There were others too... so many others, Kimmie... so many...

After a while, all I could do was laugh.

The cycle was so obvious, so fucking obvious!

Those who heard it seemed to inevitably break, coming undone at the seams when living with the echo in their minds became too much. How had no one else noticed it before? The whole fucking pursuit of that stupid song was nothing more than an elaborate suicide!

But I swore it wouldn't be me... I swore I wouldn't die, too. I...

...

The first part of the letter ends here.

It's obvious that the paper in this section was crumpled up and thrown away at some point. When I got it, it'd been meticulously smoothed out, but the creases still remain. That page of it ends there... and it begins again on a fresh, separate page.

I was scared, Kimmie.

I am still scared. I wanted to find someone who could help me. I thought maybe someone out there could.

I haven't talked much about the forums yet, have I?

They aren't very active—but there is a small community out there of people like me. People who share similar interests. Alleged cursed objects, old ghost stories, and occult memorabilia. Curiosities.

I joined up a few years ago, and I've made a few friends online. I never told any of them about what I'd found... I knew they'd want to hear it too, and I couldn't... I couldn't do that to them, Kimmie. They wouldn't have known what they were asking for.

It'd been almost a week since I'd first heard the song at that point. I hadn't been sleeping... sleeping meant dreaming, and dreaming meant music, and music meant pain.

My eyes kept drooping. I heard the song in every breath, worming its way into my brain...

But I did still ask a few of them for help.

I told them I was researching the song and wanted to find more reliable sources. I told them I wanted to understand it a little better. Most of them weren't able to give me anything I didn't already know. At best, they filled in a few of the gaps in the life of Samuel Andress—the relevant portions of which I included earlier.

But... one of them did point me toward someone that I thought might be useful.

Online, she went by OraclE, although I later found out that her real name was Charlene Simmons. She had posted a lot of details about the beliefs of Samuel Andress and Edouard Gauthier that you can find online. From what I could see, her sources seemed fairly reliable. In fact, she seemed to be pretty well-versed on the subject.

Like so many others, she too had been fascinated by The Perfect Sin.

Like so many others, she'd wanted to find it.

And like so many others, she had... but unlike them, she didn't fade away from the internet after finding it. She tried to make sense of it, the same way I was trying to. The final posts in her history were hard to decipher. I might not have understood them at all if I hadn't heard the song for myself.

I've shared one of her final (legible) posts here. I feel it says the most, more than anything else.

"I can't know how close I am. But I do believe I'm starting to make some sense of it. To understand the song, you need to understand the nature of the Perfect Sin. The act, not the song itself. I imagine it was the nature of the Sin that stuck with Samuel Andress and drove him to create the recording.

But what could be The Perfect Sin? What could be the cruelest possible action? I thought about the dreams I had. The indifferent oblivion... the inevitability of it. Perhaps that Oblivion was the sin? But no... I think that's the mistake most people seem to make at first. But it's not about something coming. Not in a literal or physical sense, at least. You see the Titan in your dreams... too vast to truly see. It has to be coming, but it's not. It's here. It cannot be escaped because it is already present. Its arrival a foregone conclusion. It does not come. It simply is. Such is the nature of Oblivion.

Oblivion always comes. If something is created, eventually it will be destroyed. And if Oblivion is a foregone conclusion, if it is the natural order, then wherein lies the sin?

I do not believe it is destruction or Oblivion... that is part of it, yes. But only the end result. The effect, not the cause.

The real sin was at the beginning.

Creation.

I finally understand it.

I finally see the point of it.

It's... it's so simple. But so easy to deny.

Existence is a firework. Beautiful for a moment and then gone. All things are born into this world only to die. Any meaning or legacy is irrelevant... and we know it... to create us, knowing of our own impermanence and insignificance... It's the cruelest thing. A cold, insensitive action carried out by a God who was either sadistic or apathetic, and I'm really not sure which one would be worse. To create that which fears its own destruction... that is the Perfect Sin. An act of true evil, and yet true benevolence. To understand the coming Oblivion, even if one cannot escape it. It is sadism and beauty in one masterful stroke of the brush... but...

But there is more.

Something else I don't understand. Something I need to piece together. I don't understand why. The simple nihilism of existence can't be it. It isn't the full song. There is something else I don't understand.

But I will."

It wasn't her final message.

There were a few other forum posts, but they were... even now, I struggle to understand them. Whether or not she figured out what I now know, I am unsure. To me, the truth of it seems so obvious, but maybe we all see different things? It is that thought which steadies my hand, but I...

No... I believe in what I've found, what I now know. I believe.

Charlene was right.

There is more to the song than the simple nihilism of our own existence. I didn't see it at first... not until I went back to it.

I thought that maybe by listening to the song again, I might be able to find that missing piece. Maybe I could free myself of it.

In a way, I have.

But as I sat and listened for the second time... then the third, then the fourth... I started to understand.

The song doesn't go away, Kimmie.

It's not supposed to.

Oh... I don't understand how I didn't see it before; it's so obvious.

As I sat and listened, it finally began to click. Finally began to make sense! It's not supposed to go away!

It's not a nightmare.

It is an invitation.

The lyrics speak of how God's grace can't save you... I used to think it was a commentary on damnation, but no. I misunderstood the warning.

Grace is not salvation, Kimmie.

But choice is.

Andress told us as much in his final verse.

Find refuge in thy slumber.

Within cold arms of stone.

Let thyself fall freely

And thou shalt find thy way home.

Slumber in cold arms of stone...

I understand now, Kimmie. It needs to be a choice. Not to live, but to die.

For so long I've thought that the song was a warning. It's not.

It's an invitation.

Heaven comes to those who want it... oh, Kimmie, I see it now... and I want it.

I won't stay here, not with the Void outside my mind. I can't. Not anymore. There's freedom in the music, I just didn't hear it before.

I'm still afraid... I'm scared, Kimmie... I'm so scared of being wrong, but in my heart I feel that I'm not. I don't pity the dead anymore, Kimmie. I know the song has set them free, and soon, I think I'll be free, too.

Please don't cry for me, Kimmie. I know you will anyway, but don't. I'm sorry for the pain I know you must have felt when you heard, and I regret that I could not see you one last time before the end. There has only ever been one person in my life I truly loved and who I know loved me back, and that was you. But I believe in my heart that we will see each other again. I know this isn't goodbye. I know it.

I've taken steps to properly preserve the recording. The cylinders weren't going to last forever... and someone needed to save them properly.

You'll find the disc with this letter.

I hope you'll listen to it. I hope you'll join me. Even if not immediately, in time. I'll see you in Heaven, Kimmie. I'll be there waiting!

Love eternally,

Rachael.

As she promised, there was a burned CD in the envelope with her letter.

I haven't listened to it yet.

I don't know if I will.

Part of me wants to. I think it might be the only way I can truly understand, because right now I'm not entirely sure if I do. Maybe if I hear it, it will make sense? But at the same time... well... I already have a good idea where listening to it leads. I already know the truth she looked for. I already know what's waiting for me.

But I still find myself curious.

If you're reading this note, then I suppose it's obvious what happened to me. I don't know what more to say beyond that other than… I hope Rachael was right, and maybe if she was, then I'm with her.

I hope so.

Either way… don't follow me.

MORE CHILLS FROM VELOX BOOKS

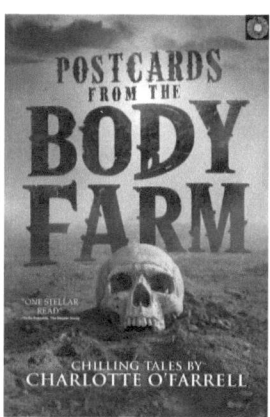

MORE CHILLS FROM VELOX BOOKS

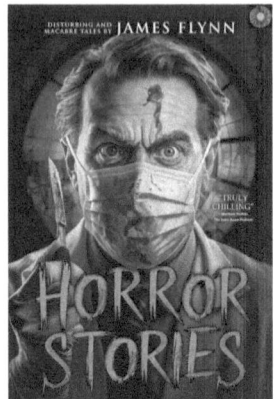

MORE CHILLS FROM VELOX BOOKS

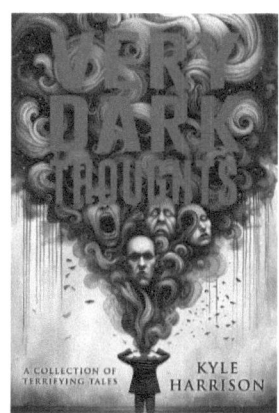

MORE CHILLS FROM VELOX BOOKS

www.ingramcontent.com/pod-product-compliance
Lightning Source LLC
LaVergne TN
LVHW040052080526
838202LV00045B/3592